WRONG
for YOU

OTHER BOOKS AND AUDIO BOOKS

BY JENNY PROCTOR

The House at Rose Creek

Mountains Between Us

Love at First Note

phil7

WRONG *for* YOU

A Novel

JENNY PROCTOR

Covenant Communications, Inc.

For my parents,
who raised me to believe in God, in family, and in myself

Acknowledgments

I WAS SITTING IN ON my daughter's viola lesson, taking notes in her binder, when the idea for this novel fell into my lap. Four brothers, a soccer field, and a girl too competitive to walk away from a challenge. It's been so fun chasing the story down and fleshing out the details. Many thanks to all those who consulted with me on matters of pickup soccer games, Puerto Rican food, small-business accounting, and the wonders of modern technology. Paul, Steve, Susan, DeNae, Kenny—thank you for helping me not sound like an idiot.

Jolene, thank you for being such a willing and intelligent sounding board. Rachel and Laura, thank you for beta reading an entire manuscript in twenty-four hours and for providing such insightful feedback. That's true friendship right there.

Emily, as always, this story is as much yours as it is mine. Thank you for endless hours of talking about people who live only in my head. Thank you for always reading first, for your impeccable notes and thoughtful compliments. Most of all, thank you for believing I'm good enough.

To my team at Covenant, thank you for taking such good care of my words and stories. Samantha, thank you for your guidance and support, your wit and wisdom. Four novels! I'm not sure I ever thought I'd get here. I'm so glad we've gotten here together.

And finally to my husband, Josh, and my spectacular children. Thank you for loving me anyway, for dealing with deadlines and distractions and a mom and wife who heeds the siren call of her stories. There is nothing in this world greater than you all, and I happily love you the most. But I'm so glad you love that I love writing too.

Chapter 1

I WAS DONE WITH ROOT beer floats.

My old singles group out in California suffered from such severe refreshment impairment that even the girls never broke out of the norm. Root beer floats and Oreos. Every. Single. Gathering. They claimed it was tradition. I claimed it was nothing short of idiotic.

I spent more than a year cursing the guy who decided mixing root beer with vanilla ice cream was a good idea and wishing I could kick him in the shins. After the kick, which I'm sure would have made me feel better, I would have drafted a letter to every Church singles group from there to Mississippi, letting them know the root-beer-float ship had sailed in 1982 and for all that was good and holy could they please make brownies or something?

I landed in Chapel Hill, North Carolina, pretty much over it. Over *all* of it.

Was I still young enough to attend singles activities?

I was twenty-five, so technically . . . yes. But who wanted to dwell on technicalities? Definitely not me. Not with root beer on the menu.

By the end of my second Sunday in Chapel Hill, I was already lined up to start teaching Sunday School to seven-year-olds in the "not for singles" family congregation, which sounded positively amazing. Before I moved in, I'd kinda hoped family-style church would be my only option, but Chapel Hill was a college town surrounded by other college towns. Three major universities and half a dozen smaller ones fed into the same body of Mormon singles, including UNC, Duke, and NC State, which made for a pretty impressive gathering. Impressive enough to warrant giving the singles their own meeting time free from hovering grandparents or noisy children. I'd felt momentarily lured to the idea of singles church when a well-intentioned woman sharing my pew had given me a flyer for the following day's singles mingle.

"My daughter is head of the social planning committee in the singles group, and they do all kinds of fun things," she'd told me. "Plus, there are lots of grad students. If you're worried about being too old, don't be. You'll fit right in."

I'd ignored the rub of her tactless observation—I hadn't said anything about feeling too old, which meant I just *looked* it—and considered the possibility of grad students. But then I'd taken a quick glance at the flyer.

Board games and . . . wait for it . . . root beer floats.

Yeah. There couldn't have been a clearer sign. I'd crumpled the flyer on my way out the door and chucked it into the trash can at the end of the hall.

Seven-year-olds? Here I come.

I'd moved into the tiny garage apartment above my grandmother's house two weeks before I was due to start my new job at the Winding Way Inn. The back side of the inn abutted my grandmother's property, and I'd been quick to make the inn's grounds my summertime haunt whenever I'd visited Granny Grace. I'd wandered through the gardens, sat on the giant porch swing, and read in the limbs of the blossoming cherry tree on the east end of the rose garden. I'd never spent any time inside—I wasn't a guest, so I wasn't allowed—but I still felt like the inn was mine. Like some cosmic force understood that simply loving a place was enough to make it my own. Which was why I'd been so excited when Granny Grace had called me to tell me about the job opening. She'd seen it in the local paper and called me right away. "You always said you wanted to run the place one day, Lane. Now's your chance."

It wasn't really running the entire inn. Just the special events. But still. Winding Way was infused with all the magic and charm of my childhood summers, with the added enticement of being back on the East Coast and closer to my family.

The Saturday before my first day at work, I stood at the foot of my apartment stairs and stretched my long arms over my head. I needed to run. Was dressed for it and everything. But it was *hot*. I was used to North Carolina's humidity. I'd grown up in Asheville, a city four hours west, but Chapel Hill was flat and relatively breezeless—too far east to benefit from the mountains and too far west to benefit from the coast.

"It's too hot to be running, Miss Lane." Granny Grace stepped out onto the porch and leaned on the paint-chipped railing, one hand raised to shield her eyes from the sun.

"It's June. It's too hot for everything."

"Not drinking sweet tea." She held up her glass. "Never too hot for that."

I didn't love stereotypes. I was a Mormon, a Southerner, and biracial—my mother was Puerto Rican, and my father was black—which meant I had all kinds of reasons to resent people categorizing me based on what they thought I was before they knew anything else about me. But as far as Southern women went, my grandmother on my father's side, Grace Ann Bishop, was quintessential. If you take everything I love about the South—the kindness, the gentleness, the food—and roll it into one person, you have my grandmother.

"You have something to drink?" Granny called. "You'll need it."

I held up my water bottle. "Just filled it up." I retied my left shoe. I was stalling, but the heat was brutal.

Granny Grace wiped her brow and stepped toward her front door. "I'm making a meat loaf later if you want some. Just knock if you get hungry."

She'd brought up a meat loaf the night I'd moved in—crispy onions on top, a tangy sauce drizzled over the entire thing, and a heaping pile of mashed potatoes to go with it. I especially appreciated Granny Grace's love for cooking because I hated to cook. *Loathed* it. Unfortunate because of how much I loved eating. It wasn't just about the food though. I loved the togetherness food brought. The family gatherings. The friendships. To have one of my favorite people living right downstairs who loved to cook *and share* was a little like a dream come true.

"I'll definitely come by," I told her.

Finally off my porch, I hit the sidewalk and ran square into the middle of what could only be described as a gaggle of women. One stepped forward. She was tiny and perky and blonde.

"Are you Lane?"

And her voice sounded exactly like her do-gooder, flyer-sharing mother. I'd been outed. "Yeah."

"Oh my word. You are just as beautiful as Mom said you were. Are those curls natural? Seriously. So gorgeous."

My hair was pulled back into a ponytail for my run, so I don't know how gorgeous it actually was, but I wasn't going to reject a compliment. "Thanks. Yeah, it's natural."

"I'm so glad we caught you." She glanced at her watch. "If we hurry, we'll make it before the game starts."

My eyebrows went up. "Game?"

Another girl stepped forward. "Trust us on this one. It's tradition. Every time a new girl moves in."

I took a step backward. "Right, but I didn't move in. I didn't really want to join up with the singles this time around."

Perky Blonde rolled her eyes. "But you're still one of us. I'm Chloe, that's Emily, Steph, and Melanie. I promise we're harmless. We can even be fun sometimes. Just come. I promise you won't be disappointed."

"I was about to head out for a run."

"And you still can." She put her tiny hands on her tiny hips. "After the game. We drove all the way over here from Raleigh to pick you up. You have to come."

I sighed. She was little, but she was fierce. "Do we have to go *back* to Raleigh? I don't know that I have that kind of time." It wasn't like the capital city was far. Maybe half an hour, but still. This was my last Saturday before work started. Time was precious.

She smiled. "Nope. Only over to Carrboro. It's less than ten minutes from here."

Hmm. Carrboro meant they were driving right through Chapel Hill to get there anyway, so it's not like they'd gone out of their way to pick me up. They would have driven *all the way* from Raleigh regardless. But whatever. I'd been looking for reasons to delay my run anyway. "Fine. But I have to be home by noon."

Chloe smiled in victory. "I promise." She tossed her keys to a brown-haired girl—Melanie?—behind her. "Start the car. I want to be there before they start warming up."

* * *

I was expecting the worst. Singles-organized, Saturday-morning badminton. Or the most cursed of all group sports—volleyball. Turned out, the game was soccer. I was willing to get behind a soccer game. Until I realized I was meant only to be a spectator.

I wasn't good at spectating. Especially when it came to soccer.

"So we just sit and watch? Who's gonna play?" I asked.

"Yes, we just watch." Chloe tugged me down onto the bleachers that lined the field. "And you'll see why soon enough. They should be arriving any minute."

It didn't look like there was going to be an actual official game. There was some semblance of a team warming up on the right half of the field, but I didn't see any refs or officials. There wasn't even a scoreboard. It looked like a casual pickup game in the park, which only reaffirmed my desire to play instead of watch. I was about to say as much when Chloe grabbed my arm and pointed. "Right there. There they are."

"There who are?" I followed her gaze across the field. Walking in a side-by-side line past the left goal and toward center field, looking a little too much like an Adidas commercial, were four men.

"We call them the untouchables," Emily whispered, her voice breathy and high.

"The what?"

"The untouchables," Melanie repeated. "The Hamilton brothers. All Mormon. All gorgeous. And all completely, irrevocably undateable."

Chloe sighed. "Sad, isn't it?"

As soon as Melanie said "brothers," I could see the common thread running through them all. It wasn't a bad thread. It was decidedly good. I mean, I wasn't going to sigh, but I also wasn't sorry I'd come along. "Why are they untouchable?"

Chloe cleared her throat. "That one on the end—Cooper—he's only nineteen and leaving for a mission at the end of the summer. The one in the blue—that's David. He's one of the twins. Not identical. He's engaged. Gray shirt, green stripe on his socks—that's Simon. He's the oldest and totally boring and has a long-distance girlfriend who lives in . . . I don't know. Somewhere far away. Overseas, maybe? I can't remember."

My eyes focused on the only brother yet to be mentioned. The other twin. "And the last one?"

Chloe wiped her palms on her knees. "That's Jamie. The best-looking of the bunch and the only one unattached."

My eyes darted from Jamie back to the oldest brother, Simon. I actually thought maybe *Simon* was the best-looking. When I said as much to Chloe, she squinted at the field for a second, then shook her head and gave me a dismissive wave. "No way. Jamie's totally hotter. Plus, the girlfriend disqualifies Simon."

I moved my gaze back to Jamie. He jogged away from his brothers, calling something over his shoulder with a grin, then turned and looked directly at us. Every girl on the bleachers gasped. Except me. I did *not* gasp. He smiled and waved.

"He's the biggest flirt," Chloe said.

"Then why is he untouchable?" I asked. "You said he was unattached."

"That's just it. He flirts, but he never asks anyone out."

I scoffed. "Has anyone ever asked *him*?"

"There are rumors it's happened." Chloe gave her shoulders a dismissive shrug. "But I think it's all talk. Everyone is too chicken."

"Because he never says yes to anyone." Steph finished her thought. "For whatever reason, he's just . . . impossible to catch."

"Untouchable," Melanie said. "Completely."

"You're lucky," Chloe nudged my shoulder. "They don't live that far from you. We're all so spread out, but you guys are almost neighbors."

Neighbors. Interesting. I crossed my arms. *No one* was impossible to catch. Maybe he just hadn't met the right girl. No. Scratch that. Maybe he hadn't met the right *woman*. Not a sideline-sitting, sighing girl but a woman. Someone willing to get in the game. Figuratively and literally. I knew life wasn't a big game of truth or dare. We weren't in middle school. I didn't have anything to prove. But sitting there watching Jamie warm up, I felt the tiny thrill of challenge that had driven me my whole life. I was a woman who went after the impossible. I was a woman who liked to win.

I stood. My running gear wasn't the greatest for soccer, but it would do for one game.

"Where are you going?" Chloe asked.

"I'm going to play."

"Play what?"

I raised my eyebrows and motioned to the field. "Soccer? It looks like they could use another player."

Steph shook her head. "You can't *play*. They get really serious about these games. Do you even . . . Have you played before?"

Ha. Yeah. A few times. "I've played enough. It'll be fine. You guys can cheer for me." I stepped off the bleachers before they could protest again and headed straight for Jamie. Untouchable? Yeah. I didn't think so.

"Hey." I stuck out my hand. "Lane Bishop. You need another player? I'm great midfield." Up close, he almost did make me sigh. Dark, short hair. Clean-shaven. Dimple in his chin. Deep-set, chocolate-brown eyes.

He shook my hand and smiled. "Jamie Hamilton. You're here with the girls from church, but I've never seen you before. That means you're new."

"I am new—just moved in a couple weeks ago—but I opted out of the singles scene this time around."

"What does that even mean? Opted out? You aren't single?"

"Funny. I'm asking you about soccer, and you're asking me very personal questions."

He grimaced. "Noted. Sorry for prying." He gave me the once-over. "You don't really look dressed for soccer."

I shrugged. "I didn't know there was going to be a game. I promise I know how to play. Maybe someone has an extra set of shin guards?"

He scratched the back of his head and looked back at his brothers. A group of guys had collected around them, but it still didn't look like enough for a full team. "I really think we're all set."

I did a quick count, then shot him a look. "Come on. You're down three men. At least let me play outside defense." I motioned across the field to the other team. "They look like they've got a full lineup. You'd rather play outnumbered than have me on your team?"

He huffed. "That's not what I said."

"Okay. I'll play, then."

He glanced back at the bleachers where Chloe and the others still sat. "Look, things may look casual, but . . . we play tough. Are you sure you won't be in over your head?"

In over my head? Sure, it had been a few years since I'd played in a real game, but who was he to discount me so quickly? I took a step backward. "You know what? You're probably right."

He held up his hands. "Look, I wasn't trying to hurt your feelings."

"Oh, no, you didn't. I totally get it."

"We can kick the ball around later if you want. After the game?"

For a second, I wondered if Chloe would have considered that a victory. It was almost like he'd asked me out. But I didn't want a sympathy sorry-I-hurt-your-feelings date. "That's kind of you to offer, but I think I'll be fine. Thanks though." With a final wave, I turned and jogged across the field right into the middle of the other team's huddle. "Okay, who's in charge over here?"

Beyond a few raised eyebrows, no one responded. I huffed. "Seriously? You're all going to stare at me, but no one will talk?"

"*Hablamos español, chica. No comprendamos.*"

I rolled my eyes. Fine. "*Quién está a cargo? Capitan del equipo?*"

At least that got a response. A guy motioned behind him with his head. "Hey, Carlos?" he said. "*Está encargado?*"

"Depends on who's asking." Carlos sat on a bench a few yards away, tying his cleats. He looked a little older than everyone else, maybe midthirties. His long hair was pulled back, and he wore a closely trimmed goatee. I walked toward him, and he stood to meet me. "Sorry. We don't let Matias out of his cage very often. When we do, he forgets how to be polite."

I stuck out my hand. "Sorry for barging in on your game. I'm Lane."

"Carlos." He smiled. "What can I do for you?"

I motioned to Jamie and the rest of his team across the field. "How hard are those guys to beat?"

Carlos folded his arms across his chest and grunted. "They've had a bit of a winning streak lately, but it isn't impossible."

"How frequently do you play?"

"Most Saturdays."

"When was the last time you beat them?"

He narrowed his eyes. "Why are you asking so many questions?"

I weighed my next words carefully. "Because I really want them to lose today. And I want to help make it happen."

A few other players moved closer.

"You, huh?" Carlos asked. "Forgive my doubts, but you're just one person."

"One person the other team isn't expecting to be any good. Jamie just shot me down like I'm still playing youth league. But I promise I'm qualified."

Carlos raised an eyebrow. "How qualified?"

"UC Berkeley. Three-time conference champions, Division I National Champions my senior year."

"Jamie—the tall one. He played in college too," Carlos said.

My confidence wavered. I had an impressive soccer pedigree, and I knew it. But ultimately, I had no idea what I was up against. I'd been riding on determination buffered with a little bit of bravado and a hope for some good luck. It didn't take much effort to imagine a smirk on Jamie's face if my plan backfired and I helped the opposing team to nothing but defeat. Still, it was too late to back down.

"Just let me play. If we don't win . . ." I hesitated. "I'll buy your entire team dinner tonight."

Carlos laughed and shook his head but then seemed to consider. "Dinner for the whole team? You're not worried we'll throw the game just to get a free meal?"

I narrowed my eyes, and a few of the players chuckled. "You wouldn't."

He rubbed his chin. "You play midfield?"

I nodded. "Center."

He ran his hand across his forehead. "Fine. But if you screw up, you're moving to the outside, and you'll never touch the ball."

Good grief. Jamie was right. These guys were serious about their sport. "I won't screw up." Did he think I'd pretended my way through four years of collegiate soccer?

Carlos's face softened. "Sorry. I didn't mean to sound harsh." He motioned to a bag a few feet behind him. "There are extra shin guards if you want them."

I pulled on a set of guards and took my place midfield. I breathed in the earthy smell of the field. It was good to be playing again. The smell of the grass. The sun on my shoulders. The thrill of anticipation. I'd forgotten how much it all felt like home.

I grabbed my ankle, pulling it up behind me to stretch my quad. I caught Jamie's eye as I released it and took hold of my other foot. He stood maybe twenty yards away, a broad smile on his face, and scratched his head. I shrugged my shoulders and waved. In over my head? *Yeah. Give me half an hour.*

My father used to say it was both my greatest strength and my greatest weakness that I was so competitive. It wasn't so much that I had to be the best at everything. I always recognized things that weren't for me and never felt badly for walking away. Ballet? Nope. Horseback riding? Not even a little. But soccer was my thing. My passion. When I was on the field, I was terrible at not winning.

Which was why it was so frustrating that Jamie was so good. Better than I'd expected. With his brothers flanking him, the four of them made playing look like a choreographed dance. It was effortless, almost magical to watch. Still, I held my own. I played hard. Ran hard. Maneuvered, twisted, danced. We were four minutes in when I scored my first goal.

Carlos gave me a high five. "Not in youth league now, are you?"

We took a break at halftime, the score tied at three. Two of my team's goals had been mine. I retrieved my water bottle from the sidelines, Chloe and the rest of her friends cheering as I approached. Swooning over guys was one thing but nothing like a little girl power to get everyone fired up.

"Seriously," Chloe said. "We watch these guys play all the time, and it's never been this fun. I hope you stomp them in the second half."

"Ooh, heads up," Steph said. "The enemy team approaches."

I turned around, watching as Jamie jogged over, stopping a few feet away. "Fine, I cave. Who are you?"

I shrugged. "I already told you who I was."

"You know that's not what I'm asking."

I kicked the ball to him, and he stopped it with his foot. "Right now, I'm just a girl who made a few lucky goals."

He scoffed. "Luck, huh?"

"Jamie, let's go!" Someone called from across the field. "You changing teams?"

He reached down and picked up the ball, then started to back away. He smiled and shook his head. "We're not through yet."

I held up my hands. "Bring it on, pretty boy."

My new friends cheered for me again as I took my place on the field. Jamie shot them a look, apparently noticing that his cheering section had changed their allegiance. It only made them cheer louder. I grinned. *Yeah. That's the way it is.*

Forty minutes later, my team was up by one, the smile on Jamie's face had long since faded, and I was *dying*. I'd been running on a regular basis, but nothing got my heart pounding like the stop and go of a soccer game. Factor in the adrenaline of competition, and it became a seriously intense workout. I was definitely feeling the burn.

But I couldn't stop. Every time I felt like quitting, the look of confidence on Jamie's face, the speed with which he'd underestimated me, flashed through my mind. We were winning, sure, but we couldn't afford to relax. I raced toward Jamie as he passed the ball to his brother, the older one, who dropped his shoulder and faked left, then surged around Carlos and made a goal.

Fantastic. Tied game.

I stopped and leaned forward, resting my hands on my knees, my breathing heavy.

Matias came up behind me. "You okay, Lane?"

I glared at him. "Oh, look. He speaks English."

He grinned. "Forgive me?"

I stood upright. "How much time do we have?"

He glanced at his watch, the only thing keeping unofficial time. "A little more than two minutes."

I nodded. "Let's do this, then."

We dug deep and kept pushing, but Jamie's defense was amazing, and we could not get a shot through. With the clock running down to the final seconds of the game, the pressure was on big time. Carlos surged forward, Matias and another player I couldn't name close on his heels. In a second of crystal clarity, I saw the play happening in my head. I ran wide to the right, then crossed over to center field in time to catch a crossover pass from Carlos. For a brief second, my path to the goal was clear, but Jamie was approaching from the left, hard and fast. In a helicopter move my old college coach would have been proud of, I maneuvered around him and sent the ball sailing toward the goal. Their keeper jumped for it, but it arced over him and hit the net. *Score!*

We'd won five to four.

I collapsed onto the field, my legs feeling like rubber and my lungs on fire, buoyed only by the exultant victory cries of my teammates.

Carlos dropped to one knee beside me. "That was some game. You okay?"

I sat up, took Carlos's offered hand, and let him pull me to my feet. "I am woefully ashamed of how out of shape I feel, but I'll be fine."

Chloe and the others were crossing the field from the sidelines, but one of the Hamiltons was on his way over too, two water bottles in his hand.

Emily reached me first. "Which one is he again?" I whispered to her, looking at the approaching Hamilton.

"That's Simon," she responded.

"The oldest, right?"

"Yep."

I brushed the grass off my palms and arms.

Simon handed a water bottle to Carlos, then offered the other to me. "Nice game."

Carlos grinned. "Lucky for us, your cocky brother wouldn't let her play on your side."

Simon looked at me, his eyebrows raised in question. "You wanted to play on our team?"

I nodded. "Jamie said I'd be in over my head."

Simon laughed. "That explains why he was so annoyed. I'm Simon, Jamie's older and much less competitive brother."

I opened the water and took a long drink. "I'm Lane." I looked across the field and saw Jamie stalking away, his bag flung over his shoulder. "Is he okay?"

Simon followed my gaze. "Don't worry about Jamie. He'll simmer down eventually."

"Yeah, and then challenge you to a rematch," Carlos said. "He is not a man who likes to lose."

"I feel him on that one." I watched Jamie until he crossed the street and disappeared out of sight.

I forced my attention back to the brother standing in front of me.

"Did you play in college?" Simon asked. He crossed his arms over his chest. He wasn't quite as broad through the shoulders as Jamie or as tall, but family genetics had still been nice to the guy.

"I played for Berkeley."

"National champs," Carlos added. His voice held a hint of pride that made me smile.

"Wow." Simon nodded. "I guess that eases the sting a little."

"You ever want to play with us again, Lane, you know where to find us," Carlos said. "Every Saturday, we're here."

"Thanks, Carlos."

He took off, waving over his shoulder. "See you, Hamilton. Bye, Lane!"

"You played a great game, Simon," Steph said.

He looked at her and smiled. "Thanks."

Emily cleared her throat. "Has Cooper heard anything about his mission yet?"

He shook his head. "Not yet. Soon, we think." He turned his attention back to me. "So I guess I'll see you around?"

I nodded. "Sure."

"It was great to meet you, Lane. Nice job today."

He turned and jogged toward the youngest Hamilton brother, who stood waiting at the corner of the field.

In a second, I realized three fundamental truths regarding my situation: Number one, I had made too big an issue about *not* joining the singles group to change my mind now, even if it did mean seeing Jamie again. Two, I really wanted to see Jamie again. And three, if that was going to happen, I needed to act. And quickly.

"Hey, Chloe, you got a pen?" The purse hanging on her shoulder looked big enough to hold an entire kindergarten classroom. Surely she had something to write with in there. "And paper too, if you've got it."

She started rummaging. "I'm sure I do somewhere. What for?"

I glanced at Simon's retreating form. "Just hurry?"

She handed over a pen and a bright-yellow sticky note. "Sheesh. Patient much?"

I took off across the field without responding. "Simon!"

He turned. I paused in front of him and scribbled my number on the note. "Give this to Jamie for me?" Had Simon not had a girlfriend, I never would have asked him to play middle man, but seeing as how he *was* attached and his brother wasn't, I hoped he'd be willing to forgive my lack of social etiquette.

He took the sticky note from my hand and studied it for a moment before looking up and meeting my gaze. "Just like that, huh?"

I shrugged and smiled. "I'm going with my gut on this one. After the sting of defeat wears off, I'm pretty sure he'll want to call me."

He shook his head with a laugh. "I'm sure he will."

I jogged back across the field and handed Chloe her pen. "Sorry. I didn't mean to be rude. I just wanted to catch him before he was gone."

Chloe eyed me, her expression wary. "No problem. What did you do?"

"You remember Simon has a girlfriend, right?" Melanie said, sounding all territorial. "We told you that."

"I didn't give my number to *him*," I said. "It's for Jamie. I asked Simon to pass it along."

Chloe's jaw dropped. "You barely even spoke to Jamie."

"What more do I need to know? He's gorgeous, loves soccer, and loves to win. Sounds good enough to me."

"But you don't . . . How can you even . . . What if he doesn't call?"

"What if he doesn't? It took me four seconds to give my number to his brother. That's hardly a serious investment." I waved a farewell to the few members of my team who were still around.

"So you won't care if he doesn't call?" Melanie asked. "You'll just be fine with that?"

"Why not? No love lost, right?"

"Can I please be like you when I grow up?" Chloe said.

Emily shook her head. "Seriously. I had to swallow rocks back there just to ask Simon about Cooper's mission. I can't *talk* to guys. No way I'd have the courage to jump into their soccer game. Or even just give one my phone number."

"Honestly, it probably won't matter anyway, right? You said it yourself. Jamie is untouchable." I said the words out loud, but in my head, I already knew differently.

Untouchable? Yeah. Not anymore.

Simon: Lane's number: 828-555-3687

Jamie: Seriously? She gave you her number? Does this mean you actually SPOKE to a woman?

Simon: Shut up. She gave it to ME so I could give it to YOU.

Jamie: Sweet. Thanks for passing it along.

Simon: You should have talked to her after the game. It was poor sportsmanship to stalk off like that.

Jamie: Whatever. I had somewhere to be.

Dave: You know he won't lick his wounds in public, Simon. He's too proud for that.

Cooper: Did you see that helicopter move she did at the end? She was RIGHT in front of you, Jamie, and then she was gone. Impressive.

Simon: Will you call her?

Cooper: If you won't, I will.

Jamie: Lay off. I'll call her.

Dave: Seriously? You never call anybody.

Jamie: You saw her, right? Seems like she might be worth it.

Chapter 2

JAMIE WAS ON MY BRAIN when I left for work Monday morning. He shouldn't have been. First day of work. Brand-new job. Brand-new city. I had plenty to think about without him muddling things up. I waved to Granny Grace, who was on her front porch watering her flowers as I left.

"First day?" she called.

I turned back. "Yep. Wish me luck!"

"You don't need luck, Lane. You'll knock 'em dead just by walking into the room." She smiled over her flowerpot. "Come tell me all about it when you get home."

"Will do. See you later!" I climbed into my Honda and started the short drive to Winding Way. Had I been willing to crawl through Granny Grace's back hedge, I could have crossed right onto inn property, cut through the back field, and made it to work in less than ten minutes. It felt silly to drive such a short distance, but 400-degree heat and the lack of sidewalks did that to me. Heels and all that grass? *No.*

I wore my favorite navy pencil skirt with a tiny kick pleat at the back and a green silk blouse that looked awesome against my dark skin. I'd had a great run that morning and a great breakfast. I felt good. Confident. Like it was going to be a good day.

All thoughts of Jamie or any kind of good day vanished when I pulled into the gravel parking lot behind Winding Way Inn. Something immediately felt off. When I'd interviewed for the job, the parking lot had been nearly full—employees of the onsite restaurant bustling in and out of the back kitchen doors, signs of life and activity everywhere. Sure, it was only 9:00 a.m., but the parking lot was empty—*completely* empty. I climbed out of my car and walked around the side of the building to the office entrance I'd been instructed to use. The door was locked.

Locked? *That* didn't make any sense. I pulled out my cell phone, wondering if I'd missed something somewhere. An e-mail, maybe? Or a phone call? I even pulled up the last e-mail I'd received regarding my employment to make sure I had the start date right. I knocked on the door and peered through the tempered glass but couldn't make anything out inside. I hurried around the building to the main entrance and climbed the wide porch steps, anxiety building with every step.

On the front door, a handwritten sign read: *Closed until further notice.*

Closed? What made an entire operation—an inn that was open 365 days a year with a full-service restaurant, twenty-five functional guest rooms, and a reservation list booked out months in advance—come to a grinding, screeching halt? Two competing thoughts ran through my brain: Why hadn't anyone told me, and more importantly, what on earth was I supposed to do about it?

I dropped onto a wood bench that sat to the right of the front door, disappointment coming on strong.

"Hello? Are you Lane? Please tell me you're Lane."

I turned around to see a woman with long dark hair and dark eyes hurrying up the stairs. She was beautiful, but with her hair pulled back into a bun and her lips stretched tight across her face, she had a look of austerity that didn't match the softness in her voice. But then she smiled, her eyes so full of kindness that the tightness I'd noticed melted away.

I returned her smile. "You found me. I'm Lane Bishop."

"Oh, thank the Lord. I wasn't sure when you were supposed to start but was keeping every part of me crossed that it would be today." She sighed. "I'm April, front of house manager."

"What's going on? I tried the back entrance, and it was locked."

"So much is going on. Let's go inside. I'll fill you in."

She pulled out a set of keys and unlocked the main doors. I followed her through the lobby and back into the inn's management offices. Hanging in the hallway, right next to the light switch, was an old photo of the inn's owner, Mr. Thomas, standing on the front porch, his hands pushed into his pockets. It couldn't have been long after he'd opened for business. Another photo not far down the hall was a close-up of a bride's bouquet. All roses and daisies.

A memory popped into my mind of a time I'd been reading in the inn's rose garden as a little girl. Mr. Thomas had led a bridal party into the courtyard for photos, stopping not far from where I sat in the low branches of a tree. I'd started to panic. I didn't want to get in trouble, so I thought it best to stay hidden, but I also worried I might ruin the pictures if I stayed where I was. Luckily the bride noticed I was there and pointed me out. Instead of the scolding I feared, Mr. Thomas pulled a daisy out of the nearest bridesmaid's bouquet and handed it to me before ushering me out of the garden with a good-natured grin.

"It's a great tree," he'd told me. "You make it yours anytime, but the first time there's a set of legs dangling down in the background of someone's photo, I'll know who to blame." I smiled at the thought. Hard to believe the same man was now my boss.

April opened Mr. Thomas's office door and looked inside, hesitating before pulling it shut. "No, not in there. That would be weird."

Weird? What would be weird? "Are we looking for someone?"

She opened a second office—Glenda's, if I remembered correctly, which meant it would be mine by the end of the week—and ushered me in. "This will be better. Gaspard should be here any minute."

"Who's Gaspard?"

"The chef."

It wasn't exactly orthodox as far as staff meetings go, but at least I'd found someone with answers.

The office was big, with a nice seating area under a large bay window. It was the perfect place to plan events—for brides, especially. The soft sofa was welcoming, and the coffee table was loaded with albums full of photos from past weddings. I perched on the edge of a wingback chair just to the left of the sofa. "So, will Mr. Thomas be joining us this morning? He was supposed to introduce me to Glenda. I think she's supposed to be training me this week. Also, why is the inn closed?"

April's face fell. "Oh. I keep forgetting how little you know."

I raised my eyebrows. "Know about what?"

She sighed and dropped into the chair across from me. "Mr. Thomas passed away. Almost two weeks ago. Heart attack. Sudden and completely unexpected. He died instantly."

My jaw dropped. Of all the reasons to close an inn, I guessed that was a pretty good one. "I'm so sorry. I had no idea."

"I suppose we were all so caught up with the funeral and everything, no one thought to call and let you know."

"So . . . everything just shut down when he died?" I couldn't hide the shock in my voice. I understood the hit it likely was for everyone to lose their boss, but to close completely? It seemed a little drastic.

April shook her head. "You've got to understand. This place was all Thornton. He was involved in everything from the restaurant to the events. He ran it all. I suppose we could have kept it going without him, but Ida couldn't bear to see people here without him. Shutting down was her doing."

"Ida?"

She reached for a framed photo sitting on the side table next to her chair and handed it over. Thornton Thomas stood in the center of the photo with what looked like the hotel's entire staff.

"That's Ida right beside him. His wife," April said. "Married forty-two years last spring. That photo was taken at our staff Christmas party last year."

I handed back the photo. "It must be so hard for her."

"It's been hard on all of us. Winding Way . . . it's not like most hotels. I've worked in hotels where the maids would be fired if they ever tried to talk to upper management. But here, everyone feels more like family. We're in it together. Running things like a team instead of the big boss telling everyone else what to do."

"It sounds amazing." Her description of work at Winding Way didn't surprise me. It was a big part of why I'd always seemed so enchanted by the place. Everyone I ever saw working at the inn always seemed so happy. My child eyes hadn't seen everything by any stretch, but I'd felt the spirit of the place. That said a lot.

She nodded. "It was. It *is*," she amended. "And that's why we have to do something."

Before I could ask her what she meant, footsteps sounded down the hall. We turned and watched as Gaspard filled the doorway. He looked exactly like his photo. Tall, bearded, forearms the size of watermelons, imposing as all get-out.

April introduced us, and he grunted a brief hello. "Nice to meet you. Now. We go to find Ida, yes?"

"Slow down," April said. "We've got to get Lane up to speed before we do."

"Fine," Gaspard said. "I'll summarize. If my staff does not start working again, they are going to find other jobs." His voice was deep, and his accent very . . . French? It sounded French. "No cooks, no food. No food? No Inn."

"So wait. The shutdown isn't permanent?" I said.

"We don't want it to be," April said. "But Ida still claims she isn't ready." She stood up, pacing back and forth in front of the window. "We were all willing to let her take some time after the funeral. It was hard canceling reservations and closing the doors, but Ida's the boss now. She wanted things shut down, so we made it happen. But it can't go on any longer. The wait staff, the housekeeping staff, they're all paid hourly. If we don't open back up, they won't stick around. Plus, there's a wedding this weekend. We can't cancel on them less than a week out."

This was all news I wanted to hear. Mostly because it meant I still had a job. But also, Winding Way was too great a place to shut its doors. At least, not without a fight.

I nodded. "I understand. So what's the plan?"

"We have to convince Ida that opening back up is the right thing to do," Gaspard said.

"How confident are we that she's going to agree?"

"It'll be easier now that you're here," April said. "With Glenda gone, Ida was afraid she'd be running that side of things on her own. Now you can do it, which strengthens our argument."

"Wait, Glenda's gone? Isn't she supposed to train me?"

April grimaced. "Yeah. She's gone. It's not her fault. She was moving anyway, but her mother fell and injured her hip, so she ended up moving a week earlier than she expected."

"So I'm on my own? With a boss who doesn't want to be involved?" It's not like I didn't have any experience. I'd worked in hotels for three years in California before making the move back to NC. But every hotel had its own set of idiosyncrasies. Not fun to imagine figuring them all out without any guidance.

"We'll all help," April said. She looked at Gaspard. "And Ida too, I hope. I don't think it's that she doesn't want to be involved. She'll just need a little time to ease back into it. She worked with Glenda a lot and probably knows the most when it comes to your responsibilities."

"Does she know anything about the wedding this weekend?" Now it was my turn to pace. I stood and followed April's same path. "Because I don't know how I feel about pulling off an event I know nothing about without Glenda here to walk me through it." I perched my hands on my hips.

"We must not get ahead of ourselves," Gaspard said. "If we cannot reopen the inn, there will be no wedding to stress over."

No wedding. The consequences of a cancellation this close to the actual event were huge. And expensive. And *terrible* for the poor, unsuspecting couple.

"Gaspard's right," April said. "First we talk to Ida. Then we worry about the wedding." She took two steps toward me and reached for my hands, squeezing them with her own. "We need you, Lane," she said. "Are you with us?"

New job. No training. A grieving, widowed boss and a wedding to pull off in less than a week? I swallowed my fears and squared my shoulders. What was life without a challenge? "Let's do it."

* * *

It took a solid forty-five minutes. And some tears. And lots of reassuring. But Ida finally conceded. The inn would be open and ready for business by Thursday when the first of the wedding party was set to arrive. After our discussion, Gaspard hurried to the kitchen to contact his staff, leaving April and me to sort through the wedding plans and figure out how everything was supposed to go.

April opened the filing cabinet behind the desk—*my* desk—and pulled out a thick, three-ring binder.

"I tried really hard to get Glenda to keep digital files, but she insisted on binders for the weddings," she said. "You're welcome to revamp the system however you want once you get going, but for now . . ." She dropped the binder onto the coffee table next to the sofa. "This is it. Smith/Callahan wedding—June 22."

I took a deep breath. "Okay. I guess there's nothing to do but dig in."

"I have to go call our department managers about getting their staff back to work," April said. "Will you be okay if I leave you?"

"I'll be great. Thanks for all your help."

I reached for the binder. An hour later, I wanted to kiss Glenda. She'd left such impeccable notes I couldn't imagine there would have been anything left for her to tell me in person even if given the chance. She'd made notes about everything from the color of the toile to the bride's walnut allergy to a physical description of a great aunt who under no circumstances was to be seated in the first three rows during the ceremony or anywhere near the head table at the reception. I was still overwhelmed, but at least I had something to go on.

There was one note, however, that no matter how hard I studied, I could not make sense of. Written in the catering notes underneath the description of the wedding cake order was a scribbled line that read "cheesecake from Joni." I had no idea who Joni was. When I went to the kitchen to ask Gaspard, he was just as clueless.

April at least offered a little bit of direction. "I don't know who Joni is, but that's Ida's handwriting. She'll know."

"Oh. Do you think she'll mind if I ask her? So soon?"

April hesitated. "She might. But honestly, what option do we have?"

Great. Way to bolster my confidence.

Even though she'd hesitated to commit, Ida hadn't denied that reopening the inn was the right decision and was precisely what Thornton would have wanted—for business to carry on as usual. But for Ida, nothing about Winding Way would ever be usual again. Somehow she had to find a new sense of normal. The longer she put that off, the easier it was to stay shrouded in her own pain, which I guessed was exactly what she wanted to do.

I knocked on the door to the main-level suite she and Thornton had occupied for the last twenty years.

"Moved in when their last kid went off to college," April had told me when we'd first visited Ida. "Said it was easier to run the place living on site."

I heard Ida's voice call from inside. "It's open. Come on in." Ida sat in the small sitting area off the kitchen next to a wall of windows looking out into a private garden space. She had a blanket stretched across her lap. It was exactly where we'd left her earlier that morning. She didn't have a book or a magazine, and the television wasn't on. She simply sat, turned away from the door, and stared out the window. She looked over as I approached. "Oh. Hello, dear."

"How are you?" It felt like a hollow question, one I immediately wished I could take back. Because, hello? How did she answer that two weeks after she'd lost her husband?

She must have sensed my discomfort. She gave me a small smile. "Don't fret for having asked. You strike me as the kind of person who wouldn't mind if I told you I needed to have a good cry on your shoulder. I don't, mind you. I think I used up all my tears this morning, but if I did, I think you'd muster up some strength and let it happen without a second thought."

I held the wedding binder close to my chest. "You can tell all that about me?"

She motioned for me to join her on the sofa. "It's in your eyes. Kindness, yes. But also . . ." She seemed to consider. "Bravery," she finally said. "You aren't afraid of much, are you?"

Heat gathered in my cheeks as I lowered myself onto the cushion beside her. "I've had my moments. But I try not to be afraid."

She reached over and took my hand. "You're going to think me an awful person, but I can't remember your name, dear. I know you've taken on Glenda's job, and I know we talked this morning, but . . ." She fiddled with the fringe of her blanket. "Oh, bother. It's completely escaped me."

"Don't worry about it. My name is Lane. Lane Bishop."

"Lane. That's right. Thornton spoke so highly of you. He was excited to have you on board. Are you from around here?"

"My father is from Chapel Hill, so I've always had family to visit close by, but I lived in Asheville growing up."

"Oh, that's a lovely part of the state. Do you have family there too?"

"Just my parents. My mother is from Puerto Rico, and most of her family still lives there. It was my father's work that took them to Asheville. He works for the university there."

"Puerto Rico is a beautiful place. We took our boys once. A long time ago."

"We used to visit every summer. But it's been a few years. I need to go back."

She nodded. "Especially if you still have family there."

"I do. My grandmother. And several aunts and uncles. Lots of cousins."

She gave my hand a gentle squeeze before finally letting go. "Then don't put it off, dear. Go see your family every chance you get."

I leaned over and picked up a photo from the side table. "This is your family, isn't it? Where do your children live?"

"Oh, far away from here, that's for sure." She sighed, and for a moment, I wished I hadn't brought them up. "Those are my two sons on either side. They're both married. One in California, one in Colorado. They were here for the funeral, but they have busy lives and work and, well, I guess I couldn't expect them to stay for long."

"And grandkids?"

"Oh yes. Three. Right there in front. Those are Jared's girls. His brother, Jacob, doesn't have children."

I put the picture back on the table. "You know, I used to hang out here, at the Inn, when I was a little girl."

"Really?"

"My grandmother is Grace Ann Bishop. She lives on the other side of the hedge that lines the west garden. I stayed with her every summer and would sneak over here to play and climb the trees."

Ida gave me a curious look. "I think I remember you. All arms and legs. And there was a boy too, wasn't there?"

I nodded. "My older brother, John."

"I know Grace Ann. Not well, but we used to go to church together. Does she still go to University Baptist?"

"Every Sunday."

"I should go back. It's just been so long . . ." She looked over my shoulder, her gaze distant, then snapped her attention back to me. "After all those years, here you are. Funny how life works, isn't it?"

"I feel very lucky. I always felt like this place was special."

"That it is." Her shoulders slumped forward, and she sighed.

She looked . . . sad? No, *sad* wasn't the right word. It didn't feel potent enough to fully encapsulate everything she'd been through the past week. "You know," I said slowly, "you could if you needed to."

"I could what, dear?"

"Have a good cry. I would stay. And listen."

She gave me a long, hard look. "I like you, Lane. I'll remember that." She patted the sofa between us. "Now. What brought you back to see me?"

I opened the binder. "I've been studying up on the Smith/Callahan wedding. It's happening this weekend, and there's a line here in the catering notes I don't understand."

She reached for a pair of glasses sitting on the table beside her and put them on. "Let me take a look."

"Right here." I pointed to the note in question.

"'Cheesecake from Joni,'" she read. She looked up. "Did I write that?"

"April said it's your handwriting. Any clue what it might mean?"

She pursed her lips, her brows drawn together, then frowned. "'Cheesecake from Joni.' I feel like I should know exactly what it means. Give me a minute." She flipped back to the beginning of the binder. "Is there a photo of the couple?"

"On the first page—right. You found it."

She tapped her finger on the photo. "Okay. It's coming back to me. I remember this bride. She's lovely, but her mother is a walking nightmare. You'll have to keep a close eye on her. Joni—she's the bride's sister. She wanted to make the entire wedding cake, but her sister wouldn't have it because Joni is also the matron of honor and will have plenty of wedding stuff to do without worrying about the cake."

"So the cheesecake is some sort of compromise?"

"It's the groom's cake. Little individual muffin-sized cheesecakes with chocolate top hats on each one."

"Sounds adorable."

"And delicious. She brought one by for us to try. I thought Glenda was going to cry, it tasted so good."

"Okay. So, she's going to bring them by the inn . . . when? Do we know that much? Or is there a number where I can reach her to coordinate?"

"Try looking on the bride's profile sheet. She should be listed with the wedding party."

I flipped to the right page. "Yes, got it. She's right here. Okay. I'll reach out to her and make sure everything is all set. What about Gaspard? He didn't seem to know anything when I asked him about the note."

Ida frowned. "Oh . . . Gaspard. That was supposed to be my job before . . . well, when Thornton . . . I guess I didn't think about it."

"Whatever it was, I'm sure I can handle it."

She shook her head. "My, we're giving you a first day you won't forget, aren't we?"

I laughed. "It hasn't been all that conventional. I'll say that much."

"You're going to do wonderfully, Lane. Thornton said he'd never interviewed anyone quite so capable."

"I appreciate your vote of confidence." I took a deep breath. "So tell me about Gaspard?"

"Gaspard." She grumbled out his name. "He's very particular about his kitchen. We generally have a strict policy about outside food and beverage—it isn't allowed, period. So we're making an exception this time around. But convincing Gaspard to let someone else—an at-home cook without a commercial license, no less—bring food into his kitchen is not going to be easy."

"Is it even legal?"

"It wouldn't be if we were selling the cheesecake, but serving it at the wedding reception won't be a problem. Gaspard will just need a little bit of sweet-talking. We have to convince him to keep his claws in, or else he'll eat that poor woman alive."

I tried to look confident. "I can talk to him."

She shot me a sideways look. "You don't know him like the rest of us do."

"It'll be fine. It has to be, right? What's done is done?"

She nodded. "If he doesn't agree, you come tell me, and I'll take care of it. He might think he's in charge of the kitchen, but I'm still the one who signs his paychecks." She frowned, and the light fell from her eyes. "At least, I am now."

It was nice she offered to toss her weight around if I needed it, but I really didn't want her worrying about a surly French chef. I reached out and touched her shoulder, then stood. "I don't think it will come to that, but thank you for offering. And for everything. For all your help."

"It was nice to feel useful," she said. "Thank you for asking. And don't hesitate to come find me again if you need me."

"I won't. Thanks again."

April met me in the hallway on my way back to my office. She held up a lanyard attached to what looked like a security badge and a key-card. "Your keys to the kingdom."

"Thanks. How does it all work?"

"The badge doesn't really do anything except make you look official. But this keycard will get you anywhere you need to go. Through the back office door, through the main door, and into any of the guest rooms."

I took the lanyard and hung it around my neck. "Sounds simple enough."

"It's cutting-edge technology around here. It's a wonder we convinced Thornton to go through with it, as old school as he was. It was literally less than five years ago that we started using key cards instead of actual metal keys to open the rooms."

"Wow. That is old school."

"Did you solve the cheesecake mystery?"

"I did. Ida was really helpful."

"She's a great lady," April said. "And she's great at what she does. I think in time she'll realize how much she still wants to be a part of things."

"Yeah, she liked that I asked her. Said it felt good to feel useful."

We paused outside my office door.

"Are you hungry?" April asked. "I'm headed to the kitchen to see what scraps Gaspard has left for us."

"Definitely. But I've got a few calls I want to make first." Mostly I just wanted to get all the cheesecake details ironed out before I went to Gaspard and told him he'd be serving someone else's dessert.

"I'll see if I can get Gaspard to bring you something. He's rough around the edges, our chef, but he's a big softy at heart. He might be feeling generous since you're new."

Yeah. New and about to make him really mad. How fun. "Anything would be great," I told April. "I'm not picky."

April would stand by me though. I could tell. For all the reasons I had for my first day at work to be flat-out terrible—finding the place basically shut down, participating in a staged intervention, and then taking on a wedding that was less than a week out—surprisingly, things still felt like they were going to be okay. The people of Winding Way were already treating me like family, like they believed in me and wanted my help. I felt completely accepted, and I hadn't been at the inn six hours.

Half an hour later, Gaspard appeared in the open doorway of my office. He held a Styrofoam to-go container and a twelve-ounce can of Coke. "April said you were hungry."

I smiled. "Starving."

He handed me the food. "Do not get used to personal delivery. It is only because you are new."

"Noted. Thanks for the special treatment."

"Now." He crossed his arms over his chest. "The rules of my kitchen: There is a refrigerator in the back. Not the walk-in. That one is off-limits. But in the back, close to my desk, there is a small one for the staff. Anything you find there, you are welcome to enjoy. Some days it will be empty, but most of the time, it is not. That's all you have access to. Understand? You eat food from anywhere else in my kitchen and you are no longer welcome."

"Understood. Staff fridge only. Kitchen off-limits."

He grunted. "How is the wedding?"

I looked over the spread of information in front of me. "It's a lot to go over, but I think we'll be able to pull it off."

"I have the original menus Glenda approved. Has anything changed?"

I shook my head. "I don't think so. I'll double-check though. If there are any changes, I'll make sure you get them."

"My order for the butcher will need to be in by 10:00 a.m. on Wednesday."

"Okay. I'll get them to you before ten."

"Before nine if I am to have time to review what to order."

Sheesh. "Right. That makes sense. By nine on Wednesday, then."

"Very good." He turned to leave.

"Actually, Gaspard, there's one more thing we need to discuss." He crossed his arms and looked back. "Not a big thing," I continued. "A tiny thing, really. Not a big deal *at all.*"

He narrowed his eyes. "For the number of times you've now said it is not a big deal, I'm beginning to think it is."

"Remember when I asked you about Joni and her cheesecake?"

He threw his hands into the air. "Ah. I was afraid of this."

"Just hear me out, okay? Joni is the sister of the bride, the matron of honor, and the maker of what I've heard are very delicious, tiny, top-hat-wearing cheesecakes."

"And she's bringing them to the wedding."

"Yes."

"And I'm supposed to serve them."

"Yes."

"Alongside the food I went to a very expensive culinary school to learn how to make myself."

"Yes?"

"You know, we have a no-outside-food-or-drink policy for a reason."

"I do know. But just this once, Ida believes we can compromise. It's important to Joni. It's an act of love for her sister."

"An act of love. How sweet. What if her act of love makes somebody sick and the blame gets pinned on me?"

"I thought of that. Which is why we should do something like this." I turned around and grabbed the tiny sign I'd made minutes before. I read it to Gaspard. "'Cheesecakes provided with love by Joni Anderson—

sister of the bride.' See? We put this on the table wherever the cheese-cakes are being served, and people know they aren't yours."

Gaspard grunted. "She is not going to use my kitchen."

"Absolutely not. The cheesecakes will arrive fully prepared and ready to serve."

"Do they need to stay cold? How much room do I need to clear in the walk-in? One shelf? Two? Should I clear an entire wall for Joni and her stupid little cheesecake hats?"

"Gaspard, I get it. It's annoying. I would be annoyed too. But there is literally nothing that can be done about it now. The cheesecakes are coming. Friday afternoon. They'll have to be refrigerated overnight, then served at the reception on Saturday. Since this is going to be my very first wedding at the Winding Way Inn and I'm trying desperately to seem like I know what I'm doing and like I wasn't just dropped into the middle of a crazy situation with no one to train me and piles of responsibilities I'm somehow supposed to know about all on my own, I'm asking for a favor." I finally took a breath. "Please. I really need you to be okay with this."

He still wore a scowl, but I could see acceptance in his eyes. "Fine. But only because this is a mess you didn't make and it wouldn't be fair for me to make you accountable."

Uh, no, it was a mess of Ida's making, surly chef dude. And she's the big boss lady now. I was pretty sure if Ida had been the one speaking to him about this, he wouldn't have responded like he did with me. Still, he'd agreed, and I'd spared Ida a little bit of drama. That was all that mattered in the end.

I opened the to-go box he'd brought and pulled out half of the sand-wich inside. "This looks great, Gaspard. Thank you."

He grunted. Again. Guess good communication wasn't necessarily a requirement for good food. He turned and headed for the door.

"Oh, hey, Gaspard?" He turned around slowly, his patience wearing visibly thin. "You know what?" I said. "Never mind. I just had one more question, but I can ask April."

"It has nothing to do with enemy cheesecake?"

I rolled my eyes. "No."

"Fine," he said with another grunt. "What's your question?"

I almost wanted to ask him something else about the cheesecake just to spite the guy. I'd never met anyone who remained in such a perpetual bad mood. But even if I needed reminders, I *was* a grown-up. I put my sandwich down. "I was just wondering if you know who is over facilities. I need to review the room set for the rehearsal dinner and reception. And also figure out why Glenda wrote a note about checking on the tent."

He scratched his chin. "Carlos is over facilities. Do not ask me if I know how to reach him. I *don't*."

Carlos. I immediately wondered if it was the same Carlos I'd met on the soccer field but quickly dismissed the thought. It wasn't that uncommon of a name. "That's fine. I'm sure April knows. I'll ask her." I popped open the Coke and motioned to the food. "Thanks again for this. I really do appreciate it."

"Like I said, it won't happen again."

One bite of the turkey sandwich and any ill will I'd felt toward Gaspard completely evaporated. I actually sighed with pleasure as I ate. Baby arugula, some sort of cranberry chutney, and caramelized onions, with smoked gouda melted all over the entire thing. Hands down the best sandwich I'd had in a really long time. I was almost disappointed to put it down when I heard my phone buzz from across the room.

But then Jamie popped into my head, and I hurried to my desk to see if the text was from him.

December 6. Cal/Penn State. Championship game.

He didn't identify himself, but I knew it was him. Who else would start a conversation with soccer stats?

I licked a spot of chutney off my finger and keyed back my response. *That was an awesome game.*

I was there. I saw you play.

I read his words once and then again. He was there? And he remembered me? *If you saw me play, then you saw us win.*

I should have recognized you, he texted back. *You were amazing.*

I hadn't thought about that game in a while. My senior year at Berkeley, we played in the championship against Penn State. It was a close game—almost too close—but we'd eked out a win in the end.

I read Jamie's text again. I *had* been amazing.

Not still licking your wounds, then, I see. Thank you for noticing, I responded.

Ha. It took awhile. I haven't lost like that in a long time.

Then you were probably due. Losing is good for us every now and then.

A full minute passed before his next message popped up. *I have a feeling you don't lose much.*

You know me so well already. I hit send, then added one more line. *I'm glad you texted.*

I'm glad you gave me your number, he responded.

I smiled. *I'm glad you're glad.*

What are you doing later?

Working. Forever working. First day today, and I'm already drowning.

How about Wednesday? he texted back. *Have dinner with me?*

Yes, please.

Pick you up at 7?

Sounds good.

Address? Also, what do you love to eat?

I texted him my address and thought about his question. I loved to eat pretty much everything, but I missed my favorite sushi place out in Berkeley and wanted to find a replacement in Chapel Hill. *How do you feel about sushi?*

His reply popped up almost instantly. *Let's do it.*

Jamie: Brothers. And by brothers I mostly mean Simon. I need food advice.
Where can I get good sushi?

Dave: You don't like sushi.

Cooper: Don't discourage him, Dave. He's finally branching out a little.

Simon: He's not branching out. He's trying to impress a girl.

Dave: The soccer chick?

Simon: Her name is Lane.

Dave: Typical. He loses like a two-year-old and STILL gets a date.

Cooper: Jealous, Dave? I'm telling Katie.

Dave: Just making a point.

Jamie: Raw animal magnetism, guys. I can't help it. Sushi. Come on.
I don't have much time.

Simon: Go to Sakura. If she asks what's good, suggest 4, 11, and 16.
Those are the best ones.

Jamie: Got it. Thanks.

Chapter 3

I DROPPED MY HEAD ONTO my desk. There was no way I was making dinner with Jamie. Wedding plans had been exploding all afternoon, and the end didn't seem anywhere near. With calls in to three different vendors and answers I needed before the end of the evening or else, I was completely tied up. I called Jamie just after five thirty to explain.

"A call this close to date time is never good news," he said after saying hello.

"I know! I'm so sorry. I'm still at work, and I'm totally swamped. I've been on the phone with linen suppliers all afternoon trying to find Wedgwood blue napkins because *our* linen supplier promised their Wedgwood blue to someone else, and all they have is navy, and the bride really doesn't feel good about navy napkins. On top of that, April overbooked the inn this weekend, so we have to relocate three guests from the wedding party to another hotel, which I'm sure is going to make everyone so happy."

"Sounds like you've had quite the day."

"For a third day on the job, it hasn't been too bad, but I don't think I'm getting out of here anytime soon. April's on her way to my office right now so we can sort out the room situation."

"What if I bring dinner to you? I'll come late. Eight o'clock?"

I considered his offer. I *would* need to eat. And by eight, we'd probably be close to finished anyway. "That sounds great. You're sure you don't mind? We can reschedule if that would be easier."

"I don't want to reschedule. I've been looking forward to seeing you all day."

My heart did a weird flutter thing, and I smiled. Bonus points for his killer confidence. "Okay. I'm at Winding Way Inn," I told him. "I'll text you the address."

At 8:02, Jamie texted. *I'm in the parking lot. Where to?*

I was finishing a work call with a neighboring hotel, so I held up my phone, showing the text to April. She nodded her understanding. "I'll go let him in," she whispered.

A few minutes later, she led him into my office, just as I was hanging up the phone. She paused in the doorway long enough to give me an appraising nod and two thumbs up. "I'm going to head out now," she said. "I think we've accomplished all we can for the night. I'll check on Ida, but then I'm out."

"Sounds good. I'll see you tomorrow."

April smiled at Jamie. "It was nice to meet you."

He nodded. "You too." He turned his attention back to me.

I was nervous. *Too* nervous. It had been so long since I'd actually done any real dating. I felt completely out of practice.

"Quiet place," he said.

"Unusually so right now. The inn's been closed the past couple of weeks."

"Really? What for?"

I filled him in on Thornton's death and my less-than-conventional start to my new job. Terrible first-date material, but at least I wasn't stuttering. Or drooling.

"And you had no idea until you got here?"

"Not at all. We open back up tomorrow. Hopefully things will settle into a normal routine soon. The past few days have been totally crazy."

We stood in the middle of my office for several seconds just staring at each other. He looked good. Dark jeans. A navy-blue polo. Hair kind of on-purpose messy.

"You look really great, Lane."

I liked the way he said my name. "Thank you. I feel a little worse for wear after my very long day, but I'll take it."

He held up the bags and motioned to the sitting area off to the side. "Should we eat over here?"

"Yeah, this is perfect."

He unloaded the bags of food, handing me a water bottle, a napkin, and a set of chopsticks. Already, I started to feel a little more relaxed. Jamie had a very easy way about him, and it quickly spilled over to me. I settled into my chair. "So I'm going to warn you," I said, pointing my chopsticks in his direction. "I'm somewhat of a sushi connoisseur. There was this place in Berkeley that was so fantastic. It's turned me into a big-time snob because nothing is ever as good."

He gave me a sideways glance. "You know I didn't *make* the sushi, right? I just picked it up."

"Yes, but you ordered it," I said with a grin. "I'm just saying. I hope you chose wisely."

"The pressure is on, then, huh?" He handed me a tray, and I pried off the lid. The roll was gorgeous. It looked like a shrimp tempura roll but fancier, topped with slivers of avocado and mango, dressed with tiny caviar and drizzled with shrimp sauce.

It took only a few bites for me to decide I was gloriously happy about my sushi. "This is amazing," I said. "What is it?"

"I only know numbers," Jamie said. "Four, eleven, and sixteen. Don't ask me which is which though." He took a bite of his sushi roll and grimaced. Like actually made an awful face.

I stared. "You don't like sushi."

He swallowed, then took a big gulp of water. "Sure I do. It's fine."

"Ha, yeah. I don't believe you for a second. Why didn't you say something?"

"I aim to please, Lane. You asked for sushi, and making you happy seemed a little more important than, um, having *cooked* food."

"Oh!" I groaned in mock disapproval. "Your disdain for this perfectly perfect meal kills me. Here—try this one." I offered him a piece of my shrimp tempura. "This one is all cooked. You might like it more."

He eyed the caviar but didn't complain as he took it and shoved it into his mouth. He raised an eyebrow while he chewed. "Okay," he said. "It's a little better."

I added a sliver of pickled ginger to my next piece. Maybe he wasn't impressed, but I was blown away. North Carolina did sushi right. "I have to go to this place in person. Seriously. You did good. This is really amazing."

He nodded. "I'm glad you like it."

I leaned back into the sofa. "So, soccer. Where'd you play?"

"University of Virginia."

"Great school. What about your brothers? Any of them play collegiate?"

"Cooper might, maybe. After his mission. And Simon could have, but he tore is ACL his senior year of high school. That derailed his college plans."

"That leaves Dave. He's your twin, right? And he's engaged?"

His eyebrows went up.

"Sorry. Chloe pretty much gave me the rundown on your family."

He put down his food and leaned back. "Knowing Chloe, it included shoe sizes and favorite foods."

"And childhood fears. Really, Jamie. Spiders? Not very original."

"Anything with eight legs should never be trusted." He grinned. "Dave went to Virginia with me. We were on the same team."

"What? Brothers on the same team? That's awesome."

"Yeah. It was pretty fun."

I leaned forward. "So here's another thing Chloe told me. *You*"—I paused. For dramatic emphasis, of course—"don't date." I crossed my arms. "They call you untouchable. All of you. It's a family description."

He ran his hand across his jaw and sighed. "Yeah, we've heard that before."

"Is it true? No one dates?"

"Fundamentally, there are problems with the assumption," Jamie said. "Because Dave is engaged, and you can't get that way without dating. And Simon has a girlfriend, which also happened *through* dating."

"True," I agreed. "But what about you?"

"I'm here, aren't I?"

"Yes, but I can only imagine how surprised that would make Chloe. What made you change your policy?"

He dropped his chopsticks and took a drink of water. "Maybe I was waiting to meet the right person."

I smiled. "And you're sure that's me, huh?"

"I'm sure I'm ready to find out."

By then the nervousness I'd felt before dinner had vanished. This guy was into me. And he wasn't afraid to say so. It was hard to keep my shoulders from doing a little victory dance.

"What about you?" he asked. "Why aren't you hanging out with the singles group?"

It was only fair. I'd brought up his dating, but . . . *ugh*. "Do I really need a reason?"

"Try me. I'm guessing I'll probably understand."

"One too many root beer floats?"

He chuckled. "I think I follow, but that answer's still a cop-out."

I shrugged. "I don't know what else to say. There was a huge singles group in California, and I guess after a little while, the whole scene made me tired. I'm not opposed to singles groups on principle. I realize there's a reason to have them. I just wanted a break."

"Fair enough," he said. "And better than a really awful ex-boyfriend story."

I laughed. "That sounded like a loaded comment. Have you heard one of those lately?"

He groaned. "Ugh, I shouldn't have brought it up."

"Oh, come on. I love a good story."

He hesitated before plowing into his story with a weird sort of fervor. "It's this girl I used to know in college. She called me out of the blue last week, started texting all the time. It's weird. We weren't even really friends. But she's been telling me all this garbage. *She* has a crazy ex story. Stalking, restraining orders, you name it."

"Wow. Why'd she suddenly start texting you?"

"I'm not going to tell you. You'll just laugh."

I forced a serious expression. "I will not. Promise."

He leaned forward, his elbows propped on his knees, and looked up at me through his very long lashes. "She said after years of chasing the wrong kind of guy, she's ready for someone with more traditional family values. Which is crazy. I didn't even know her that well. I don't know what she thinks she knows about my values."

"Whatever. You're Mormon. Does she need to know more than that?"

"It's not like Dave and I spent our weekends preaching on street corners."

"No, but you also didn't spend your weekends getting drunk and acting like idiots. Women notice that sort of thing."

He huffed out a laugh. "Don't be so sure."

"Ohhh, he has a past."

He rolled his eyes at my teasing. "We probably fell somewhere between drunken idiot and preaching on the corner. It just feels like a weird reason to reach out to someone. 'Hey, five years ago you seemed like a real family man. Want to hook up?' Plus, I'm not encouraged by the restraining order."

"Well, I promise I have no scary ex-boyfriends for you to worry about."

"Any . . . not-so-scary ex-boyfriends?" he asked.

"Nice transition," I said. "You handled that well."

He didn't miss a beat. "Thank you. It took a lot to get to that one question, but here we are."

Seriously. The guy was adorable. Confident but in a totally grounded way. That he wasn't afraid to admit he'd been digging for information made me like him even more. "One boyfriend in high school. Nice guy. Catholic. Pretty sure he's living in Asheville, working at some brewery downtown. I didn't date much in college. Just played a lot of soccer. I had one boyfriend off and on through most of my junior year," I continued. "I liked him, but he had this super traditional family and . . . I don't know. They never said anything directly, but I got the feeling they were nervous about him dating someone who wasn't white."

Jamie stared. "That's . . . I thought people were past that kind of nonsense."

I shrugged. "A lot of people are. Others, not so much."

He leaned back in his chair. "That's messed up."

"It is what it is, but I refuse to dwell on all the negative. It's out there. And, yeah, things are better in a lot of ways, but it's not going away anytime soon. The thing is, no matter how much it hurts, pain for pain won't solve anything. Being strong is moving forward, right?"

"My Uncle Anton is black," Jamie blurted. His face instantly flooded with color, like he realized how trite his words sounded halfway through saying them. "Sorry," he continued. "I said that like I deserve brownie points for having a little diversity in my family. I only mentioned it because I remember when we were growing up that . . . stuff happened. Especially within the Church—people had a hard time. I was fifteen when he and my aunt got married, and I remember sitting in the kitchen listening to Mom and Aunt Julie talking about some of the stuff people said."

"Most people just don't get it. Not because they can't but because they don't have the experience. The hard part is that being called out on that makes people defensive, and then you can't make any progress because people are too busy defending their own narrow viewpoint. It takes time. And a lot of talking. Confronting truth even when it's ugly."

"I like that. My mother used to always tell us as kids to *see bigger*. Take the blinders off, you know?"

"Yeah. It's hard though."

"I think your perspective is pretty amazing. I mean, you play it pretty cool considering how many reasons you have not to."

I held up my hands, palms out. "It's better than being angry all the time. When my mom moved to Utah from Puerto Rico to attend BYU, there were some who weren't very open-minded. My *abuela* always told her, 'When people underestimate you, smile, walk away, then blow them away with your brilliance.'"

He smiled. "That's great advice."

"Abuela is a smart lady." I nestled deeper into the cushions of my chair. "So I guess that's more history than you bargained for when you started rooting around for old boyfriends."

"No, I'm glad it came up."

I was glad it came up too. I appreciated guys willing to talk about it. "What about you? Any crazy girlfriend stories?"

"Not a one. I'm normal and boring. One serious girlfriend pre-mission. She was married before I got home. And I haven't really gotten serious with anyone since."

"Wow. That is boring."

"Right? I think so too. What about the rest of your family? Does anyone live in Chapel Hill, still?"

I took another bite before answering. "My parents live in Asheville— that's where I grew up. Mom is a psychiatrist, and Dad is the basketball coach at UNCA. Then there's just me and my older brother, John."

"Basketball. That's awesome. Do you ever play?"

I shook my head. "One soccer game the summer I turned six, and I never gave another sport a chance. Dad tried. I'm tall, even. He claimed it was a waste of good height, but nothing else ever stuck. Dad loves sports in general though, so he didn't mind too much."

"Did he play basketball? Before he started coaching?"

I nodded. "College ball—for BYU. That's where he met my mom and joined the Church."

"For real?"

"For real. His best friend growing up was Mormon. They played ball together, so John convinced him to go to BYU with him. They had a decent basketball team, so Dad went for it."

"And found more than he expected, I guess."

"To say the least. A shiny new religion and a tiny Puerto Rican wife. You should see them together. He's six foot six, and she's barely five foot four."

Jamie laughed. He had good laugh lines. Creases in his cheeks and around his eyes. And those eyes—they literally sparkled. Like he was an open book happy to let me see just how much fun he was having. And we *were* having fun. For over an hour, we continued to talk. Mostly about soccer. A little more about our families. A lot about my work. After a particularly long stretch of feeling like I'd done nothing but talk about myself, I turned the conversation back to him. It felt like he'd been avoiding the subject of his own work, which made me all the more curious to know about it.

"Okay, spill it. How does the handsome Jamie Hamilton spend his weekdays?"

He leaned back and clasped his hands, propping his elbows on the armrests of his chair. "I'm in business with David."

"Yeah? Doing what?"

"Software and app development."

"Well that's a vague, techy-sounding answer. Do you work on anything I would recognize?"

He held out his hand. "Maybe. Can I see your phone a minute?"

"Such a personal request," I teased. I used my thumbprint to unlock the screen, then handed it over. He scrolled through a few screens, typed something, then gave it back. He'd navigated to the app store and pulled up the specs for a popular logic puzzle game. Popular was kind of an understatement. The game was huge. Annoyingly huge. I scrolled over the page, trying to figure out what he was showing me, and then I saw it. The game developers were listed as David and James Hamilton.

I looked up. "You did this?"

"Don't get too impressed. Dave is the brain behind the technology. I do the marketing."

"But wait. The entire thing? LogiX? That's all you guys?"

"Maybe you should sound a little more surprised. I promise it's not hurting my ego at all."

"No! I don't mean to sound surprised; it's just . . . impressive. I don't know anyone who doesn't have this game on their phone. I'm stuck on level seventy-eight. It's driving me crazy."

"Don't tell Dave. He loves hearing that kind of thing."

"Wow. That's very cool." I placed my phone back on the table, feeling more than a little awestruck. It wasn't quite running-into-Bruno-Mars exciting, but still. Pretty awesome. Jamie had done something *big*. "How did you get started?"

"Dave went to grad school at UNC. He started working on it during his last semester and then continued after he graduated. I didn't do grad school, so I moved down here and camped in his apartment until the app launched. It was a gamble. I could have found work right after graduation, but Dave was convinced that when he finished, it would be huge. So I waited, then we launched, and here we are."

"Do all four of you live together?"

"No. Simon's got his own place. He's an accountant—graduated from Duke a few years back—and likes the quiet too much to live with us. He blames it on work and his need to focus. We just think he's boring. Cooper's with me and Dave, but temporarily. He'll head back home at the end of the summer."

"For his mission."

"Yep."

"Duke and UNC graduates in the same family," I said. "Bet that makes for lively dinner conversations."

"You have no idea. The rivalry runs deep. What about your dad? He grew up here, right? Who's his team?"

"He's totally a Tar Heel. Sometimes I think it's more about Duke *not* winning though. His team will be whatever team has the best chance of beating the Blue Devils."

He chuckled. "It's a good thing you aren't dating Simon. That man's loyalty to his alma mater is frightening."

"Where did you guys grow up?" I asked.

"Bristol, Virginia. Our parents are still there. What about you? Has Asheville always been home?"

I nodded. "As long as I can remember."

"I've visited Asheville before. Great food."

"But not great sushi, right?"

He grinned. "I wouldn't know about that."

I glanced at the clock hanging on the wall behind my desk. It was nearly ten. "I should get home," I said.

He stood and started gathering the dinner mess. "I hope I haven't kept you too long."

"No, it's been great. You're easy to talk to."

"Thanks. But we still need to talk about the most important thing." He dropped the last of the food containers into the bag and shoved his hands into his pockets.

"What's that?"

"The scheduling of our rematch."

"Ha! I knew it! Carlos told me you wouldn't be able to stand the fact that I'd won."

"I can stand it fine. I just like a good game as much as the next guy."

"Hmm. I'm sure that's all it is."

"Listen. I'm doing this youth soccer clinic with my brothers. It's through the YMCA. Simon's accounting firm sponsors it so underprivileged kids can come free of charge. You interested in helping out?"

Of course. Four handsome, sexy, soccer-playing brothers *would* run a clinic for underprivileged kids, wouldn't they. I might have rolled my eyes at the utter perfection of it all had I not been wrapping up a date with one of those handsome brothers myself. I cleared my throat, already knowing whenever that clinic was, I was *not* going to miss it. "Um, maybe. When is it?"

"Five to seven p.m. Tuesdays and Thursdays. It starts next week and runs for three weeks."

I nodded. "That might work. Really, it depends on how work is going. I can't guarantee I'll be finished in time." I almost laughed out loud at my own casual performance. I would *absolutely* be finished on time.

He took a step closer. "Don't guarantee it, then. Just . . . try."

"Where does the rematch come into play?"

He was standing close enough that I could feel his warmth, smell his aftershave. Totally distracting but in the best kind of way. "Well, I mean, we'll be *on* the soccer field," he said. "With balls and goals and everything. Once the kids leave, I'm sure we can work something out."

"Oh, I see. It makes sense you'd want to wait for everyone else to go home. That way when you lose again, it won't be so embarrassing." I reached up and gave his chest a playful pat.

"Oh, ho, ho, that's the way it's going to be, is it?"

I grinned. "What? Think you might be . . . *in over your head?*"

He laughed. "Okay. I totally deserved that."

I gathered my things and turned off the lights, then we walked together to the back door. April had locked up on her way out, so I used my newly acquired, all-powerful keycard to get us through the door and into the parking lot. Only two cars remained.

He pointed to my car. "This is you?"

"Yep. Thanks for bringing me dinner," I said.

"Thanks for letting me come." He put a hand on my arm and leaned in, kissing me on the cheek. The closeness of him, even for the briefest of moments, was enough to start my heart hammering. Jamie lingered, his body leaning into mine, and grinned. He knew exactly what sort of affect he had on me. Probably on women in general.

I rolled my eyes and pushed him away. "Okay. Enough of your spell-casting man magic."

He grinned. "I'll see you around."

Cocky jerk, I thought to myself.

I couldn't wait to see him again.

Simon: How was dinner?
Jamie: Sushi was disgusting. Company was great.
Simon: You have terrible taste.
Jamie: I won't tell Lane you said so.
Simon: In food, moron. I'm sure Lane is very nice.
*Jamie: She's going to help with the soccer clinic next week. Can you get
       her a coaching shirt?*
Simon: Will do.
Simon: Did Lane like the sushi?
Jamie: Yeah. Said it was amazing.
Simon: See? You do have terrible taste.

Chapter 4

I STOPPED BY THE FRONT desk on my way into work the next morning. "Hey, April, do you know how to get ahold of Carlos? He's the facilities guy, right? Will he be in today?" Surely he would be. The inn was officially open for business. Hopefully *everyone* would be back in.

"He's here. Somewhere outside, I think. Want me to tell him you'd like to see him?"

"Yes, please. I just need to go over a few things for the wedding."

"You got it. I'll let him know."

I turned to leave, but she called me back.

"Hey, how was your date last night?" she asked.

I gave her a casual shrug but couldn't keep from smiling. "It was fine."

"Fine? Right. I'm sure that's all it was. He's gorgeous."

"You should see him with his brothers. Seriously amazing genetics in the Hamilton family."

"Wait, there're more? Jamie has brothers?"

"Three of them. All taken though, so don't get your hopes up. Two are in relationships already, and the other is weeks away from getting his mission call."

"His what?"

"Oh. It's a Church thing. You know Mormon missionaries? Shirts and ties? Name tags? Bicycles?"

"Oh! I saw some over on Franklin Street the other day."

"Right. You don't get to choose where you go, so getting your mission call is a pretty big deal. A little like opening college acceptance letters, except you only get one, and it might send you to New Zealand."

"Wow. That does sound big. Oh, look." She pointed over my shoulder. "There's Carlos now."

I turned. "Carlos?" His hair was pulled back in the same ponytail he'd worn on the soccer field, but his shorts and jersey were replaced by a dark pair of work pants and a royal-blue polo, the Winding Way logo printed on the upper left corner.

He smiled. "Lane, from the soccer field."

I shook my head, eyes wide with surprise, and crossed the lobby to meet him. "Would it be weird if I hugged you? I'm so happy to see a familiar face!"

He laughed and opened his arms for a hug. He looked at the name badge hanging around my neck. "You work here? Welcome to Winding Way. I can imagine you've had an overwhelming start."

"To say the least," I said. "It hasn't been at all what I expected. I do have some questions for you, if you have a minute."

"Sure thing. What can I do to help?"

"It's kind of a long list, but let's start simple. What do I need to know about the tent?"

Half an hour later, Carlos had sorted out the tent dilemma, solved my where-to-put-the-DJ-if-it-rains problem, and given me specific estimates of setup/takedown times for both the ceremony and the reception for the Smith/Callahan wedding. It was the happiest coincidence of my week—having yet another person at the inn rooting for my success, especially since Chef Gaspard still seemed bugged about the cheesecake invasion and was limiting his communication with me to nothing but grunts.

It also helped that Glenda called Wednesday afternoon and talked to me for ninety glorious minutes. Anything I hadn't already figured out from her wedding file, she told me. In very specific detail. I went into the weekend feeling armed and ready to tackle the wedding like I'd been there planning from day one.

But nothing made my week better than Jamie. He texted me every day.
Questions about the wedding.
How's it going?
Great.
Is Carlos being nice to you?
Always.
Questions about me.
Any pets?
Nope.

Where does your brother live? Is he married?
Not married. He's a pediatrician living in Chicago.
Favorite food besides sushi?
Watermelon.
And my favorite question.
Can I see you this weekend?
Yes. Definitely yes.

We made plans for Sunday afternoon since the rest of my weekend was completely wrapped up in the Smiths and the Callahans and making sure Aunt Erma was seated comfortably in the fourth row.

* * *

"What exactly did Erma do?" Carlos whispered. We stood together in the back of the outdoor tent, the ceremony minutes away from starting.

"I have no idea. Her sister is the grandmother of the bride, I think. The conflict lies between the two of them. Glenda made it seem like it was a very long-standing feud."

My cell phone buzzed—a text from Gaspard. *Problem in the kitchen.*

I grumbled. "I have to go check on this," I told Carlos. "Your men are ready to go? After the ceremony, we'll bring everyone onto the back patio for cocktails while the wedding party does photos, and then—"

"We're clear to set up for the reception." He finished my thought with a grin. "We've got it under control."

"But no longer than thirty minutes. Work as fast as you can."

He smiled. "Lane. Breathe. We've done this before. Everything is going to be fine."

I squeezed his arm before walking away. "Thank you."

In the kitchen, things weren't looking quite so sunny. I found Gaspard red-faced and fuming, his arms folded tightly across his chest, nearly nose to nose with Joni—matron of honor and cheesecake maker extraordinaire.

"I don't care if there are *no* walnuts in the bride's salad. There can't be walnuts in *any* salad," Joni said. Her voice filled the entire kitchen.

"Is your sister going to be picking off of everyone else's plates? You said she is allergic to walnuts. On her salad? *I take out the walnuts.*"

"What's going on, Gaspard?" I asked.

He turned to face me. "I cannot deal with this woman telling me how to run my kitchen."

"You aren't listening to me." Joni spoke through her teeth. "If *anyone* at the reception eats a walnut and then says hello to the bride, if they kiss her on the cheek or even just breathe on her, she will break out in hives. There cannot be walnuts at the reception. End of story." She turned and looked at me. "We told Glenda this. We told her how bad the allergy is. I can't believe there are even walnuts in the kitchen."

My heart dropped. The bride was allergic to walnuts. I *knew* the bride was allergic to walnuts. I'd read as much in the catering notes. I'd even thought about it when I'd sent menus to Gaspard earlier in the week. I even remembered thinking I needed to double-check to make sure Gaspard was aware of the allergy. The *deadly* allergy. But I hadn't done it. I'd seen the note, I'd read the note, I'd assumed Gaspard had seen the same note. But I hadn't double-checked. Which meant the seventy-five already plated salads with walnuts sitting in front of us were ruined because of me. I looked at Gaspard, my eyes pleading, hoping he understood how sorry I was for making this huge mistake but also hoping he knew how important it was that he fix the problem.

I reached for Joni's hand. "You know what? You're exactly right. There shouldn't be walnuts anywhere on the entire premises. And there won't be. We're going to start from scratch and get all new salads made, and it's going to be fine. But right now you need to come with me. The ceremony is going to start any minute, and you not being there might also make your sister break out in hives, walnuts or not."

Joni took a deep breath. "Right. The ceremony." She smoothed out her lavender bridesmaid dress and glanced back at Gaspard. "But you can't just pick them out. There will be . . . remnants. Little pieces. I can't let her have an allergic reaction on her wedding day."

I reached for her arm, giving it a gentle tug. "We won't pick them out. You have my word."

She nodded again. "Okay. Things will be okay?"

"Things are going to be fine. But you need to go walk down the aisle. Right now."

I walked her back to the rest of the wedding party, intensely grateful for tiny top-hat cheesecakes, because as annoying as it was to deal with Gaspard's frustration over Joni's bringing her own dessert into his kitchen, if her presence saved us from the bride going into anaphylactic shock, it was all worth it.

Back in the kitchen, Gaspard was fuming but was at least following through with what I'd promised. All the plated salads had been dumped and removed from the kitchen, and Gaspard was starting fresh.

He glared at me hard when I came in. "I am not going to have enough greens."

"How can we fix it? We have ninety minutes until they eat. Is that enough time to buy more?"

"Buy? From where? The supermarket? This is not regular lettuce. You cannot buy it in a bag in the produce section."

I wanted to scream. Yes, we'd made a mistake, but his sarcasm was not going to help us fix the problem.

Gaspard continued to fume under his breath. "Allergic to walnuts. You would think that would be the sort of detail someone might mention to the chef."

"Her allergy was written in the catering notes. I'm willing to own my role in this. I should have double-checked, and I'm sorry I didn't. But right now we need to focus on *fixing* the problem. Please. What do you need, and where can I buy it?"

He huffed. "Spring greens. But make sure arugula is included. Don't go to a regular grocery store. The farmer's market on Estes Drive would be best."

"How far away is Estes?" I hadn't lived in the city long enough to know how to get anywhere.

"We have ninety minutes?" He shook his head. "It's too far. Try the Weaver Street Market in Southern Village. It will cost us double, but it should have what we need."

"How much should I get?"

"About twenty-five salads' worth."

It was baffling to me that he could look at a giant bowl of lettuce and tell me exactly how many salads he would be short, but I didn't have time to question. I needed to go to the grocery store.

Except I couldn't go. I was in charge of the entire wedding. If anything else went wrong, I was the only person to handle it.

I turned back to Gaspard. "Gaspard, do you not have kitchen staff who can run to the market? The wedding just started. I can't leave."

He was already shaking his head halfway through my sentence. "I am already understaffed. Not everyone lasted through the shutdown. That I even have everyone I need to pull this wedding off is a miracle." A part of me thought he really just wanted to make this my problem to fix.

I thought through the rest of the staff: April; Carlos; Sylvia, the head housekeeper. They were all swamped covering their own responsibilities. Ida crossed my mind, but seeing the inn bustling with activity *without* Thornton there to oversee everything had sent her into a tailspin, and she'd retired to her room for the day. I couldn't ask her to drive to the grocery store for lettuce. Short of pulling a gardener off the grounds, I was completely out of ideas.

My phone buzzed with an incoming text, and I cringed. If it was anyone else telling me something was wrong with the wedding, I was going to toss my phone into the koi pond in the back garden.

It was Jamie. *How's it going? Are they married yet?*

Not good, I responded. *I have a lettuce emergency.*

Sounds serious.

Feel like running to the Weaver Street Market? I need spring greens for twenty-five people.

The one in Southern Village? That isn't far from here. When do you need them?

Hope blossomed in my chest. Was he seriously offering to help? *About ten minutes ago.*

Yikes. I'm tied up in a meeting for the next hour. Simon lives close by. Want me to see if he can go?

I barely knew Simon. Hadn't seen or spoken to him since the soccer game the Saturday before, and even then our conversation had been brief. It seemed weird to ask this of him. But I was desperate. And he *was* Jamie's brother. Hopefully, Jamie was on his way to being more than a casual acquaintance, so getting to know Simon was inevitable anyway. *Do you think he would? That would be amazing.*

Hamilton brothers to the rescue. Consider it done.

I texted him the details of exactly what I needed, including Gaspard's translation of what spring greens for twenty-five salads equaled. He promised he'd get the details to Simon and let me know within five minutes if he couldn't do it. When I didn't hear back, I had to assume Simon had been willing.

I made my way back to the tent to make sure the ceremony was happening as it should. A trickle of sweat slid down my back, and I wondered, not for the first time, why anyone would want to get married outdoors in June. During the reception, we would turn on the large fans that now lined the edges of the open-sided tent, but they were too noisy for the ceremony. At least the ushers had passed out little handheld fans, and the tent provided a modicum of shade from the late afternoon sun.

With nothing amiss, I turned back and moved through the gardens to the parking lot, where hopefully Simon would be arriving soon, arugula in hand. I loved the gardens. *Loved* them. As much now as I had when I was a kid. They weren't overly manicured. They were a little wild, with foliage thick enough to create lots of hidden corners and secret spots on the path. It was literally a "winding way" that meandered all over the southeastern corner of the grounds, leading to a tiny courtyard rose garden. I wasn't sure if the garden was named for the inn or the inn led to the design of the garden. I'd have to ask Ida. Either way, it was my favorite place on the property.

A few minutes later, Simon pulled up. From everything Jamie had told me about his older brother, the dark-blue sedan he drove fit his personality perfectly. Steady. Reliable. Boring. *Nothing* like the bright-red jeep Jamie drove. Simon lifted two large paper grocery bags out of his car and handed them over.

"You are my hero." I took the bags.

He slid his sunglasses up onto his head. "It's no trouble. I didn't have to go far."

"Yeah, Jamie said you live around here, which surprised me. A Duke grad living over here in Chapel Hill. Isn't that against your code of ethics or something?"

He grinned. "I had to get special permission. It wasn't easy."

"Your neighbors must be reeling from the scandal."

"You know, you may be on to something. My house has been toilet papered twice since I moved in."

I laughed. "Completely justified. Driving around in Tar Heel country with a Duke plate on the front of your car is straight-up asking for it."

"I get the feeling you're much more Tar Heel than you are Blue Devil."

I held up my free hand in a gesture of surrender. "My dad was born in Chapel Hill. The blood in these veins runs Carolina blue."

"I'll try not to hold it against you," he said.

Simon bantered a lot like Jamie did, though he wasn't nearly as flirty. A good thing, seeing as how I'd just gone on a date with his younger brother.

But I got the impression he simply wasn't a flirty kind of guy. He clearly wasn't shy, but he wasn't a show-off either. What Jamie had described as boring, I would call . . . subtle.

I held up the bags. "I should get these inside. Thank you for bringing them. You literally saved an entire wedding reception by doing this."

He smiled, which made him look, just for a moment, a lot like Jamie. Oddly, it brought on a sudden pang of longing for my own brother. John and I had the same smile too.

"You need help getting them to the kitchen?" Simon asked.

"I can get it. Thank you though. I owe you big-time. Seriously."

"Like I said, it's no trouble."

Something was weird. The way he was looking at me, or . . . something. I didn't know. "Oh! How much do I owe you?" Maybe that was the weird thing. He was waiting for me to pay him.

"It wasn't that much." He pulled a receipt out of his pocket and held it out.

I shifted the bags so I could take the receipt, realizing as I did that I had no way to pay him back, not unless he followed me to my office, and I was on too tight a time line for that.

"Do you care if I pay you next week sometime? I'm sorry. I know this is totally rude, but these salads are literally going to be eaten in less than an hour, and I am already on the dirty list with our chef."

"Next week is fine."

"Okay."

"Okay," he repeated.

Yeah. Totally weird. Not creepy weird. Just awkward. I backed up a few steps. "Thanks again, Simon."

He waved, then climbed into his car. I hurried to the kitchen, trying to make sense of whatever it was I'd felt under Simon's gaze. It just felt different. A little too intense, maybe? Like he was looking a little too closely. Whatever it was, I forced it from my mind. I had bigger things to think about. Like a wedding and a reception and a grouchy French chef who really, really wanted his lettuce.

●●●

Simon: *Lettuce delivered. Crisis averted.*
Jamie: *Thanks, man. I appreciate you covering for me.*
Simon: *It wasn't a problem. I could walk to the inn from my backyard.*
Jamie: *Don't get any ideas.*
Simon: *??*
Jamie: *About Lane.*
Simon: *Right. Because Karen would be totally fine with that.*
Jamie: *Karen. The name sounds familiar.*
Simon: *Ha.*
Jamie: *I know I should know who she is, but . . .*
Simon: *Yeah, funny.*
Jamie: *She shouldn't be so easy to forget, man. When was the last time you even talked to her?*
Simon: *Got a letter last week. She's on a new dig.*
Jamie: *???*
Simon: *Yemen. Three months. She'll be home after this one.*
Jamie: *Until she leaves again.*
Simon: *Maybe not.*
Jamie: *It's time to give her a reason to stay, man.*
Jamie: *Carpe diem!*
Jamie: *Live like you're dying.*
Jamie: *Take the bull by the horns.*
Jamie: *Live la vida loca.*
Jamie: *Take the plunge.*
Simon: *You know you're a jerk, right?*
Jamie: *Yes. Yes, I do.*

Chapter 5

JAMIE SHOWED UP ON MY doorstep Sunday evening at 7:00 p.m. sharp. He was still wearing his shirt and tie from church, his white sleeves rolled up to his elbows, his tie loose. He held up a brown paper grocery bag. "Dessert, as promised," he said through the screen door.

I pushed the door open and stood to the side so he could come in. "You look nice." Much nicer than my jeans and loose V-neck, but since I was sure I had the edge on comfort, I wasn't feeling bad about it. "No time to change this afternoon?"

"None. I had a meeting thing after church, then I had to do this dinner thing with Dave and his fiancée, and then I headed straight over here." He held up the bags. "You ready to eat this now? If not, I can stick it in the fridge."

"The answer will always be now with me, Jamie. When it comes to food, always yes. Always now."

"Noted." He followed me into the kitchen, where he set the bag on the table and pulled out a large plastic dish with a bright-purple lid, followed by two smaller containers. "You like your cheesecake with raspberry sauce or chocolate sauce?"

I pulled a couple of plates out of the cabinet and grabbed some forks, setting them on the table beside him. "Did you hear anything I just said?"

He gave me a sideways glance and smiled. "Got it. Chocolate sauce *and* raspberry sauce coming up."

I sat down and watched as he dished up the cheesecake and drizzled it with both sauces. "It looks amazing."

"It should be for as much as Katie talked about how long it took her to make."

"Katie?"

"Dave's fiancée."

"That's right. You mentioned the fiancé dinner thing. Tell me about that."

He shrugged. "It was annoying, really. Katie's family is in town to see the venue for the wedding and finalize some stuff, and they hosted dinner for everyone. Katie's aunt lives in Raleigh, so . . . yeah. We were all over there all afternoon."

"That doesn't sound too awful. Why was it annoying?"

He grunted something noncommittal and completely inaudible. He handed me my plate. "Cheesecake?"

"Wait a minute. Not so fast. Why the grunt?"

He rubbed his hand across his jaw. "Katie has sisters. Lots of them."

"Ohhhh, it was a matchmaking party." It was easy to tell from the pained look in his eyes that it had made him uncomfortable, which made it easier to joke, but I still felt a tiny spark of jealousy flame to life at the thought. Interesting. Date *two* and I was already feeling some ownership.

"Not exactly. But close."

"Was there one for each of you? Four brides for four brothers? Ohh! Are you going to get matching cummerbunds and bow ties to coordinate with the bridesmaid dresses? Each couple could have their own color. The possibilities are endless, Jamie. Endless!"

"Are you enjoying yourself?"

I grinned. "Immensely." I took a bite of the cheesecake.

"The sad thing is you aren't far off from the truth. Minus the cummerbunds. Katie has a twin sister, and since she's the maid of honor and I'm the best man . . ."

"Wait. Katie has a twin?"

He nodded. "They're identical. Really, *really* identical. If I were Dave, I'd be totally freaked out about getting them mixed up."

"This story gets better and better."

He reached for my cheesecake. "I'm taking this back. I don't think you deserve it if you're going to keep making fun of me."

I slid my plate out of reach and took another bite. "Okay, okay! I'm done. No more teasing. She's the maid of honor, and you're the best man, and . . ."

"Nope. I'm not telling you now."

"Please? I promise. No laughing."

He put down his fork. "We have to learn a dance."

I pressed my lips together. *Hard.* But a dance? How could I not laugh at that? "Like a *dance*, dance?" I managed to squeak my words out giggle free, but it wasn't easy.

"Like a ballroom dance. It's Katie's thing. And her sister's. So we're learning this dance to perform at the reception."

I leaned back in my chair. "Wow."

He shot me a knowing look. "Tell me about it."

I took a few more bites. "This is really good cheesecake."

"You want to know the worst part? Honestly, it's not even the dancing."

"No?"

He shook his head. "It's the expectation. Cooper's off the hook 'cause he'll probably be gone before the wedding. And Simon's off the hook because of Karen. But they must have paraded Katie's sister in front of me a hundred times. It felt like one giant setup."

"Does Katie's sister have a name?"

He paused. "Elizabeth? No, wait. It's Jane. The younger one is Elizabeth."

I reached over and squeezed his arm. "Poor guy. It's a miracle you made it out in one piece."

"And with cheesecake."

"That's a miracle I'm grateful for." I nudged my plate forward. "Is there more?"

"You do like your food, don't you?"

"It's one of my favorite hobbies, yes."

"So I take it you're not the kind of girl who counts the croutons on her salad."

"Absolutely not. Unless there aren't *enough* croutons on the salad. Because croutons are delicious."

He dished up a second piece of cheesecake and slid it toward me. I took the containers of sauce and drizzled them over the top. "So how did Jane feel about the matchmaking? Was she interested? Annoyed? Embarrassed?"

"Definitely embarrassed."

"You should tell her you're seeing somebody. Then the expectations are gone and maybe you can be friends."

He dropped his fork and slid his plate forward. "Okay. You win. I can't even finish my first piece."

"This is already round two for you, right? Did you eat dessert with everyone else?"

"I guess I did. And enough dinner for three people, so maybe I'm okay letting you win this time." He stood and took the dessert containers to the sink, where he rinsed them off. Helpful but annoying. Because I'd just alluded to us having an actual relationship and he'd responded with . . . nothing.

I followed him and leaned against the counter. "So you're gonna let that one go, huh? I say we're seeing each other, and you say, 'Hey, I should do the dishes.'"

He turned off the water and reached for the dish towel hanging over the stove handle, a huge smile stretching across his face. "I wasn't going to let it go."

"No?"

He stepped closer—intentionally closer—and threw the towel over his shoulder before propping his hands on the counter, one on either side of me. Framed by his arms, I was close enough to see him, to smell him, to reach up and touch the shadowy stubble along his jawline. Our bodies were only inches apart. Maybe Jane got to be his ballroom dance partner, but it was me getting his smolder. The effect it was having on my heart was maddening.

"I *did* tell her I was seeing somebody." He reached up and wrapped one of my curls around his finger. "It made me happy to hear you say so too."

I swallowed. "Yeah?"

He leaned in just a hair, then took a step backward, folding his arms across his chest. I felt his absence immediately, a feeling I knew he was counting on. The man had flirting down to a finely honed science. I couldn't have formed a coherent sentence if I'd had to. "I also told her there was a very specific reason I have to give this relationship"—he motioned back and forth between us—"a chance."

I pushed my hair behind my ears and tried to shake the fuzz out of my brain. Stupid man and his flirty charms. I crossed my arms, mimicking his stance. "And what's that?"

"Well, I mean, somebody's gotta knock you off your soccer high horse."

"Ha!" I lunged forward and gave him a playful nudge. "How are you the man for the job? Seems like last time we played, the only person getting knocked out of the saddle was you."

His eyes narrowed. "Oh, you are so going down."

He was easy to be around. We never ran out of stuff to talk about, which saved us from any awkward silences. But mostly it was *fun*. More fun than I'd had with a guy in a long time. We didn't even do anything significant. Flipped channels. Watched the tail end of a soccer game. Made fun of all the bad hair on old-school reruns of nineties sitcoms. Around Jamie, I didn't worry about anything. Not impressing him. Not whether or not my breath was bad. He was completely comfortable. I'd never had that with a guy.

It was after midnight when he finally stood to leave. He reached for my hand and pulled me up beside him. "I'm really glad we got together," he said.

I smiled, pushing my hands into the back pockets of my jeans. "Yeah. Me too. I've never had so much fun doing absolutely nothing."

"We should do it again sometime."

"We have to keep you true to your word, after all," I said. "You did tell Katie's sister you were seeing someone."

"That I did." He tugged at my elbow and pulled my hand free, sliding his fingers down my arm until our hands were clasped.

He wanted to kiss me. I could tell by the way his eyes kept darting down to my lips. I was in—all in—but I wasn't going to stand there all pansy-eyed while he made his move. I leaned up and took hold of Jamie's tie, giving him a gentle tug. When our lips touched, he pulled me close, wrapping his arms all the way around me.

I could feel him smile as we broke apart. "You just stole my move," he said.

I grinned. "Does that bother you?"

He made a noise, something between a moan and a growl. "No. No, it doesn't."

* * *

After two hours on the soccer field with four Hamiltons and twenty-five eight-year-olds, I was maybe in love with all the brothers. The charm. The jokes. The pretending to miss goals so the kids had an excuse to dog pile them all.

It was interesting observing the personalities of each of the brothers—the similarities and differences among them. Jamie and Cooper were a lot alike. They were all about showing off their fancy footwork, which of course the kids loved. It made them fan favorites by a large margin. Dave was the technical one, creating the drills, orchestrating, instructing, keeping everyone on task and on schedule.

But it was Simon I watched the most. He spent a lot of time standing in the background with his arms folded across his chest. But then he'd cross the field and get down on eye level with one kid or another, and talk to them. *Really* talk to them. I was never close enough to hear what he said, but I saw the change in the kids after he'd finished. Chins higher, shoulders back, smiles on their faces.

I didn't have an official role, so I floated, helping wherever help was needed. But my eyes were always drawn back to Simon and his mini pep talks bestowed like happy magic all over the field.

"Hey, you're really good at this," I told him after the kids had all gone home.

He stopped in his tracks, dropping three of the four soccer balls he'd been carrying. He scrambled to gather them back up. "I'm sorry, what?"

"Sorry. I just said you're really good with the kids. I like the way you sought them out individually. I think it's good for them to be seen like that."

"Oh. Thanks," he said.

"What do you tell them?"

"Who, the kids?"

"Yeah. They're always listening so intently." I picked up the bag for the soccer balls and held it open, letting Simon drop them in before cinching it up tight.

"Thanks," Simon said, taking the bag. "It's different for each kid, really. I try and tell them something they're doing right and compliment them on that, then think of something simple they can work on that won't overwhelm them."

"I love that," I said.

"I don't know." He scratched his chin. "The last kid I talked to spit on my shoe and told me I looked like a giant booger, so I'm beginning to question my methods."

I laughed. "I guess you can't win them all?"

"Hey, Jamie!" Simon called across the field. "Can you and Coop get those cones?"

Jamie waved a hand of acknowledgment and started gathering them up.

"You were pretty great out there too," Simon said.

I raised my eyebrows. "Yeah? I've never had any coaching experience. But it was fun. Thanks for letting me come."

"You're welcome. I hope you come back next week. I'll even let you keep the shirt."

I glanced down at the bright-orange T-shirt Jamie had given me at the start of the evening. The word COACH was printed across the front in big white letters, with the name of Simon's accounting firm on the back. "I'll cherish the shirt," I joked. "Truly. I might even wear it to work tomorrow."

He laughed. "If anybody can pull it off, it's you."

I froze. I probably should have just played it off. It was nothing. A joke about a T-shirt. But the compliment still gave me pause.

"I'm sorry," Simon said quickly. "Was that—"

I shook my head. "No, it was fine. It's not—"

"Cones," Jamie said, dropping them at our feet with a flourish. "Every last one of them. Cooper didn't help though, just for the record."

"Thanks," Simon said. His eyes met mine one last time before he leaned down, organizing Jamie's haphazard pile of cones into neat stacks. Poor guy. He probably figured he'd made me uncomfortable, when really I was mostly just flattered. I mean, orange *was* a good color on me. It felt nice to think someone had noticed.

Right?

Right?

• • •

Cooper: BROTHERS. The white envelope has arrived.

Dave: Sweet. Where are you headed?

*Cooper: That's it? No ceremony? No film footage to share with all the
Internet? Just, where are you headed?*

*Simon: We know you had Mom open it and read it to you over
the phone.*

Cooper: She told you?

*Jamie: Nope. We just know you. As patient as . . . wait. There is
actually no living creature on this earth as impatient as you.*

Cooper: Whatever.

Jamie: Spill it, Coop. Where are you going?

Cooper: Sierra Leone. I'M GOING TO AFRICA, BABY.

Simon: That's incredible!

Dave: And you'll only come home with a little Ebola.

Cooper: Seriously? Is there still Ebola in Africa?

*Dave: Pretty sure missionaries have to wear masks and gloves their
entire mission. Even while sleeping.*

Cooper: Simon. Tell me Dave is joking.

Simon: He's joking.

Cooper: You're sure?

*Simon: The World Health Organization declared Sierra Leone a safe
zone awhile ago. They wouldn't send missionaries there if
Ebola was still a legitimate threat.*

Cooper: AFRICA. I'M GOING TO AFRICA IN THREE MONTHS.

Dave: You're going to be great. Dinner tonight to celebrate?

Jamie: Burgers at Simon's. I'm not cooking.

Simon: I'm working late. I can eat, but I can't cook.

Cooper: I'm feeling the love, guys.

*Dave: You're both jerks. Rib eyes. My house. 7 pm. I'll grill. Katie
will help.*

Jamie: If Katie's coming, I'm bringing Lane.

Dave: Sounds like a party.

Chapter 6

"Seriously? Your brother broke the news via text?" I walked to my car, happy to have the distraction of a call from Jamie. To say I'd had a long day was a bit of an understatement. No big events, but honestly, the small ones were sometimes more annoying. More nitpicking with less payout. The brunch for the local DAR group that filled my morning was bad enough, but then the afternoon brought in a soccer-team-sized group of six-year-olds. For tea. *With their dolls.* Never mind the fact that dolls don't drink. Or talk. Or eat teeny, tiny pastries sitting on teeny, tiny plates. I mean, sure. If the pastries are paid for, it shouldn't matter whether they are *actually* enjoyed or just *pretend* enjoyed. But it was still annoying. Add the day's pressures to two weeks of almost endless working with very little dating time, and Jamie's voice on the phone was the greatest thing I'd heard all day.

"Texting is how we communicate."

"Like cavemen?"

"No, like four brothers who are busy and wouldn't talk near as much otherwise. We've had the same group thread for years. Don't knock it."

"I'm not going to argue against the ease of communicating via text message." I unlocked my car and climbed in. "But come on. A mission call? That at least deserves an in-person announcement."

"But then the moment wouldn't be documented. All the big stuff has happened in that thread."

"Like what?" I shifted over to speaker and dropped the phone onto my lap, then started the car.

"Like Dave's engagement. Or the day we hit a million sales on the app. Or . . . Simon's house."

"His house?"

"Yeah. He's a bona fide homeowner. The real deal."

"How grown-up."

"That's Simon for you." I could hear the smile in his voice. "So, you want to come help us celebrate tonight? Just the brothers. And Katie will be there too. It'd be nice for you to finally meet her." Even with all the time I'd spent with the brothers, helping out at the soccer clinic, I still hadn't met Dave's fiancée.

"What about your parents? Don't they get to celebrate too?"

"They'll get their turn when Coop goes home. It's our turn. Come on. It'll be fun. Dave's grilling rib eyes."

"You had me at grilling. Count me in."

"Dinner's at seven. I'll text you the address."

I glanced at my watch. 5:42. If I hurried, I'd have time to go home and change before heading over.

Granny Grace was on the porch when I pulled up to the house. She waited for me, holding her hand up to shield her eyes against the bright afternoon sun. I walked over and gave her a hug. "Hi, Granny Grace."

She patted my hair. "I haven't seen you in a while. That job working you too hard?"

"Most days. I love it though. I don't mind the work."

"You feel like you're settling in?"

"It's only been a few weeks, but I'm getting the hang of it. What are you doing out here? It's so hot."

"Just watering the flowers. You hungry? It's too hot to cook, but I can make you a sandwich."

"Actually, I have dinner plans."

Her eyebrows went up. "*Man* dinner plans?"

The word *man* coincided with a twitch of her hips that made me laugh out loud. "What's gotten into you?"

"I'm just asking a question."

"Yes. Man dinner plans. His name is Jamie."

She lowered herself onto the small wicker couch pushed up under the front window and motioned for me to join her. It was out of the sun at least. "Is he a Mormon like you?"

I nodded. "He is."

"That's good. Is he nice?"

"He's very nice. He's a soccer player, Granny. Also like me."

"Does he make a good living?"

It made me laugh that dinner plans were enough to elicit so many questions. "He works in technology and makes a very nice living."

She nodded her approval. "Well, if dinner goes well, you bring him around for supper. I'll make a meat loaf and some potatoes."

"I think he'd like that." I stood. "Hey, I have to work Saturday night— the inn is hosting a Fourth of July thing—but I'll have some free time in the morning. Want me to help in the garden?"

"The first crop of beans will be in by then. You up to pickin'?"

I'd always loved working in Granny Grace's garden. The idea that with a little bit of water and sun we could grow actual things and then eat them had amazed my child mind. As I got older, I realized more of the struggle it was to keep things thriving. Gardening wasn't just water and sun. It was *work*. Not enough rain, too much rain, pests, disease, critters that snuck in and damaged the vegetables. Granny Grace once told me, "The battle never ends, Lane. There is bounty waiting if you're willing to work, but nothing comes from nothing." I'd remembered that mantra many times since then. *Nothing comes from nothing.* "I'm up for it," I told her.

She nodded. "I'll start early, before the sun gets too high."

"How early is early?"

She gave me a sideways glance. "Just come on out when you wake up. Squash beetles are easiest to find mid- to late morning, so whatever time it is, there should be something to keep you busy."

I frowned. As a kid, she'd paid me a penny for every squash beetle I'd picked off her beans. It had made the work worth it back then, but I wasn't sure sleeping in was worth getting stuck with the job *now*. I leaned over and kissed her on the cheek. "I'll be up early."

"Enjoy that dinner of yours. Don't do anything you wouldn't want to tell me about."

I laughed. "That'll never work with you, Granny. You like the dirty stuff the best."

She cackled. "That I do. That I do."

* * *

It was fifteen minutes after seven when I finally made it to Dave and Jamie's house. I'd had a slight wardrobe crisis, and my hair was uncooperative, issues I was still working to let go of when I walked up their sidewalk and rang the doorbell.

Chloe answered the door. *Chloe?* Okay, so she didn't actually answer it. It was more like she opened it, then barreled into me to give me a hug, pulling the door shut behind her. "Lane! It's so good to see you! How are you?"

I took a step backward, creating a normal-person measure of distance between us. "I'm good. How are you?"

"Totally swamped. I just started summer classes, and it's killing me. So what's up? What are you doing here?"

"Just having dinner with Jamie. I guess Cooper got his mission call today, so we're celebrating."

She grinned. "You and Jamie. So you actually managed it."

I shook my head and held up my hands. "I didn't manage anything. I gave him my number, he called me, we're dating. It's really not all that exciting."

She sighed. "It's totally exciting. You landed the big fish, Lane. It's a big deal."

It wasn't a big deal. It really, *really* wasn't. But I'd be lying if I said I didn't feel a tiny thrill of victory at her words. I was dating an untouchable brother—a guy no girl in all of North Carolina's Research Triangle had managed to snag until now. It wasn't a competition, but I still liked feeling a little like I'd won.

"It's not a big deal, Chloe. I'm not . . ."

"Is he a good kisser? I bet he's a good kisser."

My eyebrows went up.

"Wait. No. You don't have to answer that. That was totally rude. He is though, right? I'm just really guessing he probably is."

Before I could respond, Jamie thankfully pushed open the front door. "Hey, Lane. You're here." He stepped outside and slipped an arm around my waist. He looked at Chloe. "Oh, hey, Chloe. What are you doing here?"

"I brought cookies over to congratulate Cooper."

"Oh. Cool," Jamie said. "Do you want to stay and eat dinner with us? Dave's grilling."

I could see from Chloe's expression what it meant to her that she'd been invited, but her elation quickly morphed into a frown. "I so wish I could!" She pulled out her phone and glanced at the screen. "I have class in forty-five minutes." She leaned forward to hug me one more time. "Seriously though," she whispered in my ear. "The two of you. It's so perfect!"

We watched as she hurried to her car and pulled down the drive, waving before she turned and disappeared from view. I followed Jamie inside, stopping at the entry table where Chloe had left her plate of African-shaped cookies. I picked one up, careful not to smudge the icing that lined the continent and highlighted the region where Cooper would be serving. "Wow," I said. "She had a busy afternoon."

"That's Chloe for you," Jamie said. "She's always doing stuff like this."

"I think maybe she has a little bit of a crush on you."

He lifted his shoulders in a playful shrug. "Who doesn't?"

I rolled my eyes. He was ridiculous. He put his hands on either side of my waist, pulling me toward him. Ridiculous, but that didn't stop me from enjoying the feel of my body pressed against his. He leaned in for a kiss but froze inches from my face when his brother called to him from the kitchen.

"Jamie? Where are you?" Dave yelled.

Jamie frowned. "Seriously? I've been gone twenty seconds."

I grinned. "Come on. I want to meet Katie."

"Hey, Lane," Dave said when we entered the kitchen. "I'm glad you're here. You can help too." He grabbed a couple of spoons out of a drawer to the left of the stove and dipped them into the saucepan sitting on the front burner. A woman I assumed had to be Katie stood beside him. Her straight brown hair was piled high on top of her head, and she wore a striped apron that made her look as if she belonged in the kitchen. It almost made me wish I liked to cook. *Almost.*

"Don't make them taste it," Katie said. "It's fine."

"Taste what?" Jamie asked.

"Whatever it is, it smells delicious," I said.

"Here." Dave handed us each a spoon. "It's caramel sauce for the bread pudding. She says it needs something, but we can't figure out what."

I took the spoon and blew on the still-steaming sauce, my hand cupped underneath in case it dripped.

Jamie swallowed his down and tossed his spoon into the sink. "Tastes good to me."

Dave rolled his eyes. "Says the guy who thinks Cocoa Puffs make a good dessert. Lane? What do you think?"

I tasted the now-cool sauce, holding it on my tongue long enough to really get the flavor. "I'm not a chef by any stretch," I said, "but I think maybe it needs a little more salt."

"Salt!" Katie said. "I forgot the salt!" She reached into a cabinet over the sink and pulled out the salt shaker. "Thank you," she said to me over her shoulder. "I can't believe I forgot something so simple. I'm Katie," she added.

"Oh, right," Dave said. "Sorry. Katie, Lane. Lane, Katie."

"It's nice to finally meet you," I said. Jamie leaned against the counter next to his brother. For a split second, I recognized how much the two of them looked alike. They weren't identical by any stretch, but if they dressed the same and fixed their hair the same way, they might be able to convince people they were. Jamie was slightly taller and a little broader through the shoulders. And Dave wore his beard trimmed close. But their eyes were the same—a deep-chocolate brown. And the way they held themselves was *exactly* the same. It was a little disconcerting.

"Do you want us to stand side by side? Give you profile shots for comparison?" Dave asked.

"Sorry. I didn't mean to stare."

Katie set her wooden spoon on the stove and turned around. "Once, when Dave and I first started dating, I saw Dave standing in the hallway at church and waltzed right up, lacing my arm through his, and snuggled up close. Only it was Jamie. I've never been so horrified."

"Serves you right," Dave said. "The number of times you and Jane messed with guys growing up."

She grinned. "Ah, those were the days."

Ha. I liked her already. "I loved your cheesecake," I said. "It was really delicious."

She wrinkled her brow for a moment, then glared at Jamie. "So that's why you stole so much cheesecake! You were going to see Lane."

"Busted. But it was for a worthy cause, Kate. I fed her good food, and she agreed to go out with me again." Jamie moved closer. "Thanks for blowing my cover," he whispered in my ear.

"Anytime," I whispered back.

"It's all right," Dave said. "Everyone understands Jamie needs all the help he can get when it comes to women."

"I'm a man who has accepted his limitations," Jamie said. "I do the best I can with what I've got."

I rolled my eyes for the second time that night. What he *had* was enough to make him the talk of every Mormon singles group for a hundred miles in three different directions. "I admit the food helped your wooing," I said, "but the soccer is what sealed the deal for me."

"Got it. So you like dating someone you can wipe the floor with," Dave said, a big smile on his face.

"Watch it," Jamie said. "She wiped the floor with you too."

"Floor wiping not required," I said. "I just like a man who loves the game like I do. Besides, that day was mostly luck."

"That wasn't luck," Dave said. "It was sheer brilliance and skill."

"We'll see about that next Thursday," Jamie said with a huff. I glanced at him out of the corner of my eye. I might have been making it up, but he actually sounded a tiny bit annoyed. Not pretend annoyed, but legitimately bothered.

"What's happening on Thursday?" Katie asked.

"A rematch," Jamie said, his arms folded tightly across his chest. "Next week, after the last clinic."

Truth? I'd been avoiding the idea of a rematch. On purpose. The first couple times Jamie talked about it, it was fun and flirty and seemed like it wouldn't matter. But then he got a little more serious. Like the outcome was really important. Like he wanted to beat me just to prove he could. It was a little unsettling. I understood competition. I'd carried the title of most competitive ever on the planet my entire high school and college soccer careers. But this was different. Jamie and I were dating. And I had no idea how the outcome of a rematch, whether I won or lost, would affect our relationship. The fact that I even had to wonder had me worried.

"Sounds exciting," Katie said. "Who's playing? Should I bring popcorn?"

"We're still working on the teams," Jamie said.

"You should let Lane have Simon," Dave said. "He's the strongest player next to you. That way when she wins, you'll be able to nurse your ego with the fact that her winning was probably because of him."

"She should have Simon on her team," Jamie said, "so that when *I* win, I'll rest easy knowing it was an absolutely fair match up."

"Such a sweet-talker," Dave said. "I can tell your girlfriend is putty in your hands right now."

"She can handle it," Jamie shot back. "She's the one who started this whole competition in the first place."

Two things battled for space in my brain: One, Jamie hadn't even flinched when his brother had called me his girlfriend. And two, was he sure I could handle it? 'Cause he was kinda freaking me out a little. His playful banter had an undercurrent of serious even *I* didn't like. And that was saying something.

"I don't know," I said. "I think for the health of our relationship we might need to stay off the soccer field."

He dropped an arm over my shoulder. "Are you really worried about that?"

"She's met you, Jamie," Dave said. "She has every reason to be worried."

Katie clapped her hands. "Enough soccer talk. Where'd Cooper sneak off to? And where is Simon?"

"I'm right here," Simon said from the doorway. He set a briefcase onto the floor. "Sorry. I came straight from a meeting. Cooper's on the front porch with a plate of cookies."

"Alone?" Katie asked.

Simon nodded. "He's on the phone."

"Not anymore. I'm back." Cooper appeared in the doorway behind Simon, throwing his arm over his brother's shoulders. "Just another lady friend calling to congratulate me and say they'll write me while I'm gone. Ah, the ladies. They can't help themselves."

Simon grabbed Cooper's arm and pulled, twisting his body so that in a matter of seconds he had the youngest Hamilton brother in a headlock. Cooper grunted and tried to pull free, but Simon was a few inches taller and wider through the chest. "If only *the ladies* could see you now."

"You're just jealous." Cooper's voice was strangled and tight. "'Cause no girls ever pay *you* any attention."

Simon finally let him go. "I only need one to pay me attention. She's all that matters." Our eyes met for the briefest of seconds, and my heart jumped. No. It wasn't a jump. More like a tiny fraction of a . . . shift. Because Simon making my heart jump while I was standing there with *Jamie's* arm around me would be weird. Plus, I knew who Simon was talking about. Jamie had told me all about his dinosaur-bone-digging girlfriend, Karen. *She* was the she. Not me. My heart was just being stupid. I leaned closer into Jamie's side. "Hey, come talk to me," I said to Jamie.

He followed me into the living room. Once we were alone, I leaned up and, with a hand on either side of his face, pressed my lips against his. He was surprised at first, I could tell, but he quickly warmed to the kiss, pulling me closer with an arm across the small of my back.

"What was that for?" His words were soft, close to my ear.

"I don't know, I . . . Dave called me your girlfriend earlier. I mean, I know he was joking, but you didn't correct him."

He cocked an eyebrow. "Is it too soon? I know it's only been a couple of weeks."

I bit my lip. "And four days."

He still held me close, my hands pressed against his chest. "I can tell you this," he said. "I don't want to be seeing anyone else."

I shook my head. "I don't either."

"So . . . we keep dating, then. Only each other." He smiled.

This. This was what it felt like. Not stupid little heart jumps over weird, unintentional eye contact. Chloe was right. I had landed the big fish. There was no way I was screwing that up. I leaned up and kissed Jamie again. "Yes. Good plan."

...

Jamie: Dude. I need help.
Simon: Are you texting just me?
Jamie: I want you to keep this between us.
Simon: Okay. You have my attention.
Jamie: I need help with Lane.
Simon: Explain.
Jamie: We went out last night. Dinner and then to the bookstore.
Simon: And?
Jamie: She's a book person.
Simon: Okay.
Jamie: I'm not a book person.
Simon: She seems to like you the way you are.
Jamie: But if books are important to her, I feel like I need to try.
Simon: So ask her what she likes to read, then read those books.
Jamie: But I want her to think I know books.
Simon: I'm not helping you pretend to be something you're not.
Jamie: Not what I'm asking. Can you just tell me a book to read? One she might think is impressive?
Simon: I don't know her, Jamie. I have no idea what books she likes.
Jamie: She was talking about this one book. Something historical. About cathedrals, maybe?
Simon: Pillars of the Earth?
Jamie: Yes! That's it.
Simon: Ken Follett. Great book.
Jamie: If that's what she likes, what else could I read?
Simon: Look up Ariana Franklin. And Bernard Cornwell. You should also read everything Khaled Hosseini has ever written. If Lane's a big reader, she's probably read them.
Jamie: Got it. Thanks.

Chapter 7

The "Macarena."

I'd heard a lot of crazy requests in three years of event management but walking down the aisle at your wedding while doing the Macarena?

I stared at Evie, the bride-to-be, her face all aglow with excitement. She was serious. Actually, legitimately, for real *serious*. Was it possible I'd misunderstood? "We're not talking about the reception, right? During the actual ceremony, that's the song you want playing?"

"I know it sounds cheesy, but it's such a significant part of our history. It's our song, our dance, our happy-couple music. It's the perfect song to usher me right into my future husband's arms."

My pencil froze over my notepad. She'd really just said that sentence out loud. The "Macarena" was the perfect song to usher her into her future husband's arms. I dug deep to find my business-professional face before I looked up. I could make it through this without laughing. *I could.*

"Okay. The 'Macarena' it is. Is anyone giving you away?"

"Giving me away?"

"A father, maybe? An uncle?"

Evie blinked.

"Walking you down the aisle. The symbolic 'giving away'?"

"Oh, right. That. My father's dead, and I don't have any uncles, so I'm dancing down the aisle on my own. That's not a problem, is it?"

"Definitely not. Your wedding, your dreams. We're just here to make it happen." It was a canned line. Not even a good one. But it was a great fallback when brides started to get weird about their plans. Rule number one of successful event execution? Offer your own opinion as infrequently as possible. Preferably never. Because if you have *no* opinion, nothing is ever your idea and thus can never be your fault.

I jotted down a note for our audio-visual guy. A DJ would handle the reception, but he wouldn't show up until after the ceremony was over, which meant the ceremony's music fell on us. It killed me to think I'd be party to such an outlandish wedding march, but what was I gonna do?

"What does the groom think about the music?"

"About the 'Macarena'? He doesn't know. And I want it to stay that way. It's going to be a huge surprise, and he's going to love it. Trust me. When he sees me line dancing down the aisle, he'll flip." She squealed and clapped her hands. "Ahh! I'm so excited!"

I suddenly had an overwhelming desire to call Randi. She'd love the "Macarena" story. My freshman year at Berkeley, Randi had been my first roommate. After five minutes of hanging out, we'd discovered we were both from the East Coast, on the soccer team, and hospitality majors. Weird but totally convenient and fortuitous. Up until college, I'd never been great at making friends. Not for lack of caring—I was just busy. And incredibly passionate about soccer, which probably gave me a little bit of tunnel vision. Save my teammates, I rarely had much of a spare thought for anybody. If I was going to have a friend, I kind of needed her to fall into my lap. Randi had.

"Did you get that last part?"

I looked up to meet the bride-to-be's expectant gaze. She'd asked me something. And I'd heard it. I knew I had. Something about dancing and bridesmaids and . . . "Yes!" It finally came to me. "I did get it. And we can absolutely widen the aisle so your bridesmaids and groomsmen can line dance in as well."

"It'll need to be at least twelve feet. Can the ballroom accommodate twelve feet?"

I wrote another note—*twelve feet for line-dancing wedding processional.* "It might cut the number of seats by a dozen or so, but based on your guest list, I don't think that's going to be a problem," I said.

She leaned back into the sofa and grinned. "I can't believe this is really happening."

I glanced at my watch. "It's about time to meet with the chef. Is anyone joining you for the sampling?"

She nodded. "My maid of honor and my mom." She pulled out her phone. "Actually, they just pulled up. I'll go out and meet them."

Except for her terrible taste in music, Evie was a pretty cool bride. Though anything would seem cool after the Antiquing Club we'd had staying with us all week. Their first day, they'd inspected every piece of furniture on the property and declared anything manufactured after 1957 "absolute rubbish."

I finished a few more notes, then grabbed my phone, tapping out a quick text to Randi. *The wedding story to top ALL wedding stories? The Macarena. DOWN THE AISLE. We need to catch up. I have a new job. And a new man. Call me soon?*

I slipped the phone back into my desk drawer, then headed toward the lobby to find Evie and the rest of her group. I was waylaid by April hurrying down the hallway. "Hey, Lane, how are you with numbers?"

"Are we talking how-many-points-did-they-score numbers? Or what's-the-square-root-of-seventy-four kind of numbers?"

"How about profit-and-loss-statement kind of numbers? Didn't you get a minor in business or something? I feel like that was on your résumé."

"I did, but I promise it doesn't qualify me for much. I had to retake my accounting class twice, and I still barely passed."

She motioned for me to follow her. "Still. You're more qualified than me."

"Qualified for what?"

We stopped outside of Thornton's old office. April sighed. "Ida's going over the inn's financials. She says she's fine, but I'm not so sure she has things under control."

An uneasiness grew in the pit of my stomach. I'd had my suspicions. Ida had seemed less than comfortable when I'd turned over a stack of bills from various vendors the week before. She'd insisted she knew what she was doing as she'd taken them to Thornton's office, but I'd recognized the uncertainty in her eyes.

"What all should Ida be handling?"

"The better question is what isn't she supposed to be handling?" April said. "Thornton pretty much did everything money related. I run deposits to the bank, and Gaspard handles the ordering for the restaurant. But everything else was Thornton—vendor payments, record keeping, taxes. All of it."

"What exactly do you want *me* to do?"

"I don't know. See if you can help her make sense of things? We had a vendor call this morning wondering why they haven't been paid yet. Someone has to help her sort things out. We have to pay people, Lane."

"I've got a bride meeting with Gaspard in two minutes. You know I can't leave anyone unsupervised with that man."

"True. How about I handle Gaspard? I'll take the bride, you take the money talk? Please?"

"Fine," I grumbled. I handed her the notebook. "Bride's name is Evie. Mom and maid of honor are joining her for the tasting. They should be in the lobby."

"Got it," April said. "Anything I need to know going in?" She started to back up down the hallway.

"Just don't make fun of the 'Macarena' and you're all set."

She paused midstep. "I'm not even going to ask."

I knocked on the door to Thornton's office before opening it slightly and sticking my head inside. "Hello? Ida? It's Lane. Can I come in?"

Ida sat behind Thornton's desk, a sea of papers spread out in front of her. She looked up. "What? Oh, sure, sure. Come in." I walked across the office and sat in the same chair I'd occupied when Thornton had interviewed, then hired me two months before.

Ida smiled, but it was weary. "How are you, Lane? Is there something I can do for you?"

"Actually, I'm wondering if there's anything I can do for you." I glanced at the mess on the desk.

She shook her head and sighed. "Thornton had a way about doing things. I figured it would be easy to sort it all out, but I'll be honest. I'm not sure what's up or down at this point."

"Did Thornton work with an accountant?"

"No. Not even at tax time. He prided himself in handling all the financials himself." She sank back into her chair. "It wasn't right, him carrying all the responsibility like that, but I think he liked being the one who kept everything running. He was the keeper of the keys, so to speak. He liked having ownership like that."

"That's understandable," I said. "Do you mind if I take a look?"

"Oh, I don't want you to trouble yourself with all this. I'll figure it out eventually."

"Are you sure? I've got a minor in business. I'm not an expert by any means, but I might know a little something that could help. At the very least, let me help you sort through everything."

Ida relented. "I guess a little help wouldn't be such a bad thing. It's kind of you to offer."

Two hours later, I'd sorted the papers scattered across the desk into something that was almost organized. Thornton had been completely old school. He'd kept all his books and records by hand in thick black ledgers, one for each year. I'd created a stack of bills from vendors and food suppliers, a stack of bank statements from two separate accounts, and another stack of stuff I couldn't make sense of but figured probably had something to do with . . . *something*.

The longer I worked, the more questions piled up. I still hadn't come across any utility bills for the hotel. Power, phones, Internet. They were all still functioning, so that was encouraging, but I'd been working at Winding Way nearly a month—more than enough time for something like a utility bill to make its monthly appearance. It was possible there was an e-mail address Thornton used to receive digital copies, but it hardly seemed likely that a guy who balanced his bank statements in black hardbound ledgers would receive and pay bills online. There were other expenses too. Expenses I knew must have existed but that I couldn't find any record of in the papers Ida had collected. The linen service that brought in fresh sheets and towels every day. The landscaping crew. The company that provided banquet staff when we had events too large for our own wait staff to handle. The list went on and on.

"Ida, did you say Thornton handled the payroll as well?" As soon as I'd asked the question, I knew the answer had to be no. I wasn't an hourly employee, so I never had to clock in or out, but I'd seen other employees using a computer in the staff lounge to do just that. And we'd all still gotten our paychecks, even with Thornton gone. I'd set up the direct deposit for mine my first day at work.

Ida leaned back in her chair. "He used to. Had this big book and would write out the checks by hand. But then, a few years back, April set him up with a payroll service that handles it all."

Well, that was comforting. At least through any potential turmoil we would all keep getting paid. Or would we? I picked up the most recent bank statement from what I assumed to be the inn's main account. I didn't know the exact amount required to pay the inn's employees every two weeks, but my hunch was that it was more than what was in that account. Without knowing what deposits were expected, I couldn't know for sure how serious the problem was or if it was even a problem at all. But I did know one thing. I was in way over my head.

"Ida, I think we need an accountant."

"An accountant? Oh, Thornton would never have been okay with that. He hated the idea of anyone but him having any sort of hand in the money pot. Said you couldn't trust anybody these days."

"Not all accountants are bad. And I'm not sure how else we'll ever sort through all of this." I opened the current year's ledger. Thornton clearly had a system. Each entry was notated, but he used some sort of shorthand that was impossible to understand. At least for my nonaccounting brain. At the root of it, I knew it was basic. Money comes in, money goes out. But figuring out *how* Thornton had kept those records in order, then figuring out why a vendor wasn't getting paid and why the bank account didn't look like it was going to make payroll? Yeah. It was definitely accountant territory.

Ida pulled off her glasses and rubbed her hand across her face. "You know we bought this old place and started things up, just the two of us? We only opened a handful of rooms—the rest were in terrible shape—and only offered breakfast at first. Thornton cooked. I ran the front desk and cleaned the rooms." She chuckled. "We were so crazy. Doomed to fail. That's what everyone said. But then people kept coming, and, well, forty years later, here we are."

"I love the history of this place. I always have."

"Did you know this building used to be a hospital?"

"I did know that. I must have read the historical marker plaque in the garden a thousand times as a kid."

Ida shifted a stack of papers, straightening their edges. "Thornton loved this inn. It was everything to him." Tears welled up in her eyes. "Honestly, I don't know if I can do it without him."

"We can do it, Ida. All of us. You don't have to manage it all on your own."

She shrugged her shoulders and huffed. "I know. But all this?" She motioned to the desk around her. "This isn't anyone's burden but mine."

I stood. "You and a good accountant. And I think I know just the guy."

"You do? Who?"

"His name is Simon Hamilton. He's a friend from church. I don't know him well, but I know his family, and I know he's trustworthy. Do you want me to reach out and see if he'd be willing to look things over?"

Her shoulders slumped, the lines in her face drawn down, but then she shook her head and breathed out a resigned sigh. "You're right. I can't do this on my own. Go ahead and call him. If he's willing, I could clearly use the help."

•••

Jamie: Hey. Lane needs a favor. You game for offering some accounting advice?

Simon: Probably. What's up?

Jamie: It's the inn. The owner died and left the finances in a mess. They need help sorting it out.

Simon: That sounds like more than advice.

Jamie: Yeah, probably. I'm going to give Lane your number. Okay if she calls?

Simon: Sure. I'll do what I can.

Jamie: Feel free to do a little recon work while you're with her.

Simon: ??

Jamie: Talk about books. Music. She mentioned Emily Dickinson the other day. Heard of her?

Simon: She's a poet. If she's telling you what she likes, why not Google it? You don't need me to spy.

Jamie: Maybe not. But it'd be cool to name-drop someone she already likes before she ever mentions it.

Simon: That's ridiculous.

Jamie: But you'll still help, right? Just pay attention is all I'm saying.

Chapter 8

"You know I'm dying to hear about the 'Macarena,' but I want the man news first." Randi didn't even say hello when I answered her call in the middle of my drive home, just launched right in.

"How can man news be more exciting than a bride and her entire wedding party doing the Macarena down the aisle?"

"I can't even wrap my brain around how ludicrous that is. Stay focused, Lane. I have twelve minutes until my cream puffs are done, and I need to know details. Name? Profession? Is it serious? Is he gorgeous? Is he Mormon?"

I laughed. Randi wasn't Mormon, but she knew me well enough to know it was something that would matter to me. "His name is Jamie Hamilton. He works in app development. Grew up in Virginia. He *is* Mormon. He has a twin brother."

"Hold up. Back up and tell me what that means."

"It means when his mother was pregnant, instead of having one baby, she had two."

"Thanks for that, Lane. Your faith in my intelligence is astounding. *App development.* What does that mean?"

I pulled into my driveway and turned off the car, then grabbed my purse and headed up the stairs to my apartment to change clothes. It was the last day of the soccer clinic, and the evening of the now-infamous soccer rematch. "You know the game LogiX? The puzzle game thing you can put on your phone?"

"No."

"Seriously?"

"Seriously. I also don't play Candy Crush or Farmville or Words with Friends. *I know.* I'm a walking freak show."

"What *do* you do with your spare time?"

"I cook."

"And the world is better for it."

"Clock's ticking, Lane. Get to it."

"He and his brother run this company that designs and develops apps. It started with the two of them, but I think they've hired a few other people now, and . . . I don't know too much about the logistics of how it all works. They've been in talks with this company in California, and if stuff works out between them, Jamie says it's going to be huge."

"So he's stable and responsible and makes a nice living for himself," Randi said. I thought of her college boyfriend who'd spent an inordinate amount of time bumming around our living room, skipping class, talking about the next big break he knew he was moments away from discovering. It took Randi six months to decide the guy was too lazy to ever discover anything but the underside of our couch cushions. Their breakup ratcheted up Randi's vigilance in making sure guys she dated—and I dated—were far away from the "maybe I'll still be living with my parents in five years" track.

"Yes. This guy's definitely a grown-up."

"How does he feel about soccer?"

Ha. She *did* know the right questions to ask. "He plays. That's how we met. And he's good too. Played in college and everything."

"Sounds like a great match."

"I think so. It's a good story too. He totally blew me off when we met and didn't want me on his team. It was only a pickup game in the park, so I approached the *other* team and played for them instead."

"You did not. Oh my word, please tell me your team won."

"Let's just say it was my *third* goal that gave us the victory."

"You are so hard core. Okay. Soccer, money, good job, Virginia, twin brother. What else?"

"Hold on. I'm texting you a picture." I sent a photo I lifted off Jamie's Facebook profile, then switched over to speaker phone so I could dig through my laundry to find my shorts. Me and laundry. We hadn't been getting along lately.

"Oh. My. Word. You have met the perfect man."

"Right? I can't wait for you to meet him."

"Ugh. It'll never happen. That would require me to leave the kitchen and have a social life."

"How's it going?" After college, Randi decided her true passion in life was pastries. She'd gone back to culinary school and become a pastry chef for a fancy restaurant in Atlanta. She complained about the hours, but I knew in her heart she loved it.

"It's going. Just got one of my original desserts added to the menu, so there's that." A buzzer dinged somewhere in the background. "Gotta go," Randi said. "That's the cream puffs."

"Hmm. Enjoy one for me."

"Will do! Love you. Talk again soon!"

* * *

I'm not going to lie. For a minute, I considered letting Jamie win. He'd been acting like the stupid rematch was *so* important, which bugged. But once I was on the field, my competitive edge took over. I mean, we were all still smiling the whole time, but there was no way I was coddling Jamie's ego. The rematch was his idea. If he won, fine. But it wasn't going to be because I held back.

I really did end up with Simon on my team and a few other guys who had been helping out with the clinic. But Jamie kept both Cooper *and* Dave on his team. It was maybe a slightly unfair advantage, but my team won anyway. So much for worrying about *that*.

After the game, everyone congregated on the sidelines. "Ready to admit defeat?" I asked Jamie, my tone playful and light. "Bow to my skill and prowess? Kiss my cleats, maybe?"

He rolled his eyes. "I have never seen Simon play like that."

I crossed my arms across my chest. "Oh, I see how it is. Simon gets the credit for winning, huh?"

"No. You were amazing. Of course you were amazing. You guys beat us fair and square. But seriously. Simon was . . ."

"What was I?" Simon joined the group, grabbing a water bottle out of the cooler at Jamie's feet.

Jamie turned and rummaged through his bag, pulling out a miniature soccer ball—gold with black detailing that looked like it had all but completely flaked off. It looked like a Nerf ball I would have played with as a kid. He tossed it at Simon. "Take it, man. You earned it."

"Behold," Dave said, his voice hushed and reverent.

Cooper copied Dave's tone. "The king has been dethroned."

I looked from Jamie to Simon, then back to Jamie again. Finally, Dave had mercy on my confused state. "It's Hamilton family tradition," he said. "That gold soccer ball has been passed around from brother to brother since we were all playing youth league soccer at the YMCA. When one of us had a good game, scored a hat trick, made it to a championship game, or whatever, the ball was ours."

"Until someone else did something amazing," Cooper said. "Then it was passed on."

Okay, that was an adorable tradition. The fact that as grown men the brothers still passed it around? Also adorable. "So why is Jamie the king?"

It was Simon who answered. "Because no one's had this thing as frequently as he has. And it's been years since it's changed hands."

Jamie reached for a water bottle, grabbing a second one and handing it to me. "Enjoy it while it lasts," he said to Simon. "Next time we're on the field, I'll get it back."

Dave started to cough—a loud, fake cough. "Dude, I think I'm getting sick. I don't think I'll be playing soccer again for a long time. How are you feeling, Coop?"

Cooper threw his hand to his forehead. "I think I'm coming down with something too. And wait . . . look . . . yep. I think my ankle's broken." He started hoping on one foot, hanging his arm over Dave's shoulder. "I'll be out for weeks, months even."

Jamie sloshed the contents of his water bottle toward his brothers, splashing them both. Cooper dodged most of the spray, even standing on one foot. "Simon?" he said. "How are you feeling?"

Simon looked at his brothers, his face passive. "I feel great," he said.

"Thank you," Jamie said. "At least I have one brother who isn't an idiot."

"But I'm pretty sure I'm working that day," Simon said.

Jamie rolled his eyes. "You're all morons." He looked my way. "You want to get out of here?"

"Sure. Is food involved?" I said.

"I could eat," Cooper said. "Are we going to go eat?"

Dave elbowed his brother, then said something under his breath too quiet for the rest of us to hear. Jamie didn't even respond, just scooped up his bag and offered his free hand to me, leading me toward the parking lot.

"It's cool," Cooper called after us. "I'll just get something at home, then. Y'all have fun."

Jamie chuckled. "The youngest Hamilton isn't always the most astute."

"He's kind of cute in his innocence." I turned my head and caught a glimpse of Simon climbing into his car on the other side of the parking lot. I waved. "Great game, Simon," I called.

He nodded and waved back. "You too."

"Seriously," Jamie said, repeating his sentiment from earlier. "I don't know what got into him tonight. He was amazing."

"He did play some incredible defense."

We stopped, standing between his car and mine. "Want to ride with me to get a burger or something?"

I glanced down at my clothes.

"I can take you home to change first if you want."

I shook my head. "No, it'll be too late. I'm fine if you are. Let's just get fast food somewhere."

"Sounds good."

It was weird. No, not weird. It was incredibly comfortable and easy and *not weird*. We were smelly and sweaty from our game, I had grass stains on my shirt, my hair was probably frizzy and ridiculous, and I totally didn't care. Maybe that was the thing that was weird. Even though we'd only been dating a month, I was completely relaxed around Jamie. There was a casualness to being around him that was super easy. It reminded me of all the guy friends I'd hung out with in high school, which, upon further reflection, made me a little uncomfortable. Friendship was a good thing—a good way for relationships to start. But not if that was all there ever was. I thought about the thrill I'd felt when Jamie had kissed me for the first time. That didn't feel like friendship, so why did I still feel uneasy?

...

Jamie: Did Lane ever call you about the inn?
Simon: Yep. Just waiting to hear back about when her boss wants
          to see me.
Jamie: Since you're helping her, I'll let you keep the golden soccer ball a
          little longer.
Simon: Sure. Because that's exactly how it works.
Jamie: I'm just saying.
Simon: I earned the ball. Get over it.
Jamie: Who were you trying to impress that night, dude?
Simon: No one. It's been awhile since you've played against me. We're
          usually on the same team.
Jamie: Whatever. I still say you were showing off.

Chapter 9

I MET SIMON AT THE back office door of the inn. I pushed it open and moved to the side, letting him pass me as he made his way into the dim interior, a contrast to the late August sunshine outside. He wore a suit, looking all businesslike and professional, which was good. It would only help Ida feel better about her decision to let him help.

A month. An *entire* month. That was how long it had taken for her to finally let Simon come. Apparently she'd had a conversation with one of her sons—Jacob, I think—who wasn't comfortable letting some stranger get his hands on the financials of the inn when no one but his dad had ever had anything to do with it. He'd offered to look at the accounts himself, but he was all the way on the other side of the country. Without access to Thornton's handwritten ledgers, there was little he could untangle. Why this made perfect sense to *me* and everyone in the Thomas family didn't see it, I had no idea. At one point, I suspected Jacob knew of some sort of tax evasion or fraudulent behavior he didn't want anyone digging up. In the end, it seemed more like a control issue and a worry about someone taking advantage of his mom. At least, I hoped that was all it was.

I motioned for Simon to follow me. "I really appreciate you coming to help."

"It's no problem," he said. "How are you? How's Jamie?"

Jamie.

Jamie was good. Great, even. We saw each other a few times a week, went out every weekend. The Friday before, we'd run into one of the developers from his and Dave's company, and he'd introduced me as his girlfriend without hesitation. So that felt significant.

"I'm good," I answered. "You're not seeing Jamie much yourself?"

He shook his head. "Not lately. I think he's saving all his spare time for you."

"He's had so *little* spare time. All the buyout talk is keeping him busy."

"I guess that's a good thing. The opportunity," Simon added. "Not the spending time away from you."

"I knew what you meant." The company in California had thrown some pretty impressive numbers at Jamie and Dave over the past couple weeks. I didn't know all the details, but Jamie seemed excited about the offer to move their company—which they were told the brothers would still operate independently—under the larger company's corporate umbrella.

I stopped and turned to face Simon. "Do you think it's a good idea?"

"What? Selling LogiX?"

"Yeah. I mean, surrendering control. Isn't it risky to pull others in like that? It seems like Dave and Jamie have a good thing going on their own." I wasn't necessarily opposed to Jamie's selling his company. The way he talked, it seemed more like a merger than an actual buyout because he and Dave would still be involved. It's possible I was just worried it would all end with Jamie moving to California, which left me . . . well, not with Jamie.

"There's always risk," Simon said. "But it could also mean more capital to invest in developing new apps and new software. It means access to better marketing and input from some of the country's best developers. They would likely still be successful if they stay on their own, but from what I've been told, this deal would launch them into a higher level of business. I think it's smart."

"Hmmm." We continued to walk, stopping outside Thornton's old office, where Ida was waiting inside.

"That sounded like a loaded 'hmmm,'" Simon said.

I smiled. "No, I was . . . thinking about Jamie's options. That's all."

"About moving-to-California options?"

Dang. Perceptive. I shook my head. "It's too soon to think about that."

"You know they might not decide to move. So much work can be done remotely these days." It was sweet, his trying to reassure me, but I'd seen the fire in Jamie's eyes when he talked about it. He'd served his mission in California and described the place as both a land of incredible business opportunity and the home of the very best people on the planet. "I think he really wants to go," I said. "He loves it out there."

"Didn't you go to school in California? How did *you* like it?"

"Berkeley was great. I loved it. But I'm a sucker for North Carolina."

He nodded. "Yeah, I feel that way too. Virginia, North Carolina. I don't really care where, as long as I'm close to the mountains."

"Yes! I grew up in Asheville and literally lived minutes from the base of Mount Pisgah. The mountains have always felt the most like home for me."

"I've hiked Mount Pisgah. It's beautiful up there."

"We hiked it every year growing up. Mostly in October, to see the leaves."

"Sounds amazing." He held my gaze for a long moment, and something crackled between us—a spark of connection that I felt in my fingertips and all the way down to my toes. Simon's eyes said he felt it too, a realization that brought a different conversation I'd had with him into sharp relief. When he'd saved the wedding my first weekend on the job and we talked in the parking lot, I'd felt uneasy, like there was more to his look and I didn't know what. It was the same look he was giving me now, only I wasn't uneasy anymore because I felt the same spark.

Except, *no.* Simon had a girlfriend. And *I* had a boyfriend. Sparks were for people not already in relationships.

Time to change the subject. I reached for the doorknob. "Are you ready?"

He nodded. "Lead the way."

* * *

Ida warmed to Simon immediately. There was nothing flashy about his demeanor, from his simple dark suit and pinstriped tie to his conservative, short haircut. But he was still a Hamilton. And when Hamilton men smiled, polite professionalism morphed into full-on charm, even if, in Simon's case, it was completely unintentional. Simon was different from Jamie in that regard. Jamie knew how to work it, to play his strengths for greatest impact. Simon seemed utterly clueless about how charming—and handsome—he was.

It took about ninety minutes to work through everything and give Simon the information he needed to tackle the job. By the end of our meeting, Ida looked exhausted. She pushed the stack of Thornton's old ledgers toward Simon. "I sure do appreciate your help, though I have no idea how you're going to sort any of this out. We maybe ought to burn it all and start from scratch."

Simon smiled. "I don't think it will come to that." He shuffled together a stack of papers and dropped them into his briefcase, then slid the ledgers into an outside pocket. He reached over and shook Ida's hand. "Are you comfortable with me discussing my findings with Lane? If I have questions or need more information?"

Ida looked at me. "Oh, of course. Some days I think she's more invested in this inn than I am. Whatever else you need, just let her know. I'll help her track it down."

We said our good-byes, and I followed Simon into the hallway, shutting the door behind me. "So what do you think?" I asked him.

His eyes shifted to the closed office door like he wasn't sure if Ida could hear us.

"Here." I moved across the hall and opened the door to my own office, then stepped to the side. "This is my office. We can talk in here."

He followed me in. "Wow." He gestured to the large sitting area in front of the big bay window. "You get the bigger office, huh?"

"Only because we do all our consulting for events in here."

"And that's your responsibility?"

"Pretty much."

He walked over to a bookshelf against the far wall and scanned the shelves. It was mostly stuff that came with the office. Thick product catalogs, sample books, and a few historical volumes of Orange County, North Carolina, history. I'd at least added a few personal things on the middle shelf—a picture of my family, a couple of my favorite volumes of poetry, the cheesy paperweight my last boss had given me when I'd left California.

"Are these yours?" Interesting. He'd reached for the poetry first. Most people went straight for the family photo.

"Yeah. Those are my favorites."

"I love poetry," he said. "I know Billy Collins and Longfellow, of course, but I'm not familiar with Nikki Giovanni."

"Oh! You should be. She's incredible. Revolutionary. Groundbreaking. Brilliant." I leaned against the back of the overstuffed armchair that flanked the sitting area. "What I love about Nikki Giovanni is that her language isn't so obscure or flowery that you have to search and dig and ponder to understand. It's simple and yet still so evocative and moving. Her word choice is brilliant. And so multilayered. I don't think she's ever written anything I didn't love."

He flipped through a few pages, then took a step forward. "Here." He handed me the book. "Read me your favorite."

"Really?"

"Yeah. I mean, only if you want to."

It suddenly occurred to me that hanging out with my boyfriend's older brother, reading poetry alone in my office, might not be the greatest idea. But he seemed so earnest. And interested. And poetry wasn't something I got to talk about often. The downside, I guess, to a soccer player dating another soccer player. Jamie and I spent a lot of time talking about soccer. Somewhere in the back of my mind it occurred to me that Simon was *also* a soccer player. But I didn't feel up to dealing with the implications of that observation. I flipped the book open, searching the pages for something I could read.

I settled on "A Poem on the Assassination of Robert F. Kennedy." Moving but not quite as evocative as my actual favorite, "Love Is." Considering my audience, the assassination poem felt like a much safer choice.

"Okay. This one isn't my favorite, but it's still a good one." He nodded his encouragement, and I started to read.

Simon was silent when I finished, just standing there, his arms folded across his chest, leaning slightly against the bookshelf. "That was . . ." He cleared his throat. "That was nice."

I put the book back on the shelf. "Does Karen like poetry?" Karen? Yes. Dinosaur-bone-digging Karen. That felt right.

"Yes, she does. It's one of the things I love most about her. She has a deep appreciation for literature."

A blush of heat crept up my neck at his words. He loved her. *Of course* he loved her. Jamie said they'd been together a long time. I don't know why it embarrassed me to hear him say it. "It must be nice to have that in common," I said. "I don't think Jamie cares for poetry much."

"I don't know," Simon said. "He might surprise you."

I raised my eyebrows. Jamie liking poetry would *definitely* be a surprise. "I don't know. It's fine though. He's got a lot of other redeeming qualities." I moved toward my desk. "So . . . the inn? Do I need to start searching for money under the mattresses?"

"I don't think things are quite that bad, but it's hard to say at this point. I'll need to spend some time with the numbers to know for sure."

"Any idea what the problem is? The inn is busy. Almost too busy. It seems like we shouldn't be struggling to pay vendors, and yet, since Thornton died, it's like we're always a couple weeks behind. Waiting for payments on the next event so we can pay bills related to the last one."

He scratched his jaw. "I'm going to have to break things down a lot further to have a clear picture, but my gut is telling me this is a classic case of mismanaged growth."

I dropped into my chair and motioned for him to sit. He settled into the leather chair across from me, his briefcase sitting at his feet. "What does that mean?" I asked.

"Sometimes when businesses start and their operations are smaller and easier to manage, financial systems are put in place that easily accommodate a smaller business model but don't necessarily accommodate potential growth. If the business does grow and the financial management doesn't grow with it, it's easier for funds to be mismanaged because, though well-intentioned, owners make decisions without a clear picture of how their business is really doing."

"When Thornton and Ida opened the inn, it was a much smaller operation," I said. "Just a handful of rooms. Ida did all the cleaning herself."

"Right. So Thornton handling all the finances made complete sense. But then the business started to grow."

"And his financial strategies didn't."

"Exactly. Think about it this way," Simon said. "At a large hotel or any other multifaceted operation, there are individual profit-and-loss statements for each component of the business—the hotel restaurant, event services, room revenue. At any given moment, you can see what parts of the hotel are profitable and what parts aren't. If you're losing money on breakfast. If weekday bookings are down, creating a drain on the accounts. Maybe the restaurant loses money during the week but makes up for it during Sunday brunch when everybody brings their grandma in to get a mimosa."

I smiled. I knew the exact Sunday brunch crowd he referenced.

"It doesn't look like Thornton was itemizing out the costs of running the inn, at least not on paper. His ledgers list every expense, but they're all jumbled together. Like the only numbers he paid attention to were the biggest ones. Money in. Money out."

"But if there's always enough money coming in, things have to be okay, right?"

"In the simplest sense, yes," Simon said. "But that's just it. It doesn't look like there *is* enough money coming in. Like I said, I need to dig into the numbers to know for sure."

"How is that even possible? The inn is still open and functional. We're all still getting paid."

"Unfortunately, if things continue like they are, I don't think you'll be getting paid much longer."

My heart rate spiked. Gaspard. April. Me. Not to mention dozens of other employees. We all relied on the inn. But it was more than just a paycheck for Ida. It was everything she and Thornton had built together—his entire legacy. There had to be a way to fix things. I drummed my fingers against the desktop and forced out a frustrated breath. Simon was so calm, but there was a lot at stake, and thinking about it was stressing me out.

He reached across the desk and touched my forearm, his fingers light but somehow still steadying. "Lane. I don't want you to worry. I'll make this my top priority, okay? I'll find you some answers. Soon."

I took a deep breath.

"Okay?" he asked.

I nodded. "Okay." I wanted to believe him, but it was hard not to feel like his measured diplomacy was a cover to keep from telling me the inn was two months shy of not making payroll. Or worse, shutting its doors altogether.

Simon moved to the door. "I assure you I'll be as transparent as possible when I know how things stand."

"Thanks, Simon. I appreciate it."

He was out the door when I realized we'd never discussed his fee. He'd probably send us a bill, but I wanted to be sure he knew we were expecting it and not trying to freeload off a boyfriend/family connection. He was almost to his car when I caught him.

"Simon!"

He turned. "What's up?"

"We never talked about your fee. I hope you're planning to send us a bill for your time."

He ran a hand across his jaw. "I'm going to do this one on the house."

I put my hands on my hips. "No way. You can't do that."

"I'm the boss. I can do whatever I want."

"But you shouldn't do it, Simon. It's not fair. I never expected you to help out as a favor. I wouldn't ever ask that of you."

"I know you didn't. But just the same. I'd like to do this for you."

Something akin to discomfort settled in my gut again. Not full-on discomfort. More like a distant cousin. A niggling. A tiny seed of a thought that, spurred by our earlier nanosecond of connection, was beginning to take root. I'd like to do this . . . *for you*, Simon had said. *For me.*

"Hey, can I ask you a question about Jamie?" I blurted out.

Simon paused, one foot already in his car. "Sure," he said.

It was impulsive. But somehow in my messed-up brain, it felt like mentioning Jamie would make the weirdness in my gut disappear. "I, um, do you know of any restaurants he likes? He's been working so much, I thought I might take him dinner this week. Surprise him, you know?"

Simon nodded. "I'm sure he'd appreciate that. Let me think a second." He shrugged out of his suit coat, which had to have been hot in the early August heat, and laid it across the backseat of his car. "Oh, I've got it. There's this Vietnamese place over on Franklin Street. I don't remember the name, but I could look it up for you. I don't think Jamie's ever been there, but a client recommended it to me the other day."

"And you think Jamie would like it?"

"Yes. Absolutely. All Jamie talked about when he first got home from his mission was pho. I bet he'd love it if you took him some." Jamie had served in Anaheim, primarily among the Vietnamese who lived in the area. Funny we'd never talked about the food. I guess not liking sushi didn't necessarily mean a distaste for Asian cuisine in general.

"That is an amazing idea."

"Good. I can text you the name of the place if you want."

"Yes, please. That would be awesome."

"Will do," he said. He waved one last time as he pulled out of the parking lot, the loose gravel crunching under his tires.

I watched him drive away but wished I hadn't. I wished I'd turned and gone back inside without giving him a second thought. Instead, he was getting a second, third, and fourth thought. It wasn't good. I stood in the center of the sidewalk just outside the inn's office entrance and forced Karen into my mind, imagining her and Simon together. I didn't know anything about her, but it was easy to picture her as beautiful and intelligent and totally worthy of a Hamilton brother's affection.

I walked back into my office focused on that image. I imagined them laughing and talking, even reading poetry. The longer I imagined, the quicker my misguided feelings dissipated. I didn't feel anything for Simon. A spark maybe, sure. But sparks didn't have to turn into flames. They could be squelched in a second, put out with nothing but a drop of water or a tiny puff of air. I took a deep, cleansing breath. It felt good to be in control.

I turned my thoughts to Jamie. Surprising him. Taking him food I knew he'd appreciate. Feeling his arms around me and his lips on mine . . . *yeah*. I was good. I had the right Hamilton brother—no doubt about that.

Simon: Nikki Giovanni. Billy Collins. Henry Longfellow.

Jamie: ??

Simon: Those are poets Lane likes. You know, you could have just looked at the books on her office shelf. No real sleuthing necessary.

Jamie: Excellent. Guess I should have thought of that.

Simon: Don't name-drop Giovanni. Lane wouldn't buy it. Collins you can probably get away with, but Longfellow has been around the longest, so he's your safest bet.

Jamie: Got it.

Simon: Also. I did some research. Nikki Giovanni is on the faculty at Virginia Tech, and she's doing a signing at the university book store in September. That's not too far away.

Jamie: This is very good information. Lane's birthday is in September.

Simon: Well, there you go.

Chapter 10

I PULLED INTO THE PARKING lot of Jamie's office just past 7:00 p.m. *Office* being a relative term. It was more like a giant warehouse. One large room. Exposed pipes and large steel beams running across the ceiling. Giant windows. I stepped off the service elevator that had clanked and clunked up to the top floor and stood at the edge of the massive space. A cluster of desks sat in the middle of the room. They were all empty, desk lamps turned off and chairs pushed in, save two on the end, where Jamie and Dave sat. Dave had his feet up on the desk, his head leaning back in his hands, while Jamie leaned over his laptop, his face close to the screen.

At the sound of the elevator, they both looked up.

Jamie smiled. "Lane?" He stood and walked toward me, meeting me in the middle of the room. He leaned in to kiss me on the cheek. "What are you doing here?"

"I brought food. When you said you were working late, I figured, well, a guy has to eat, right?"

He looked at the bag, then looked back at me. "Do I smell . . ."

"Pho? Yeah. It's this new place on Franklin Street. Have you tried it?"

"I haven't. I could seriously kiss you right now," he said. "You brought me pho."

"You should kiss her right now," Dave said, coming up behind him. He held his keys in his hand. "Pretty sure it's part of the deal."

"There's enough for both of you," I said, looking at Dave. "I wasn't planning on staying."

"Nope. I'm done for the night. You kids have fun though."

Jamie took the bags from my hands and walked back toward his desk. "Do you have to leave?"

"Not exactly, but you're working. I don't want to keep you."

"How about you stay long enough to eat with me, then you can go, and I'll get back to work."

"Fair enough," I agreed.

I'd been to Jamie's office twice. Once because he had wanted to show me around and introduce me to the rest of the people he worked with, and a second time when we'd met the week before and gone out to dinner with Dave and Katie. We'd all come from work, so we'd parked in the office parking lot and ridden together to the restaurant. But I'd never been there at night. With just the two of us sitting in the tiny pool of light his desk lamp created in the otherwise dark and cavernous room, it almost felt . . . I don't know, creepy?

"I don't know how you work in here alone. Especially at night."

"You get used to it," he said.

"How did you end up with such a giant space? You're not even taking up a third of the room."

"It was Dave's doing. He knows the guy who owns the building. Some guy rented the space and paid two years in advance but then bailed three months in. So the owner's letting Dave and I finish out the term for nothing but the cost of utilities. It's a sweet setup."

"Sounds like it. I guess free space is the best option, even if it is scary at night."

Jamie pulled all the food out of the bags and opened the containers. I'd never had anything Vietnamese. There was pho, but then there was another container of what looked like a giant herb salad Jamie set between us. He handed me a set of chopsticks and a spoon.

"You're going to teach me how to do this, right?"

He grinned. "You've never had it?"

"I had to Google it to know what it was," I said.

He proceeded to give me a rundown of how to best savor the pho, first by drinking the broth, then by trying the noodles, then by adding an assortment of the various herbs sitting on the desk to the broth and getting a bite with all three elements together. The magic was in recognizing the simplicity of the flavors on their own but then getting the complexity of them all working together when combined. I couldn't decide if I was more thrilled to have finally experienced pho or more disappointed that I'd gone so long without it.

"Hey, what are you doing the last weekend in September?" Jamie asked.

I leaned over my bowl and took another sip. "I don't know. I'll have to check my work schedule. You have something in mind?"

We both sat behind his desk, me in Dave's chair and Jamie in his. He reached across the armrests between us and took my hand. "I want you to come home with me to Bristol. For Cooper's missionary farewell."

I fiddled with my chopsticks. It was a big step. Going home to Bristol meant meeting his parents. Seeing his childhood home. Spending time with his entire extended family as they sent Cooper off on his mission. It felt involved. Intimate. Important.

"Wow. Are you sure? It's only been a couple of months. I don't want to impose on your family's time together."

Jamie leaned back in his chair but didn't let go of my hand. "We've been dating two and a half months. And it'll be almost four by the time we head to Bristol. In Mormon dating time, that's the equivalent of at least two or three years."

I rolled my eyes. "That's not how it works."

He smirked. "I'm not asking you to marry me, Lane. Just come home with me. Meet the family. I want you to be there."

It was classic Jamie. *Impetuous* maybe wasn't quite the right word. That implied a lack of forethought or carelessness, and Jamie was not careless. But he also never gave more than two seconds' thought to any decision he made. He trusted his gut implicitly. No long pondering or careful consideration required. When we'd eaten with Katie and Dave the week before, Dave had confirmed Jamie's quick decision-making went far beyond stuff like what to eat for dinner. It played a huge role in what made him so great at business. He was determined. Resolute. Committed. And he had good instincts. "He's a little overbearing when he can't rein it in," Dave had said. "But we love him anyway."

"Can I tell you something about me?" Jamie asked.

"Okay."

"When I was in college, I dated a lot of different women. I mean *a lot*, a lot. I had this reputation of being a player, but that wasn't . . . I wasn't trying to hurt anybody. I just knew what I wanted. And it never took me long to figure out whether or not a girl was someone I was interested in."

He shifted, leaning forward and taking my other hand as well. "I didn't like what people were saying about me. That I played with people's emotions.

Led people on. So around the time I graduated, I backed way off. Stopped dating. I figured when I met the right person, I'd know."

I tensed. He was sounding serious. More serious than I felt. But he also sounded genuine and real and like a guy who was trying really hard to lay his heart out on the table. I tried to relax. This was good. Real. And come on—Jamie was amazing. There wasn't a good reason to shy away.

He squeezed my hands. "Don't freak out. I'm not trying to freak you out. I'm just saying I like you. I want you to come to Virginia. Meet my family. Help us give Cooper a proper send-off. It'll be fun."

Curse those eyes. "You're very convincing, Jamie Hamilton."

He leaned forward and kissed me. "Only when I want to be."

* * *

"Granny Grace? Are you out here?"

"Lane? Back here." She held her hand up, just barely visible above the tall rows of corn that filled the back third of her garden. I passed the tomatoes and cucumbers, then stepped over the cantaloupe and watermelon before I found her. "You just getting home from work?" she asked.

I yawned, pausing at the end of the row. "Yeah. We had a bridal shower in the dining room this morning."

She was leaning over, pulling weeds out from in between the tall, yellowy stalks. She grunted, twisting the thick stem of a weed and yanking it out of the ground. "You've been working lots of Saturdays lately." She stood, pulling off one glove before wiping a hand across her forehead.

"That's the nature of the business," I said. "Have you seen this watermelon? It's gorgeous."

"It's not ready yet." Granny came up beside me. "Still too green."

"How do you even know that?"

"Oh, it's complicated," she said, her tone serious. "Here. Lean in real close." She motioned me forward. "Lean right down close to the watermelon." I was almost almost bent in half as it was. "Closer," she said. "Now close your eyes and take a deep breath."

I did as she asked, standing stone still, my eyes closed. Until I heard her laugh. I stood, my hands pressed to my hips. She was almost doubled over in laughter, her arms held to her sides.

"Seriously?" I said. "I get this kind of treatment from you? You're worse than Dad!"

"Where do you think he gets it, child?" She continued to laugh but leaned over and rolled the growing watermelon up on its side. "See? Still too green. You have to wait till the underbelly turns a little yellow."

"You're funny, Granny Grace. Truly."

She swatted at me with her gardening glove. "You want to help me get the beans in? All these weeds have about done in my back."

I groaned. "Didn't we pick all the beans the last time we were out here?" It felt like all I'd been doing in her garden was pick beans.

"We did. And the time before that, and the time before that," she said. "Don't begrudge a good harvest, Lane. A full freezer is never a bad thing."

"I think I'm too busy smelling the watermelon."

She laughed again. "Now you sound like your mama. How about you pick 'em, I'll cook 'em, then we both get to eat 'em."

"Fine. If you're offering to cook, I'll pick. Do you mind if Jamie eats with us? He's coming over later. We were going to go out, but if you're cooking, I think I'd rather ask him to stay."

"That's fine with me. Just be sure to pick enough for three." She crossed to the gardening hutch at the back of the house and pulled out a basket. "Here. Use this."

I took the basket from her outstretched hand. "I won't stop till it's full."

She rinsed her hands in the deep sink next to the hutch, then dried them on her apron. "You're getting serious with that boy, aren't you?"

"With Jamie? Yeah, I guess so."

"You told your mama about him?"

I sat on the porch steps, the empty basket resting on my knees. "Not too much. I mean, she knows I'm seeing someone. But . . . I don't know. Anything I tell her, she tells her mother, and I don't think I'm ready for those phone calls yet." My Puerto Rican grandmother. Fierce. Stubborn. And devastated that I wasn't married by my twenty-second birthday. Even three years later, she was still giving my phone number to every missionary who served in all of Puerto Rico.

Granny Grace chuckled. "If you're getting serious with Jamie, that will help things, won't it? You've found a nice man. She'll be happy for you."

I stood back up and moved toward the beans. "I know. You're probably right. But you know how Mama is. She overanalyzes everything. I never know if I'm having a conversation with my mother or with Dr. Bishop, who might launch into a psychoanalysis every time I turn around."

"You're overgeneralizing. Your mother isn't that bad. Wanting to know the details of your life is not the same as wanting to offer a diagnosis."

"Things are easy right now, Granny. It's nice not worrying about all the complicated family stuff. It's only been a few months."

She didn't say anything in response, but I could feel her stare.

I stopped and turned around. She stood there, her look intense, her hands on her hips. "Are you playing games with this boy?" she asked.

I huffed. "No. Why would you say that?"

"He's taking you to meet his family, isn't he?"

"Not until next month."

She grunted something incoherent.

"What? So you're grunting your opinions at me now?"

"Listen. I'm not trying to meddle. You're a grown woman, and I know you're going to do what you're going to do. But the way I see it, you're keeping this man at a safe distance. I'm wondering why that is."

Stupid grandmotherly perception. I'd been dancing around the same realization myself for days. I'd agreed to go to Bristol with Jamie because I wanted to go, but thinking about it made me panic a little. Every time I thought about our relationship growing more serious, a tiny flame of fear flickered in my belly. "I'm being cautious," I said. "Is that really such a bad thing?"

"Is that why you can't tell your mama? You're being cautious."

"She called you, didn't she?"

"It doesn't matter if she did. I'm still speaking the truth."

"It's not a bad thing to be careful, Granny. I don't want Abuela getting her hopes up until I'm sure this is the real deal."

She lowered herself onto the back-porch steps. "What makes you think it's not the real deal?"

I couldn't explain my hesitation, really. "It's not that I think it's not. I'm just trying to take it slow." I dropped a few more beans into the basket.

"I think that's smart. But if you're being cautious while he's holding you close? Sounds a little like dancing with one shoe off."

"What does that even mean?"

"It means you're in it but not really in it. And at a much higher risk of getting stepped on. Best mind your toes, Lane. Or in this case, *his*."

I saw her point. Keenly. And spent the next twenty minutes of bean picking in quiet introspection. When I'd dated my only serious college boyfriend, we'd fallen in love pretty fast. There was intense chemistry between us—all kinds of sparks even from simple stuff like hand-holding. But the relationship didn't have a ton of depth underneath all those sparks. When things had gotten tough in the form of family disgruntlement, we hadn't had the roots to weather the storm.

I didn't want a relationship with no spark, but I also didn't want one that was all spark if it meant a lack of depth underneath all that chemistry. It was why I appreciated the easy comfort I felt around Jamie. It made relationship building easier. It was true that Jamie did seem a little more serious about things than I did. But it wasn't because I wasn't on my way there. That he was a little farther along didn't concern me. I'd never been one to jump into stuff quickly, and he *was*—in every sense of the word. I felt pretty confident I would catch up eventually.

The beans grew well over my head, their leafy vines climbing up and around the thick twine Granny Grace had secured between sturdy bamboo poles. After half an hour, my back and arms ached. I dropped the half-full basket onto the ground between my feet and pulled out my cell phone for a quick break.

I had a text from Jamie. *We still on for tonight?*

Granny Grace is cooking. You up for coming over instead of going out? I responded.

Sure. Can I bring anything?

Nope. Only your appetite.

Okay. Be there at seven?

Sounds good.

Granny Grace's warning about playing with Jamie's feelings echoed in my head. But I wasn't playing. I keyed out another text, this one maybe more for my own benefit than his. *I can't wait to see you.*

Simon: How are things with Lane?

*Jamie: Good. We talked poetry. I mentioned Billy Collins.
        She was impressed.*

Simon: Good.

Jamie: How's Karen?

Simon: Your guess is as good as mine.

Jamie: Still haven't heard from her?

Simon: Not a word.

Jamie: Sorry, man.

*Simon: I had to stop by the inn the other day to get some forms signed,
        and Lane was drinking hazelnut hot chocolate.*

Jamie: In August?

*Simon: I know. I said the same thing. She said it was her favorite no
        matter the time of year.*

Jamie: So weird.

*Simon: I'm telling you because it might be useful. Isn't her birthday
        coming up?*

*Jamie: YES. Thanks for the reminder. That poetry thing in Virginia.
        When is it?*

Simon: Dude. Look it up.

Jamie: What was the poet's name?

Simon: Nikki Giovanni.

Jamie: Got it. Looking it up now.

Jamie: Score. The signing is ON Lane's birthday.

Simon: Lucky for you, then.

Chapter 11

I'D ALWAYS BEEN CERTAIN MY parents had the fastest courtship and engagement of any couple I'd ever heard of. Dad had fallen for Mom and proposed three weeks after they met. She'd said no, of course. He'd had to ask three more times before she'd finally agreed, but the fact that he'd been so sure after such a short amount of time blew me away. Still, it was nothing compared to the speed of Chloe's whirlwind engagement. It hadn't been three full months since she'd kidnapped me on that fateful Saturday morning and taken me to my first Hamilton brothers' soccer game, oohing and aahing over the "untouchable brothers" everyone dreamed of dating.

And now she was engaged. To some new guy—Chad something or other—who was days away from starting pharmacy school at UNC and probably hadn't even finished unpacking his apartment before he and Chloe had been shopping for wedding rings.

Which was why I found myself on the longest Tuesday morning of my life working through the details of Chloe and Chad's wedding reception. Because the gardens at Winding Way were *perfect* for Chloe's wedding photos. And the ballroom at Winding Way was *perfect* for the dance party she wanted her reception to be. And the terrace at Winding Way was *perfect* for her bouquet toss, and the food was *perfect*, and the main staircase was *perfect*, and by eleven thirty, I was pretty sure if I heard the word *perfect* one more time I was going to quit my job and move to Tahiti.

At least I wasn't the only one overwhelmed by Chloe's enthusiasm. Her mom hugged me on their way out the door, giving my shoulders an extra squeeze. "Thank you for being so patient," she said softly. "Hopefully she'll mellow out a little by October."

I smiled. She probably wouldn't. But it's not like I could complain. She loved everything about the inn. That made my job really easy. After seeing Chloe and her mom out the door, I headed to the kitchen in search of lunch but was waylaid by a call from my mother. I hesitated before answering. I hadn't talked to Mom in . . . days? Weeks, maybe? Granny Grace's words flashed through my brain. Maybe it was time to finally fess up a few details. I answered the call.

"Hi, Mom."

"Well, bless me, the daughter I thought was lost to me has finally answered the phone."

"Very funny. How are you?"

"Busy. Have you talked to John lately? *He's* not answering my calls either."

"Not since last week. I'm sure he'll call you when he's got some free time." John was in the throes of a pediatric surgical residency. Which generally made his "I'm busy" excuses much more convincing than mine.

"I hope he does. I want him to come home for Thanksgiving this year."

"Have you heard from Abuela? Is she going to come?"

"She's coming. I bought her plane ticket this morning."

Thanksgiving with Abuela. It had been too long since we'd been together. At the same time, thinking about Abuela made a knot form in my chest. Her presence at Thanksgiving meant pressure. It meant questions about why I wasn't married and when I was going to get married and had I heard from Elder Hansen whom she'd met and given my number to? My mother had no trouble reading my prolonged silence.

"Lane. You know her concern is out of love."

I did know. And I understood. My grandmother was one of seven daughters. All lived in her hometown of Arecibo. All had multiple children and grandchildren, and most even had great-grandchildren. But my grandmother only had Mom. And it had nearly killed her. Emergency surgery after she delivered her first and only child saved her life but ended any hope of more children. Then Mom moved far away and only had two kids, both of whom persisted into adulthood so far unmarried and *without* children.

"You mean her love for great-grandchildren."

"I can't say I blame her there. It might be nice to have a few grandbabies of my own."

"I'll get right on it, Mom. Should I go now? Find the first available man?"

"Don't be smart with me. You *are* dating someone, aren't you? You told me you were."

"Yes. I'm dating someone. Haven't quite gotten to the how-many-kids-we'll-have conversation, but dating, yes."

"Have you gotten to the bring-him-home-for-Thanksgiving conversation? Because bringing a boyfriend to meet your abuela . . . Oh, Lane, she would be so happy."

Maybe. But was I ready for that? "I'll think about it."

"You do that. And if you talk to John before I do, will you tell him about Thanksgiving? It would be so nice to have us all together."

"I will, Mom. Listen, I'm at work. I need to run."

"Love you, dear. Your father says hello."

April was already leaning into the staff fridge looking for leftovers when I finally made it to the kitchen. "What did Gaspard leave for us today?" I asked.

She pulled out a container and lifted the lid, sniffing the contents. Her eyes went wide. "It's bisque." She turned around, holding the container like it held liquid gold. "He *actually* left us some bisque."

I was already reaching for bowls. "Is there enough for all of us?"

April glanced around. "There's enough for two of us. Please don't say we have to share it."

I jerked my head toward the door. "Let's eat in my office. You warm it up, I'll sneak us some fresh bread, and we'll meet there in five."

"You're my best food friend, Lane," April said, her face solemn. "May the bread gods be ever in your favor."

Gaspard's crunchy french bread was his pride and joy and one of his most acclaimed specialties. I didn't believe it at first. Bread? Most acclaimed? But then I'd had some. And vowed I would never doubt Gaspard's abilities again.

It was not, however, easy to get my hands on a fresh loaf. Generally, employees were swatted away like pesky children. And rightly so, really, seeing as how customers paid for it and all. But that bread dipped in the best crab bisque I'd ever tasted in all my very foodie life was worth a little schmoozing.

"Hi, Gaspard." I leaned onto the stainless-steel surface of his workstation adjacent to the stove. He hovered over a pot of simmering tomato sauce.

"Ahh, no." He slid a clean spatula under my elbows and lifted them up, then tossed the spatula into a bin behind him. "This space is for food. Not your germ-covered arms."

I wrinkled my forehead. "I do not have germ-covered arms."

"No? Then maybe you should go out into the dining room and let people use them as plates. If they are so clean that they can clutter up my workspace, they must be clean enough for our guests."

I took a step back and rolled my eyes. "Fine. My arms are nowhere near your food or your countertops or you. Happy?"

He gave me a dry look. "Immensely."

Mission Bread Retrieval was off to a roaring start. Time to pull out my power weapon. I'd been saving it for a while—well over a week—but I *really* wanted that bread. "So. Gaspard. You busy next Sunday?"

He paused. "What do you want from me?"

"What makes you think I want something? I'm just curious."

He leaned forward, wafting the steam over the pot toward his nose, then breathing in deeply. "More garlic," he said. "I don't believe you. You have never been curious about my Sunday plans. Why start now?"

Good grief. He was not going to let me be diplomatic. "Fine. You want it straight? I have two tickets to see Francesca Maren next Sunday night in Raleigh. I don't love Francesca Maren. But word on the street is you do."

He froze midstir. "How did you get tickets to that show? It's been sold out for months."

"It doesn't matter. All that matters is that I'd like to give the tickets to you. Tenth row. Pretty great seats for a sold-out concert. What do you say? You want them?" I folded my arms across my chest. I could tell I had him just where I wanted him.

"Plates up," a voice sounded behind him.

He turned, giving a final glance over an order on its way out to the dining room. He adjusted the garnish on one plate, then added additional sauce to another before waving them away. When he turned back to me, his face was stern. "What's in it for you?"

"Nothing. I *want* to give you the tickets."

He shook his head. "No. There is fire in your eyes, Lane. You're after something."

I stuck out my chin. "Fine. You get the tickets, I get fresh bread whenever I want it for three months."

He narrowed his eyes. "Two months and not a day longer. Leave the tickets on my desk."

I rolled my eyes. "You didn't even give me a chance to counter."

He dropped a loaf of bread into my arms. "My bread. My terms."

I huffed. "Isn't it technically Rodrigo's bread? He's the one who makes it now anyway. Maybe I ought to give the tickets to him."

Rodrigo breezed past, a tray of fresh loaves ready for the oven in hand. "Hey, thanks, Lane," he said with a grin. "I'd love the tickets. I'll slip you some bread whenever you want."

Gaspard stalked off after Rodrigo, muttering something I couldn't understand. Probably something French. I chuckled on my way out, the booty of my conquest wrapped safely in my arms. My first couple of months at Winding Way I'd been terrified of Gaspard, but really, when you got through all the bluster, he had a pretty decent heart. Not a generous heart. But a decent one nonetheless.

* * *

"How on earth did you wind up with tickets to Francesca Maren?" April dipped a huge chunk of bread in her soup before taking a bite.

"I booked the library for a bridal shower. The mother of the bride is the station manager for WKIX in Raleigh. There was an issue with dates and availability, but I managed to shuffle stuff around and get her the date she wanted, so she sent the tickets over as a thank-you."

"Wow. Some thank-you."

"Maybe if I liked Francesca Maren."

"Does *anyone* like Francesca Maren? Besides Gaspard?"

"I have no idea. They've been giving tickets away on the radio for months, so someone must."

"Or no one does," April said. "And that's why they're giving away all the tickets."

I reached for the bread and tore off a chunk. "Don't you dare say that out loud. I just secured our bread source. You really want to risk it now?"

My cell phone rang from inside my desk drawer, the ringtone faint but not faint enough that April couldn't hear it. My cheeks flamed red, and I lunged for my desk, grabbing the phone and silencing the call.

April held up her finger and pointed at me, shaking her head. "No way are you getting off without an explanation."

I dropped the phone back into the drawer and slammed it shut. "I have no idea what you're talking about."

"You have a BOYBAND 2.0 ringtone *on* your cell phone. You! A working professional. An adult. A classy, put-together woman has a ringtone that plays 'You'll Get Me Back' by BOYBAND 2.0."

"Maybe we need to talk about the fact that *you*, also a working professional woman, recognized 'You'll Get Me Back' in less than five seconds."

She paused. "Maybe so, but it's not my ringtone."

I dropped back onto the sofa across from her. "It isn't generally my ringtone either. Only when Randi calls."

"An old friend from high school?"

"College. My freshman roommate. We didn't know each other, but then we discovered we had all this random stuff in common, including an intense and deep-seated love for all things BOYBAND 2.0."

She shook her head and laughed. "This is seriously the best thing I've ever heard. Did you ever see them in concert?"

"Oh, you have no idea."

"More than once?"

I raised my eyebrows.

"Twice? Three times?"

I shook my head and bit my lip, holding up my hand, fingers spread.

April's eyes went wide. "You saw them in concert *five* times? What, did you follow them all over the country?"

"No! More like . . . all over the Eastern Seaboard."

"Oh, this is so awesome. I mean, I liked their music. I even had a few of their albums, I think, but you . . . This is 2.0 dedication I'm not sure I've ever seen before. Do you know the dance? What am I asking—of course you know the dance."

I scoffed. "What do you take me for? I don't just know the dance. I stood on stage inside Philips Arena in Atlanta, Georgia, and *did* the dance. *With* the band."

"You did not."

"Oh, I did. They pulled me out of the second row and brought me on stage—Dustin on one side and Jeremy on the other." I sighed. "I high-fived them both. It's probably still on YouTube somewhere."

April messed with her phone for a second, then set it down on the table, the opening bars of "You'll Get Me Back" emanating from the tiny speaker. She kicked off her shoes and moved to the middle of my office, motioning for me to join her. It was totally ridiculous, doing this in the middle of my office, in the middle of a workday, years after I'd even thought about the cheesy dance steps that went along with BOYBAND 2.0's biggest hit. But that song was such a huge part of my teenage experience. I couldn't *not* dance.

So I did.

In my conservative black skirt, tapered jacket, and business hair. I kicked off my low-profile business-y shoes and danced like I was a sophomore in high school, the flame of love for Dustin and Jeremy and the rest of 2.0 burning bright.

I'd just completed the most difficult of the crisscross leg jumps followed by a spin and semi-inappropriate hip thrust when I turned and saw Simon standing in the doorway of my office, a bemused expression on his face. Never had I wanted to crawl under the floorboards and hide quite so intensely as I did right then. Of all the people I could have embarrassed myself in front of, why did it have to be Simon? With his professional demeanor and grown-up mortgage and reasonable car.

Simon stood there watching while I scrambled to put my shoes back on and smooth the flyaways back into my bun.

"Sorry," he finally said once I was mostly put back together. "Your door was open. Should I come back another time?"

I ushered him into the office. "This is fine. April and I were just finishing lunch. Just give me one quick second."

April looked like she was going to cry from the effort of holding in her laughter. I shot her a scolding look, then ushered her out the door, the remnants of our shared lunch gathered in her hands. I followed her into the hallway, closing the door behind me. "I am so not sharing my bread with you ever again," I muttered under my breath.

She smirked. "Oh, I'm pretty sure the look on your face when you saw him standing there is well worth the sacrifice."

"I have no idea why I agreed to be your friend."

"Who is he?"

"Jamie's older brother, Simon. He's the accountant who's reviewing the inn's financials."

"Oh! I can see the family resemblance. You were not wrong about Hamilton family genetics. You're sure he's not single?"

"Nope. Happily taken."

"Hmm. That's too bad."

"Okay. I'm going to go talk to him now."

She nodded while backing away. "Good luck."

"You're not going to tell anyone about my BOYBAND history, right?"

She paused. "Oh, no. I won't tell *anyone*. I'll tell *everyone*."

Ha. Funny.

Back in the office, Simon had taken a seat under the bay window. A sheet of paper lay on the table in front of him—a list of some sort.

I sat across from him. "Sorry about that."

He looked up from his phone and turned it off, setting it facedown on the table. "It's no trouble. I know I wasn't expected."

I'd gotten to know Simon well enough to know that if I didn't mention the dancing, he wouldn't either. But I couldn't let it go. "It was an impromptu thing," I said. "I don't generally turn my office into a dance club."

His lip twitched. "Perhaps you should. You seemed . . . enthusiastic."

It was official. I'd never been quite so embarrassed. Why I felt like further explanation was going to help my cause, I had no idea. "It was just this cheesy boy band I liked growing up. They had this dance that went along with one of their songs, and April didn't believe I knew the entire thing, and then she started playing it, and I . . . I am so embarrassed."

"Don't be," Simon said. "If it makes you feel better, I went through this phase in high school where all I listened to was Francesca Maren. I haven't heard any of her songs in years, but if one came on the radio right now, I'd probably have a hard time not singing along."

My jaw dropped. "For real?" Admitting to a Francesca obsession for anyone other than sixty-year-old French chefs was brave.

Simon held up his finger. "Don't mock. You have no room to talk."

"Oh, whatever. I'm like you. I haven't listened to BOYBAND 2.0 in years."

"Years, huh? So if I were to steal your keys and go out to your car, I wouldn't find a single 2.0 CD?"

I shifted in my seat and reached for the sheet of paper on the coffee table. "Tell me why you're here again?"

"Oh, no." He pulled the paper out of my grasp. "I'm not letting you off that easy."

I crossed my arms. "Fine. Yes. But only their greatest hits. And I don't listen to it all that often, and why am I telling you any of this?"

"I have no idea, but I'm so glad you did." He leaned forward and propped his elbows on his knees, the light catching the blue of his eyes. They were so different from Jamie's dark brown—almost a translucent blue with a little rim of yellow-gold right around the edges. We were two beats past awkward when I realized I was staring. I leaned back, giving my head a little shake. "You, uh . . . were saying . . . about the inn."

"I wasn't saying. Not yet. But I guess I should." He glanced at his watch. "I've got another appointment in half an hour, but there're a few things I need from you. Since I live so close, I thought it would be easier to bring over the list in person."

"That's right. I forgot you live close."

"I could walk if I wanted," Simon said. "There's a gate at the end of my property that cuts through to the gardens."

"I could walk too," I said. "I keep telling myself I will once the weather cools down."

"*If* the weather ever cools down," he added. "I hate September because it feels like it should be fall already, but it never really is. It's still hot."

"I hear you there, but I love September anyway. It's my birthday month, which means it has to be my favorite."

"Yeah? You got any big plans?"

"All I know is Jamie has made me promise to take the entire day off. He won't tell me why or where we're going."

A split second of awareness flashed across Simon's expression. He *knew*!

"You know where he's taking me, don't you?"

He cleared his throat. "I think we need to talk about the inn."

"Oh, come on. One little hint?"

"Never," he said. He held out the sheet he'd stolen from me moments before. "Come on. I've got somewhere I need to be. You need to look at this."

I snatched the paper back with a huff. "Fine."

"There are a few more things I'd like to look over if you can help me gather them. Three more years of tax returns—I only have two years, and I'd like to go back a little further than that—and an employee history, if Ida has one."

"What does an employee history entail?"

"How many employees does the inn currently have? How much is each employee paid? Records of hires, terminations, that sort of thing. Hopefully

Thornton kept a human resources file that kept track of the details. If not, we can pull records from payroll and piece things together as best we can."

"I can do that. This afternoon, even. I'll see what I can find in his office."

"That'd be great. The only other thing I need is a little more sensitive in nature. And it's going to have to come straight from Ida."

"Okay. What do you need?" I said.

He cleared his throat. "In putting together the whole puzzle of the inn's financial situation, I'm finding gaps. Chunks of money that are coming from somewhere but not any of the business accounts Ida turned over in the original info I was given. My hunch is that Thornton probably had some personal accounts involved in the running of the inn—which happens sometimes in owner/operator businesses—but without access to those personal accounts, I can't really get a clear picture of what's happening."

"Do you mean like a personal checking account?"

"Sure. Or personal credit cards he might have used for business expenses."

"Oh! That reminds me. Ida brought this file by and asked that I give it to you." I hurried over to my desk and picked up a heavy file with a large yellow rubber band wrapped around it. "I haven't had a chance to look through it, but it might be exactly what you're looking for. She said it looked like account statements of some sort." I handed him the file.

He looked through the first few sheets, then nodded his head slowly, his eyebrows drawn together. "These are definitely helpful."

"Your face looks like it isn't good news. What do they say?"

"I need to pull back and factor this into the big picture. But initially, it's confirmation of what I suspected."

"What do you suspect? We're not talking anything criminal, are we?"

He hesitated. "No. Not criminal. More . . . negligent. Like Thornton was in over his head, but instead of asking for a life preserver, he kept treading water, hoping he could build a boat with one hand while keeping the business afloat with the other."

I sank back into my chair. "Thanks for the visual."

"I don't want you to completely lose hope. But you might want to prepare yourself for potentially bad news. The sum total of everything I'm discovering doesn't look good."

If he wasn't so well-intentioned and also working for *free*, I might have been annoyed by his pessimism. Winding Way was a thriving business. It was busy. Active. Beloved by so many people. There was no way it could fail. "Thanks for all you're doing, Simon. I really appreciate your help."

He stood. "It's not a problem. So I'll wait to hear from you, then?"

"Of course. I'll talk to Ida this afternoon and look into the employee history as well. I'm sure she'll help with whatever you need."

"Sounds good. Thanks, Lane." He walked to the door but paused before leaving, turning back to face me. "Jamie says you're coming up to Bristol for Cooper's farewell."

"Oh yeah. I guess I am."

"I'm glad you're coming. It's crazy—all of us together at home—but it's fun too."

The warmth and sincerity in his voice was a little disconcerting. Awesome. But disconcerting. "Is, um, Karen going to be there?"

The light dropped from his eyes the second I said her name. The change was so visible I immediately wished I could take it back. He shook his head. "No. She's still overseas."

"Oh. Sorry. That must be hard."

"Yeah. We've gotten to talk on the phone a couple times this week, but I haven't seen her since April."

"That's really tough."

Any further response he might have given hardly mattered the second "You'll Get Me Back" started playing from inside my desk drawer. Curse Randi and her incessant calling. Twice she was going to embarrass me in one day? Also, *why* hadn't I silenced my entire phone instead of just the one call?

Simon's lip twitched into a tiny hint of a smile. "You better get that."

"I swear that's not my regular ringtone. It's my college roommate. The band . . . It was kind of our thing." For Randi to call instead of text was weird. To call twice in a thirty-minute period? Far outside of the ordinary.

"Yeah, that's what they all say," Simon said.

I shooed him out the door. "Don't you have somewhere to be?"

He grinned. "Bye, Lane."

I answered my phone just in time. "Seriously? Are you trying to make sure every person I work with knows of my BOYBAND 2.0 obsession?"

"You're the one who set the ringtone. You can only blame yourself for that one. Plus, if you'd *answer* your phone, I'd only have to call once."

"It's a Tuesday afternoon. I'm working."

"Working, schmerking. A ring on my finger is worth the interruption, don't you think?"

"What? Are you serious?"

"As a caramel cream puff."

"Oh, I'm so happy for you, Ran." She'd been serious with her boy-friend long enough that it was more a question of when they were getting engaged than if. But it was still exciting. "Have you picked a date yet?"

"Probably not until next summer. We're thinking a destination wed-ding. On a beach somewhere, maybe. And I'm already planning my wed-ding cake. Simple white cake, a lavender honey glaze . . . I can see it in my head. Taste it, even."

"I want you to tell me all about it."

"That you would even say so when I know you're working is a tes-tament to how much I know you love me."

"I do love you."

"There's a 'but' in your tone. Are you about to say 'but'?"

I sighed. "Maybe?"

"I know, I know. Work hours."

"I just have this really tedious event résumé I have to work through and price. It was supposed to be finished yesterday, so I'm already behind, and now I have to gather all these financial documents for our accountant, and then there's this anniversary party in the ballroom this weekend . . ."

"I get it. You gotta work. When's your meet-the-boyfriend's-family trip?"

"Not till after my birthday. And I'm just meeting the parents. I already know everyone else."

"You nervous?"

"Not really. I mean, I want them to like me, but Jamie says his par-ents are great, so I'm sure it'll be fine."

"How are things with Jamie?"

I hesitated a fraction of a second before saying, "Good. They're good."

"Uh, no. You hesitated. Why did you hesitate?"

I sighed and sank into my desk chair. "I don't know. Jamie is amaz-ing. Literally. In every sense of the word."

"But?"

"But I guess sometimes I feel like our relationship is a little one dimen-sional. We both love soccer, so we talk about it a lot. And he's so easy to talk to. But there's more to me, you know?"

"And you don't think he sees that?"

"That's just it. I'll start to think that, and then he'll do something that totally contradicts that impression. He brought up poetry at dinner the other night. Mentioned Billy Collins by name and everything."

"You love Billy Collins. That sounds awesome."

"Right? It is. At least it should be."

"So maybe you need a little more time to get to know that side of him."

"I'm sure you're right."

"Don't rush it," Randi said. "You Mormons always like to rush into relationships, but sometimes they take time. You don't have to be perfectly convinced right from the very start. This guy sounds great for you, Lane. I think you need to stick with it and see where it goes. Focus on the good stuff."

"Yeah. I'm trying. I hope you get to meet him sometime soon."

"Me too. Okay. Go work. But I want an update after your birthday next week. Full details. Which means we're talking, not texting. I give you the wedding cake scoop, and you give me the birthday surprise scoop."

"You got it. Tell Victor I said congrats on the engagement. I'm happy for you guys." I hung up the phone and pulled my chair up to my desk, opening the offending event résumé on my computer screen. Another friend married. Or at least on the way there. For once in a really long time, I was in a relationship that had the potential to land me in the same space. I should feel good about that. I *did* feel good about that. Didn't I?

...

Simon: Did you know your girlfriend has a long-standing obsession with BOYBAND 2.0?

Jamie: She what?

Simon: BOYBAND 2.0. They were big when we were in high school.

Jamie: Oh, right. I think I saw their CD in her car. Annoying.

Simon: Why is it annoying?

Jamie: There's a lot of good music in this world. Why waste airspace?

Simon: If she likes it, it isn't a waste of her airspace.

Jamie: Simon the diplomat.

Simon: They're doing a reunion tour.

Jamie: Who?

Simon: BOYBAND 2.0

Jamie: So?

Simon: You asked for help, dude. This is a good idea.

Jamie: No. Not taking Lane to a BOYBAND 2.0 concert.

Simon: She's got other friends. Old roommates maybe?

Jamie: But if I get her tickets, she might want me to go.

Simon: You'd go if she wanted you to. You're not a jerk.

Jamie: If I don't get her the tickets, there's no risk.

Simon: Whatever. I'm not invested either way. You said you wanted my advice. I'm giving it.

Jamie: I'll think about it.

Jamie: How did you know there was a reunion tour?

Simon: The radio.

Jamie: How did you know Lane liked them?

Simon: Saw her at the inn today. Work related.

Jamie: How's that all looking?

Simon: Nightmarish. Old-school owner. Scattered paper trails. Almost finished though.

Jamie: Don't dash my girl's hopes. She loves that inn.

Simon: Noted. But it might not matter.

Chapter 12

WANT TO GO TO CALIFORNIA for the weekend? Jamie's text popped up just after lunch. That was if a granola bar and apple crammed down in between appointments qualified as lunch. We were days away from the biggest wedding the inn had hosted since I'd come on board, and I was swamped.

I glanced at the time, then leaned back in my chair. I had five more minutes before the wedding planner was due for a final walk-through. That was long enough for a quick conversation.

I keyed out a response to Jamie. *Want to come to the inn and help me run a wedding this weekend?*

He responded almost instantly. *Boo. No last-minute getaway, then?*

Nope. I'm slammed through Sunday. Why the sudden trip?

More business merger stuff. It's good news though. They're bringing in their top developer to kick around some ideas.

So you think it's for sure going to happen, then? I was torn. I wanted him to say yes because I wanted good things for his business, but I also wanted him to say no because I didn't want him to move to California.

I'm pretty much sold, he replied. *But Dave still needs convincing. If there's a meeting that will do that, it's this one.*

I told myself if the merger happened, they might still live in NC. But I wasn't an idiot. From everything he'd told me, moving was the best possible thing for his business. If that was true, I probably should have been happier for him.

When are you leaving? I asked.

Tomorrow morning.

Tomorrow morning. *Wednesday morning.* Which meant he'd never really planned on me going along after all. Because Wednesday wasn't the weekend. He had to know I couldn't get off work in the middle of the week and skip out on four full workdays. So he'd asked so I wouldn't feel sad about his leaving. So I knew he'd love to have me with him if I could be. Which was sweet. Sort of.

Wednesday is way more than the weekend.

I know. It was a pipe dream to have you tag along. But I had to ask. I'm happier when you're with me.

Well, okay, then. That sounded better. *Will you be home in time for next Tuesday?*

Of course, he responded. *I wouldn't miss it.*

My birthday. And the surprise whatever-it-was we were doing all day.

Travel safe, I texted.

Will do. I'll call Thursday after the meeting.

And so began another week without my boyfriend. It seemed like that was happening more and more lately. It was already September, and we'd been together only three or four times since the beginning of the month. It felt like I was seeing more of Simon, what, with how much work he was doing for the inn. I understood and didn't fault Jamie for how busy the merger was making him, but it wasn't fun.

* * *

"You look tired, Lane," Carlos said late Friday morning. The outdoor tent and chairs for the ceremony were finally set up and ready for the following morning. Since Carlos was shorthanded, I'd wound up helping.

I smiled. "I'm not used to chair duty." I pulled up my phone and looked at my event notes. "The florist is going to be here at 6:00 a.m. to start setting up," I told Carlos. "Can you be here to oversee that?"

He nodded. "Sure thing."

"I'll be in by eight thirty. I don't think the DJ will be here before then, so, really, you'll only need to handle the flowers. Oh, and the doves. They're scheduled for delivery between seven and eight."

"Where do the doves go after they're released?"

"I think they fly home. The bird people always leave with empty cages, so I assume the birds know where to go."

"Smart birds."

A text buzzed on my phone. Gaspard. I groaned. Texts from Gaspard this close to wedding day always made me nervous. "I gotta go check on the kitchen."

Carlos nodded. "Wait, Lane. Tomorrow, I'll be here through the morning but need to leave at noon for Javie's soccer game. I'll come back after to oversee the takedown. Will that be a problem? I'll make sure Chris is on standby to help with anything you need while I'm gone."

I wasn't Carlos's superior in any way. As head of facilities, he had more employees that answered directly to him than I did. But with Thornton gone and Ida mostly absent, we'd all sort of developed this group accountability system to keep everything running like it needed to run. It wasn't so much that Carlos was asking my permission. It was more like he was making sure the day could happen like it needed to without him around.

"It should be fine," I told him. "How's Javie doing? She did great when she came to the Hamilton's soccer clinic."

"She scored two goals in her last game." He beamed the way only a proud dad could.

"Yeah? Like father, like daughter."

"When will we ever see you on the field again? Are you giving up your cleats?"

"Never. I've just been so busy. It's not easy to get weekends off from this place."

"Easier for me than for you, I guess. I haven't seen any of the Hamilton brothers either. Last weekend, only Simon played. I had to send some of my guys over to play on the other team."

"I guess everyone's been busy. Dave and Jamie are working on this business thing. It's taking up a lot of their time."

"Cooper leaves soon too, right? For his missionary service?"

I nodded. "The first week in October."

Gaspard buzzed through again. "Hey, text me Javie's schedule," I said to Carlos. "I'll come watch her play sometime."

He smiled. "She'd like that."

Fortunately, Gaspard's needs were mild. Raspberry honey sauce with the coconut shrimp appetizer instead of blackberry. Since the printed menus read "berry honey sauce," I figured no one even needed to know we'd replaced one with the other. Those were my favorite kinds of problems. The ones that didn't involve seeking out already stressed bridal party members or very busy wedding planners.

Gaspard clearly had a handle on everything in the kitchen. April and Ida were managing check-in for the few wedding guests still trickling in. And everything outside, at least everything that could be done ahead of time, was ready to go. Which meant . . . I was technically done for the day. I glanced at my watch. At twelve thirty.

My phone buzzed with an incoming text, this one from Simon. *Had an appointment cancel, so I'm suddenly free. Do you have time to look over inn financials?*

Oddly, my afternoon is clear as well. Meet here? Or I can come to you this time.

I'll come there. See you in a few.

I headed back to my office to wait for Simon. He knocked on my door a few minutes after I got there myself.

"Come on in," I called.

"Looks like you're throwing quite a party out there," Simon said. He closed the door behind him before walking to my desk, where I'd just sat down.

"We have a wedding tomorrow morning, which is why it's so weird that I have nothing to do this afternoon. Normally I'm working like crazy to get everything finished."

"Was this one easier?"

"Not really. I just spaced the work out a little better. That, and Jamie's been in California, so I've worked late the past two nights."

"Ah yes. I know well the perks of a long-distance relationship. No reason to ever leave work."

"How's Karen doing? Has the dig been successful?" We'd talked about her a few different times in our various interactions. Enough that I felt like I'd gotten to know her a little. I hoped I could meet her one day. If she ever came back to the country, anyway.

"I think so. They've discovered a cluster of what they think were ninth-century homes. They're finding cookware, different forms of pottery. She texted me a few photos. It's pretty interesting stuff."

"That's got to be rewarding work. Uncovering things people haven't seen or touched in centuries."

"Have you heard from Jamie? How did the meeting go?"

"We only spoke briefly, but it sounds like it went pretty well," I said. "I'm sure he'll have more to say when he gets home."

"You'll probably be excited when all of this is decided and behind you."

I shrugged. "It's fine. I know he's excited. But it will be nice to talk about something other than the merger. And soccer."

"Oh, the soccer talk. He's the worst at that."

"Does he . . ." I hesitated, suddenly wondering if hitting up my boyfriend's older brother for information was a good idea. "No, never mind."

"What? You can ask me. It's fine."

"I was just going to ask what kinds of things Jamie was interested in growing up. Besides soccer, of course." Since I'd admitted my doubts to Randi and claimed our relationship felt a little one-dimensional, the thought had been bouncing around my brain more than I cared to admit. If I could find a few other things I knew Jamie was interested in, maybe I could build a little more commonality between us. "Did he like anything else? Books? Music? Movies?"

"Honestly, it was mostly about soccer for him. He has terrible tunnel vision. Which is great when you want to be successful at one thing but doesn't help if you're trying to be a well-rounded individual."

I frowned.

"Wait. Sorry. That came out wrong. I'm not trying to dog on him. There's absolutely more to Jamie than soccer. He's great at his business. And I know he really cares about you."

I nodded and smiled. "I know."

"And I . . . uh . . . I think he's been getting into poetry lately too," he added, though it sounded a little like an afterthought. "Maybe you inspired him in that regard."

"Yeah. He's mentioned it a few times. It's been sweet."

He motioned to the chair across from my desk. "Should we do this here? Or . . ." He looked back to the couch and chairs under the window.

"No, let's move. It's more comfortable by the window." I stood and followed him over, trying to shake off the weirdness of our exchange about Jamie. I kind of wished I hadn't asked. Nothing made it easier to feel like my relationship was one-dimensional than to have someone tell me my boyfriend really *was* one-dimensional.

Rather than take the chair like he always did, Simon joined me on the couch. It felt more personal, and I wondered if it was intentional, like he wanted to soften the blow of telling me my place of employment was about to burst into a giant ball of financial failure flame. "So?" I finally asked.

"So," he began, but then a knock sounded on my door, interrupting him. We both looked to the door.

"Sorry," I said. "I'm not expecting anyone. Just give me a minute."

I crossed the office and opened the door to a man I'd never seen before. Actually, not quite a man. More like a man-boy. He could have been twenty, but had he told me he was still in high school, I would have believed him. "Hi. Are you Lane?"

My suspicions were instantly raised. Eager. Fresh-faced. Super clean-cut. I was almost afraid to admit my identity for fear of what I knew was coming next. "Yes, I'm Lane."

He fidgeted, shifting his weight from one foot to the other, pushing his hands into his pockets, then pulling them out again. "I'm sorry. I . . . this is really awkward. The woman at the front desk told me I could come back to your office."

"It's fine. What can I do for you?" I probably should have invited him in, but if I was right about where the conversation was headed, he wasn't going to be hanging around long.

"Well, I'm Jason." He extended his hand, which I shook. "I, um, so I met your grandmother on my mission. I got home a few weeks ago, and she suggested I look you up." He closed his eyes and gave his head a slight shake. "Did that sound as stupid to you as it did in my head?"

Poor guy. He wasn't the first victim of my grandmother's scheming. "It didn't sound stupid."

He perked up. I didn't want to encourage him, but he'd made quite the effort. To be carelessly dismissive didn't feel right either. "She said she would mention me to you?" he said, his voice still hopeful.

I grimaced. "She didn't mention you. I'm sorry, Jason. Do you want to come in a minute?"

He followed me into my office, where I introduced him to Simon. I'm not sure how much Simon had overheard, but I could tell he was enjoying watching the entire scene play out.

It took about three sentences of explanation for Jason to recognize my not-so-interested status.

And my almost-twenty-six status.

And my I-might-disown-my-grandmother status.

He was gracious and understanding considering how embarrassed he must have felt. Luckily, he was on his way up to school at Southern Virginia University from his home in South Carolina, so he'd made only a small detour to swing by the inn. It was still awkward, but at least a little less so knowing he hadn't done something as dramatic as fly across the country to see me.

"Man, I'm kinda wishing I'd just texted," he said as I walked him to the door. "I guess I thought showing up might be a nice gesture."

"It was very sweet," I told him. "I'm sure your gestures will be appreciated by the right girl someday." I said good-bye and closed the office door, leaning against it with my eyes closed. I should have expected it. It had been a particularly long dry spell since I'd heard from one of Abuela's knights in shiny returned-missionary armor. I thought maybe my living on the East Coast was making it harder for her. Not as many missionaries left from the eastern states. But she'd still managed to find one. *Of course* she had. She was nothing if not determined. I stayed there, my hands pressed against the smooth wood of my office door until Simon cleared his throat. I opened my eyes to see his grin spreading from one ear all the way to the other.

"There's got to be a story," he said. "And I bet it's a good one."

I shook my head, crossing back to the couch, where I collapsed onto the cushion beside him. "You don't know the half of it."

"So I take it the grandmother he referenced is not the one who lives here?"

"No. My mother's mother. She's still in Puerto Rico. And maybe just a little meddlesome."

"Sending returned missionaries to your place of employment is a *little* meddlesome?"

"Okay, maybe a lot meddlesome. But . . . she means well."

"Has this ever happened before?"

I nodded. "Four times. Only one other time in person. The other guys called or texted."

His shoulders shook. "This is so awesome. I really want to meet your grandma."

I snorted a laugh. "You'd probably like her. She's funny and spunky and has this great personality. Everyone loves her."

"Do you mind if I ask you a personal question?"

"Sure."

"Why is she so concerned about you getting married? I mean, she must be to be sending these guys to see you."

I explained Abuela's family situation. "She always wanted a big family," I said. "And she never got it. She'll be eighty-four in January, so I think she's feeling her age and wanting me to give her a great-grandbaby before I'm thirty."

"Is this a family responsibility you carry alone? Propagating the next generation? No siblings to help out?"

"I have an older brother, John, and Abuela definitely made an effort to pair him off. For a while, anyway. But then John finally told the family he's gay, so that ended her matchmaking."

"Yeah, I guess that would do it. Was that hard for John? For your family?"

"Hard for him, I'm sure. I think my parents suspected for years before he actually said anything, so when he came out, it was like we all breathed a collective sigh of relief that we could finally talk about it."

"What about your grandmother?" Simon asked. "I might be reaching here, but she seems pretty dedicated to the idea of a traditional family."

"Really, she's just dedicated to *her* family."

"You know, I think it's pretty special she's so invested."

"She wants me to be happy. I know that. Sure, it's been annoying to have random guys show up ready to declare their intentions, but . . . I don't know. It's not like I've managed to get hitched on my own. And really, I'd love the same thing—to find someone, to settle down and have a family."

Simon dropped his gaze to his hands and shifted just slightly away from me.

"I'm sorry. Was that too personal?"

"No." He cleared his throat, looking back up to meet my eyes. "No. I think it's nice." He held me there, his pale eyes I couldn't help but keep noticing locked on mine.

"So, um . . ." I swallowed. "The inn."

"Right." His voice cracked as he spoke. "The inn." He pulled a binder out of his bag and handed it to me, then gave his head a little shake as if to clear his mind. I recognized the gesture because I was doing the same thing to clear *my* head.

What had just happened?

I focused on the binder as Simon started in on his findings. "There are a couple different problems that have contributed to the financial position the inn is now in. Part of the problem is that Thornton was a really nice guy. The rest of it was just as I had originally thought—mismanagement of growth and some generally bad accounting."

"He was a nice guy? How is that a problem?"

Simon reached over and turned a page in the binder. It was full of charts and graphs and paragraph after paragraph of analysis. "If you flip over to the second page," he said, pointing about halfway down, "that's a graph showing the average number of employees at similar inns of this size. And that blue bar is how many employees Winding Way has had over the past five years."

"It's almost double."

"Exactly. The extras are almost entirely within the housekeeping and grounds-maintenance departments. Numbers were also slightly high for the kitchen and wait staff, but those numbers are debatable depending on who you talk to." He leaned forward, propping his elbows on his knees. He seemed so earnest, so genuine. "Now, things aren't quite as bad right now as they were before Thornton's death because several employees left the inn when everything shut down. But the payroll is still too big, and it's cutting into the profit margins."

"I remember thinking it was odd that even after so many employees left, we still didn't need to hire anyone new. Though Gaspard did say he was a little understaffed in the kitchen."

"And that may be true," Simon said. "But I'm guessing housekeeping and grounds haven't had any trouble keeping up with their responsibilities."

"Why would Thornton have hired more people than he needed?"

"I had that same question. But then I ran into Darcy in the parking lot the last time I was here."

"Housekeeping Darcy?"

He nodded. "I asked her how long she's been an employee at Winding Way, and she immediately teared up. She said Thornton gave her a job two years ago when no one else would, letting her work around her son's school schedule. Her sister, Lisa, has been here for almost ten years. She asked Thornton to give Darcy a job."

"Which he did," I said.

"Right. And it seems like the same scenario played out more than once. There are four separate sets of siblings who work in housekeeping or in maintenance and three husband/wife pairs."

"So he was giving people jobs because they needed them, not necessarily because the inn needed someone."

"I don't think we can be entirely sure about what his motives were unless we pull in all of those employees and ask them about their experiences getting hired, but that's what it seems like to me. On top of that, he's paying people way too much—far more than what they would receive at a comparable job somewhere else."

"Which makes his employees loyal but doesn't do anything to make his business successful." I took a deep breath. "Okay. Too many people on the payroll. What else?"

"Honestly, that's the biggest factor. The largest part of any hotel's revenue goes to staffing, but Thornton took things to a new level. There are a few smaller things, slow bleeds that have made a difference over time but aren't quite as significant on paper. The restaurant, for example, is losing money. Breakfast and lunch don't bring in enough, and dinner, though it's profitable on its own, isn't quite profitable enough to compensate for the breakfast/lunch losses. The linen service contract is another. When compared to what other area hotels of similar size pay, it's way too high."

I leaned back, my shoulders feeling heavy and low. "Tell me the good news."

"I'm sorry, Lane. I wish things looked different, but numbers don't lie."

I flipped through the binder of information Simon had provided. Charts noting the inn's total revenue, expenses by department, analyses, projections. To say it was extensive was an incredible understatement. It was likely thousands of dollars' worth of work he had done all for free. "Simon, I can't believe you did all of this. This feels like so much more than number crunching."

"That's why I get paid the big bucks."

I closed the binder and swatted at his chest. "Except you aren't letting us pay you the big bucks. This is crazy."

He smiled. "Strategic management accounting is what I do. It's numbers, but it's also figuring out what management decisions would make the numbers look better."

"Which means you're also going to be able to tell us how to fix things?"

He frowned, running a hand over his jaw. "Lane . . ." He forced out a breath. "I'm not sure the inn is worth fixing. At least not for Ida."

My heart sank into my stomach. "Why? It wouldn't be hard to turn things around, right? We let some people go, we shut down breakfast and lunch. I get the problems are big, but they still look fixable."

"On the surface, they appear to be. But the problem is much deeper than that."

"Okay. Explain."

"Rather than fixing the aspects of the business that were failing, Thornton did what he could to stay afloat, relying on credit. Lots and lots of credit. He used his business card until it was maxed out and then switched over to two different personal cards that are in his and Ida's names together."

"Did Ida know about them?"

"I don't think so. The address on all three accounts is a post office box in Carrboro. My hunch is that Thornton used a PO box so Ida wouldn't see the statements. It was lucky I found a note about it in the back of his most recent ledger. It took a little bit of searching to find the right post office, but I finally found it and took the liberty of checking his mail. All three accounts are in arrears. The collection letters are piling up."

"How much debt are we talking about?"

"In total? $175,000."

I closed my eyes. "Oh, geez."

"Yeah. Not great numbers for a small operation like this."

"There's got to be a way to fix this. Maybe Thornton had a life-insurance policy. Maybe if we shave expenses way down, we can slowly pay the debt and get the inn back on its feet."

"I'm afraid it's not that simple."

"It has to be that simple. People love this place. We can't just give up."

"I think you're misunderstanding me, Lane. I'm not saying Ida should board up her doors and shut down. I think she should sell. She'd make enough to pay off her debt and still have a little left over for a modest retirement. Business wise, it's a smart decision."

"Ida will never sell. Thornton *loved* this place."

"Are you sure that's how she feels?"

Doubt flooded my mind. The truth was Ida had been pulling away from the operational side of things for weeks. Occasionally, she'd rally and jump into one project or another, but her stamina never lasted long. She just seemed spent. Like the burden of ownership was really weighing her down. I could easily see her wanting to sell. A surge of panic swelled inside. She couldn't sell. Winding Way would never be the same.

"What if we don't tell her how bad things are?"

Simon raised his eyebrows. "Why would we do that?"

"To buy us some time. We can make some changes, try to increase revenue, and get things under control without Ida having to worry about it."

He shook his head. "You know I can't do that."

My shoulders slumped. "Why not? I know this place matters to her. We just have to get her through the rough spots."

"I can't do it because it's not good advice. She deserves to have all her options presented. If she wants to try to save the inn, I'll help her do it. But as a business professional, I can't lie about what I've discovered or about what I think is her best option."

"What if it's what *I'm* asking you to do? Will you at least delay a little while? For me?"

"No, Lane. I won't do it. And you shouldn't ask me to."

I huffed. "Of course that's what you'd say."

"What's that supposed to mean?" he asked, the measured calm in his voice finally giving way to something a little more defensive.

I stood, walking to the window, my back to him. I took a deep breath, then turned, my arms folded tightly across my chest. "Jamie was right about you. You really are all books and no passion."

Simon: Jamie. Text your girlfriend. You can't go out of town and never communicate with her.

Jamie: I've called her. But I'm busy. And so is she. It's hard to sync up.

Simon: Try harder. Even just a few more texts will make a difference.

Jamie: Where is this coming from? Did you talk to her?

Simon: About inn stuff. She mentioned she hasn't heard from you much and seemed disappointed.

Jamie: Got it. Thanks for the heads up. I'll call her now.

Chapter 13

GRANNY KNOCKED ON MY DOOR a little before 10:00 p.m. I could see her shadow illuminated against the bright porch light at the top of the stairs. Even though I was far from in the mood for company, I'd never not answer the door for her. Especially not while living in her house. I paused the movie I was watching, stretching my arms far over my head on my way to the door. My muscles still ached from all the stupid chairs I'd set up that morning. Which was dumb. How far I'd fallen if setting up chairs felt like a workout.

Granny held a casserole dish covered in tinfoil with a bag of rolls resting on top. "I come with food."

I smiled. "You're welcome anytime without it. But . . ." I peered toward the dish. "Since it's here, I'll go grab a fork." I motioned her into the apartment as I walked toward the kitchen to get utensils—enough for both of us. If I knew Granny, she wouldn't watch me eat alone.

"It's just leftover lasagna," she said. "And my homemade rolls." She set the pan on the coffee table in the living room and sat down in a chair.

"*Just* lasagna and homemade rolls?" I called from the kitchen. "Granny, you have no idea how happy you've made me."

"You didn't eat tonight?"

Back in the living room, I put her fork on the coffee table, pulled the tinfoil off the top of the pan, and took a big bite. It was still warm. I moaned with pleasure as I dropped onto the sofa. No one induced food comas like Granny did. She stood and walked to the kitchen, shooting me an it's-a-good-thing-I-love-you look as she passed by.

"Utensils but no plates," she mumbled under her breath. "Kids these days." I reached up while taking another heaping bite, and she dropped the plate into my hand before sitting back down.

"Thank you," I mumbled through a mouthful of food. I reached for my water bottle sitting on a side table and took a long swig. "I didn't eat." I scooped a serving of lasagna onto my plate, then dished some up for her as well. "I had a decent lunch, but then this thing happened at work, and I got annoyed and came home and . . ."

"Drowned your unhappiness in Kit Kat bars?" Granny looked at the floor in between the couch and the coffee table, the detritus of my pity party covering the carpet.

I tore off a piece of roll. "Stupid, I know. Fun at the time though."

"What's going on at work? You care to tell me about it?"

I breathed out a sigh. "It's not good. Simon thinks Ida should sell the inn. I guess there's all kinds of debt she didn't know about, so he thinks that's her best option."

"Jamie's older brother Simon?"

It still made me wince to think about Simon. My words had been harsh. *Too harsh.* "Yeah. He's the accountant who's been helping sort through all this mess."

"Right. I remember you telling me that. Why are you scared about selling? If somebody buys the inn, they'll still need someone to throw the parties."

I shrugged. "Maybe. But what if someone buys it so they can bulldoze it and build a row of condominiums? Or a mini mall?"

"Do they even build mini malls anymore?"

I grumbled something unintelligible.

"Lane. Tell me what's going on. You're sad about something bigger than the inn."

Sad wasn't the right word. More like disappointed in myself. "I am not."

"Mm-hmm. Sure, you aren't."

I wasn't talking to her about Simon stuff, so I relied on my feelings regarding the inn. She had to buy that. It's not like my feelings weren't real. "I just feel derailed, you know? You know how strongly I felt about coming here. I felt pulled here, like I was supposed to be at Winding Way. For what? For this? For them to sell it out from under me three months after I start?"

"You helped Ida find an accountant who sorted out her problems for free, didn't you? Maybe you were here for that purpose. And you've made some nice friends and spent some quality time with your grandmother. I don't see the problem."

"I'll have a problem if I lose my job."

"Is that really all this is about?"

"It feels like giving up. That's hard."

She picked up her fork and took a bite of lasagna. "Is that really all this is about?" She repeated her question.

I huffed out a breath. "Of course it is."

She pointed her fork at me. "I don't believe you. Did something happen with Simon?"

My eyes flew to hers. *Curse the woman for knowing me so well.* "What? No."

She grunted. "You sure?"

"Fine. I said something that was really mean. But I didn't mean it. I think he probably knows I was emotional and upset about the inn, but I'm still going to apologize. The next time I see him."

"I see. I guess that explains all the Kit Kats."

"It seemed like a good idea at the time."

"You know he came by here the other day?"

I froze. "What? Who did?"

"Simon. I met him. Both brothers came by on the same day, actually. Isn't that funny? They weren't together. Jamie came first, on Wednesday morning. You'd just left for work."

"That was the morning he left for California."

"Later that afternoon, Simon came by. I told him you were working late, but we had a nice little visit anyway."

I went to the kitchen and filled a water glass for Granny. Why had Simon stopped by? What had they talked about? And why hadn't he mentioned that day that he'd been hanging out with my grandmother? I hurried back to the living room and sat a little closer this time, perpendicular to Granny's perch on the overstuffed chair. "What did you talk about?" I asked.

"Oh, nothing, really. Gardening. Families. He came out back and helped me pull out all the dead tomato plants." She giggled. "Wearing a shirt and tie, even. I don't know how he'll manage to get the dirt off his sleeves."

I shook my head. "Why didn't you tell me? I saw him today. I could have said thank you."

"I told him thank you well enough. He was helping me, not you. Besides, I'm telling you right now."

I picked up my lasagna plate. "Simon is a very nice man. I'm not surprised he helped you." A new wave of guilt washed over me—shame that I'd spoken so carelessly.

"Mm-hmm. Nice to look at too."

I nearly choked on my lasagna. "Sounds like you have a crush, Granny. Would you like me to tell him for you?"

She held up her hands, a wicked gleam in her eye. "I'm too old for that nonsense. But are you sure *you* don't have a crush?"

I lowered my fork, sliding my nearly empty plate back onto the coffee table. "Why would you even ask that question? You've met Jamie. You know I'm dating him."

"I know you are, and that's fine. But I also know I hear Simon's name almost as frequently."

"It's just because he's been helping out with the inn."

She leaned back in her chair, her arms crossed over her chest. "I'm going to say one more thing."

I stood. "It doesn't matter what it is. You're crazy. And you're wrong about this."

She shrugged. "Maybe so. But you're going to listen anyway 'cause I'm old and I brought you food. So sit back down and hush a minute."

I dropped back into my seat. "It's so not fair you get to play the *old* card."

She laughed. "I'll take every advantage I can get."

"Fine. I'm listening."

"Two men came to see you on the same day, Lane. Two nice, kind, respectful men. But only one hung around long enough to talk to me. Only one offered to help in my garden. Why do you think that is?"

"Jamie was on his way to California. He couldn't have stayed."

"I'm not talking about why Jamie didn't stay. I'm talking about why Simon did."

Well then. Admittedly, I'd felt a little bit of spark on more than one occasion with Simon. But it had been easy to douse out any chance of it developing into anything because, Karen. And Jamie. And Jamie. And Jamie. But Granny's observation functioned like a burst of oxygen to my teeny tiny spark, and for a brief moment, it flared. Was it possible there really was something there? That he felt the same spark I did? I forced the thought away. It was ridiculous to even entertain. "Simon has a girlfriend, Granny. Did I tell you that? Her name is Karen, and things are pretty serious. Jamie thinks they'll be engaged soon."

She raised her eyebrows. "Is that right?"

"Of course it is. I wouldn't lie about something like that."

"I guess that changes things, then."

I folded my arms. "I don't understand. What does it change?"

"Well, I was about to tell you I thought Jamie was the one who's wrong for you and you ought to be seeing Simon instead. But a girlfriend . . . that changes my whole theory."

"Jamie's not wrong for me, Granny." It felt affirming to say it out loud.

She stood and moved to the front door. "Be sure and cover that lasagna before you put it in the fridge."

"I will. Thanks for bringing it up."

She paused a moment longer. "Lane, if Simon has a girlfriend, you'd do best to keep your distance. I saw the way he got under your skin tonight. And I heard the way he talked about you when he was pulling up my tomato plants. If you spend too much time with him, child, especially if you're meant to be falling in love with his brother, it's only going to lead to trouble."

"But it's not like that, Granny," I said.

"And it won't be so long as you mind me and keep your distance. Jamie and Simon are *brothers*. That's a relationship that lasts forever. You want to keep out of trouble with the one? If I were you, I'd stay far away from the other."

Jamie: I'm taking Lane to the poetry-signing thing up in Virginia. For her birthday.

Simon: So you said. I'm glad. She'll like it.

Jamie: I also bought her the concert tickets, just so you know. I'll kill you if she wants me to go.

Simon: Just be in California when it happens.

Jamie: Good plan. Then she'll have to take someone else. Dinner suggestions?

Simon: You don't need my help with dinner.

Jamie: Yes, I do. This night really matters. We haven't been together in a long time, and I want things to be perfect.

Simon: I'm sure they will be.

Jamie: I'm NOT sure. Come on. Help a brother out?

Jamie: Simon. Come on. Don't leave me hanging.

Simon: She likes food, right?

Jamie: Yes. All kinds. Especially fancy kinds.

Simon: If you're driving all the way up to Virginia Tech, research the area. Find someplace local that has a unique specialty. Pick a separate place for dessert. A local bakery or something. Be intentional. Not like you happened upon it and picked it because it was on the way. She'll appreciate that you planned ahead and gave thought to what she might like.

Jamie: Got it.

Simon: And talk about something other than soccer.

Jamie: For real?

Simon: In fact, talk about everything BUT soccer. Books. Music. Movies. Politics. Philosophy. No sports.

Jamie: Ugh. I'll try. But I'm not making any promises.

Chapter 14

LATE SEPTEMBER WAS NOT SUPPOSED to be warm. It was fall. Officially, on the calendar and everything. And yet at 9:00 a.m., it was already seventy-five degrees. I shrugged out of my sweater, realizing I'd probably end up carrying it around all day anyway, and opened my front door, tossing it back inside onto the couch. I wanted to need it. Stupid North Carolina. It always hung on to summer as long as it possibly could.

Jamie waited for me at the bottom of the stairs. We'd only texted briefly the night before. He'd gotten in after midnight, too late to have much of a conversation, but he'd promised he'd pick me up at 9:00 a.m. sharp for my birthday . . . for whatever it was he had planned. He leaned up against his jeep, looking all cool and stud-like. California looked good on him. He'd been gone less than a week, but somehow he'd managed to get a nice tan and what I swear looked like actual, for-real highlights. I reached up and touched his hair. "Did you . . . ?"

He shrugged away like he was embarrassed. "It looks stupid, right?"

"No! I wasn't saying that. It looks nice. I just didn't know you were a salon kind of guy."

"I'm not. But Byron's sister was at the beach house where we all stayed, and she owns this salon, and she thought it would be a good idea. I didn't want to be rude about it, you know? She did Katie's hair too while we were there."

So Katie had gone to California with Dave. Technically she was a little more invested than I was, what, with an engagement ring and everything, but it still stung a little that she'd managed to make the trip while I'd stayed behind. Also, five days at a beach house sounded very different from five days of hanging out in a hotel while Jamie worked. "I wish I'd been there."

He reached out and put his hands on my waist. "Me too."

"Byron. He's the head guy? The merger guy?"

"Yeah. He owns a house in San Diego. Right on the water. We're talking an incredible house—huge. Big enough for all of us to have our own space. He brought in all the key players from his development and design teams so Dave and I could get a feel for how they work. It was intense but amazing."

"Sounds like it."

"How was your weekend? Good wedding?"

"The bride fell as she walked down the aisle, but otherwise a perfect day."

He pulled me a little closer. "So, birthday girl, are you ready for *your* perfect day?" He kissed me, and I leaned in, wanting to feel like I still had some connection to him and his new California life. I believed him when he told me he wished I could have been there. But I still felt . . . removed from it all. Wishing me present didn't change the fact that we'd barely talked the entire time he was gone. One conversation to tell me Dave was convinced and they were working on final negotiations. And then one voice mail telling me he missed me. That was it. Didn't make me feel very essential. At least the kiss was something tangible I could hold on to. I pulled him closer, deepening the kiss and slipping my hand to the back of his neck, my fingers tangling in his hair.

"Wow," he whispered when we finally broke apart. "That was . . . wow."

"I missed you."

He kissed my forehead. "We have to get on the road."

I climbed into his jeep, wondering for the fiftieth time where he was taking me at nine in the morning on a Tuesday.

"So where are we headed?"

He grinned. "North."

"North? That's all I get?"

"For now. That's it."

We settled into the drive, conversation coming the same easy way it always did. Somewhere right after we crossed the Virginia border—Virginia? He hadn't been joking about heading north—I brought up the merger, more specifically the likelihood of the merger bringing about a move. He was frustratingly vague in his responses. "Byron likes the East Coast," he said. "Maybe we'll wind up staying out here." I reminded myself that we'd been together only three months. That wasn't a long time—not long enough to necessarily justify my involvement in his decision-making. But I wasn't great with unknowns. The fact that he avoided discussing what might happen to *us* if he moved made me really uncomfortable.

All the stuff Granny said about Simon didn't help either. It wasn't like I thought I could just switch brothers. But I also couldn't deny that had I met Simon under different circumstances . . . I squashed the thought before I let it go anywhere. There was no undoing his very legitimate brotherly connection to my current boyfriend or his very legitimate relationship with Karen. For that reason, it was a nonissue, and Granny was right. I just needed to stay away from him. An easier prospect now that his work with the inn was mostly finished.

Thinking about the inn brought up a new wave of emotion. Sadness, regret, disappointment. Simon had gone straight to Ida after he'd left my office on Friday afternoon. Ida had called down and invited me to join them, but I hadn't had it in me to listen to his explanations again. I'd made some excuse about the wedding and needing to take care of something and made my escape—to my garage apartment and forty thousand Kit Kats. So healthy.

In hindsight, I wished I'd gone so I could know how Ida had taken the news. I'd looked for her at work Monday morning, but she'd stayed in her rooms all day and asked not to be bothered. For sure I could ask Simon. He'd tell me. But the last time we'd talked, I'd insulted him. Which meant the next time we talked, I needed to apologize. Mix that with all the feelings Granny's suggestion stirred up and talking to him suddenly felt like a much bigger hill to climb.

"You okay over there?" Jamie asked.

I turned, startled by his voice. "What?"

"You've been silent for twenty minutes. I thought you might stare a hole in the dashboard."

"Sorry. Thinking about the inn."

He slowed the jeep and exited the highway. "I am sorry about the inn." I'd given him the rundown earlier in our conversation. "I know you love it there. But maybe change wouldn't be a bad thing. There are a lot of great hotels that would be lucky to have you on staff. Hotels everywhere, you know? All over the country." He gave me this knowing look that made my stomach tighten and my heart skitter all over my chest. We might not be having the conversation about California, but that didn't mean he wasn't thinking about it.

"So," he said. "Ready to get some lunch?"

"Where on earth are we?" I asked.

"Blacksburg, VA," he answered. "Home of Virginia Tech, the famous Cabo Fish Taco, and Carol's donuts, both of which are on today's menu. And home to your birthday surprise."

I shook my head. "I am so confused."

"You'll have answers soon enough," he said with a grin.

Lunch was amazing. Good tacos and great donuts. But everything was even better because I could tell Jamie had done extensive research regarding where we should go and what we should eat. Careful consideration wasn't in his typical arsenal, so it meant a lot that he'd slowed down enough to think about what I might enjoy.

We walked hand in hand down a sidewalk in downtown Blacksburg.

"What are you smiling for?" Jamie asked.

I looked his way. "What?"

"You're smiling. We're walking, and you have this goofy grin on your face."

I squeezed his hand. "I'm just happy." I was happy. *Really* happy. Jamie was being thoughtful and kind, and it was stupid I'd doubted what I had in front of me. With *him*. Suddenly I didn't want there to be anything going on with Simon. No confusion. No . . . potential for sparks or whatever. If I was going to take Granny's advice and put him out of my mind, then I wanted to clear the air and be done with it.

"Hey, I think I need to tell you something," I said to Jamie as we climbed back into the car.

"Okay."

"I said something really mean to Simon the other day. I'm going to apologize, but I sort of maybe pulled you into it. So I just wanted to tell you what I said. In case it ever comes up."

"What did you say?"

"You have to understand where I was coming from. Simon was just being so logical and unemotional. And I was the exact opposite. He'd just told me he thought the inn needed to be sold, and I lashed out. He didn't deserve it though. It wasn't fair or kind."

"What did you say?" Jamie asked again. There was a tiny edge to his voice, which only served to remind me that Simon was his brother to whom he was very loyal. *He* could hurl insults at him all he wanted because that was the kind of relationship they had, but clearly he wasn't crazy about the idea of those insults coming from me.

"I told him you were right about him. He really is all books and no passion."

Jamie immediately started to laugh. "That's all? I tell him that all the time."

I relaxed. "I know. But I don't. And the way I said it . . . It's fine. I'll call him tomorrow and apologize. I just wanted you to know too. Since I dragged you into it all."

Jamie picked up my phone from where it sat on the center console between us. "Here. Call him right now."

"What? No. Today is about us, Jamie. I don't—"

"Listen, if I know Simon, those words you said are eating him alive. He hates for people to be disappointed in him. Just call him. It'll make him feel better."

"I haven't even thought about what I'm going to say."

"Just tell him what you told me. I'll even get out and give you a minute of privacy." The jeep idled in the parking lot of the donut place where we'd gotten dessert. "Go ahead. I'm going to buy a few more donuts for the trip home."

Simon answered on the first ring. I realized I'd never actually spoken to Simon on the phone. We'd only ever texted. He had a nice phone voice.

"Do you have a minute to talk?" I asked him.

"Sure," he said.

"I just wanted to apologize for the way I reacted last Friday." My words tumbled out so quickly they sounded more like an incomprehensible heap of syllables rather than an actual meaningful sentence.

Luckily he understood anyway. "You were angry, Lane. I understood."

"But I had no right to be angry. It wasn't personal, and I took it personally. After all you've done to help, it was childish of me to attack you like that."

"It wasn't childish at all. I appreciate how committed you are to a place you love. That's nothing to be sorry for or ashamed of."

"Thank you for saying so," I said. "But I still stand by my apology."

"Then I accept it. Thank you."

There. Done. Time to move forward. In the end, I was glad Jamie had suggested I go ahead and get the apology over with.

Jamie climbed back in the jeep.

"Things okay?" he asked.

I nodded. "Much better. He was really nice about the whole thing."

"He's a decent guy, I guess," Jamie said with a teasing grin.

"Just decent, huh?"

"Fine. Maybe a little better than decent."

"How highly you praise him," I joked.

"You want the truth? Mom thinks he's the best of us, so decent might be an understatement."

"She actually said that? He's the best of you?"

"I don't mean she loves him more. That's me. She definitely loves me the most," he joked. "But growing up, Simon was good, even when the rest of us were totally rotten. He had good perspective. Though sometimes I think that was both a blessing and a curse. He spent a lot of time analyzing situations, trying to decide if stuff was worth going for. Is it worth the risk? Worth caring about? Will others suffer for my actions? It's a great quality to have, but that kind of perspective is a curse when you're a kid because you can never just go for something because you want it, regardless of what other people think. Sometimes you have to eat the last Pop-Tart, you know? Because you're hungry and everyone else can deal. He was never the kid who would eat the last one."

I chuckled. "I can totally see that about him."

"So you talked, and you're good and he's good?" Jamie asked.

I nodded. "Yeah. We're good."

Our next stop was the university bookstore on Virginia Tech's campus. Jamie gave me a mischievous smile. "Ready?"

"My birthday present is at the Virginia Tech bookstore?"

"Trust me. You're going to love it."

Halfway through the store, I saw a poster. *Nikki Giovanni. Poetry Reading and Book Signing, 2 PM.* I turned to Jamie. "Are we . . . Did you?"

He cocked his head, motioning to the back of the store. "Come on. I think she's back here."

Only a few chairs on the back row remained empty. We took our seats and looked to the front, where Nikki Giovanni herself sat quietly waiting for her introduction. Several bookstore employees bustled around her. One leaned in and whispered a question, which made her smile and nod.

I turned to Jamie. "I can't believe you did this. How did you even know how much I love her?"

A flash of discomfort flitted across his face, but it was gone so quickly I almost wondered if I'd made it up. "I saw her book on the shelf in your office. I figured if you had her collection, she must be a favorite. That the signing was on your actual birthday was really just a stroke of luck."

I shook my head. "She *is* a favorite. She's amazing." I reached for his hand. "Thank you. This is the most incredible present anyone's ever given me."

He leaned over and kissed my cheek. "I'm glad you like it."

For the next hour, I was riveted on Giovanni and her poetry. I hung on every single word. Most of what she read I already knew, but to hear her reading was miraculous in ways I couldn't describe. We waited in line after she finished, then we purchased a copy of her newest collection, which she signed for me. In every sense, it was an entirely perfect afternoon. Back in the car, I stared at my new book, running my hand over the cover.

"Jamie, thank you for this. For today."

"You're welcome." He smiled and reached for my hand. "I'm glad you're happy."

"Yes. Very happy." And I was. Hesitations, distance, disconnectedness. All gone by the end of the day. Yet again, the second I'd started to doubt, Jamie had swept in and reminded me why I'd fallen in love with him.

The thought gave me pause. Had I fallen in love with him? I'd never said it out loud, but after the day we'd just had, I felt it. Keenly.

It was nearly dark when we made it back to my apartment. Jamie shifted the car into park and leaned over, resting his hand on the back of my seat. "Happy birthday, Lane," he said softly.

I grinned. "Thank you very much."

"What would you say if I told you the excitement isn't over yet?"

My eyebrows went up. "I'd be curious, I think. Unless you're planning to take me to the soccer field for another rematch. In which case, I'm much too tired and you win."

He chuckled. "No more rematches. I promise. Just"—he switched on his stereo and slid in a CD—"this."

BOYBAND 2.0 started blasting from his speakers. I started to laugh. "*What* are you doing?"

"I'm jamming down to some awesome music," he said, his face a mask of mock seriousness.

"You are making fun of me, and I am not amused."

"You're right. I totally am. Maybe you'll forgive me when I give you these." He handed me an envelope.

I opened it. And then I screamed like a teenage fangirl.

Two tickets. Third row, center at Philips Arena in Atlanta. To the BOY-BAND 2.0 Reunion Tour. I leaned over the center console and wrapped my arms around Jamie's neck. "Seriously. This is the most ridiculously stupid but still incredible thing ever. I am so embarrassed that I am so excited to go, but gah!" It was hard to keep from squealing. "I am *so excited* to go!"

"I thought you would be."

"Have I even told you about my BOYBAND obsession?"

"You mentioned it in passing. When you were talking about things you and Randi had in common."

"That's right. I did. Ohh!" My eyes opened wide. "The concert's in Atlanta. I could take Randi!" I looked back at Jamie. "Wait. That's crazy. You have to come with me."

"I . . . have to be in California that weekend. You can take Randi."

I looked back at the tickets. "October 31. Halloween. That's the Thursday before Dave and Katie's wedding. You have to be in California two days before your brother gets married?"

He looked trapped, his eyes wide, his mouth hanging open.

My jaw dropped. "You just lied to me so you wouldn't have to go to the concert."

He grimaced. "Yes? I did?"

I swatted at him. "You are a terrible human being."

"Come on! I bought the tickets. I support your obsession. I just don't want to be a part of it. I love you, Lane, but I'm only willing to go so far."

I froze. *I love you, Lane.* He must have sensed my sudden discomfort because he reached for me, his hand cupping my cheek. "Sorry," he said softly. "That's not how I'd imagined saying it for the first time."

I closed my eyes and took a deep breath, leaning into his touch. I closed the distance between us and kissed him, then brushed my lips across his cheek, hovering next to his ear. "I don't want you to go to my concert anyway," I said. "But . . . I love you too."

* * *

Later that night, I called Randi to hash out all the delicious details of my day. From the book signing to the concert that, yes, she could attend with me to the end-of-the-day *I love you.* We covered everything.

"Confession?" I asked toward the end of our conversation.

"Okay. Hit me."

"When he first said 'I love you,' I panicked a little."

She hesitated a beat or two before responding. "Like, for real panicked?"

"No. I mean, it only lasted a split second. He didn't even realize anything was wrong. But in my head, I was freaking out."

"You said I love you back, Lane. Did you not mean it?"

"I think I did. I do love him . . . I think."

"You think. How compelling."

I sighed and collapsed back onto my bed, stretching out full length. "I do love him. After today, especially. He orchestrated this incredible day, acknowledged parts of me I didn't even know he'd noticed. It was a big deal."

"Maybe that's the part that's freaking you out. Suddenly things seem really serious."

"Maybe that's it."

"Don't run from this guy, Lane." Randi had on her bossy voice. "I know I haven't met him, but he sounds really amazing. And he's been so good to you. Thoughtful. In tune with you, and that's saying something."

"You know I spent a lot of time with his older brother?"

"Simon, right? He was helping you with money stuff at the inn."

"Yeah. Granny thinks he has a thing for me."

"Oh no, no, no, no. You are not thinking about your boyfriend's older brother. You stop right now. Stop and run the other direction. Run hard and fast and far, far away from those feelings."

"I don't have *feelings*. All I said is that I spent time with him and maybe *he* has a thing for *me*."

"Right. I'm sure you mentioned it because you haven't felt even the tiniest of connections."

"I haven't felt a connection. I mean, maybe I did at first. But he has a girlfriend, so it absolutely doesn't matter. Also, the last time we talked, he infuriated me and I insulted him. See? There are a lot of reasons for this to be a nonissue."

"Then why did you mention it?"

I groaned. "Uggh. I don't know. Maybe because it's weird thinking there might be something there? I mean, how do I act the next time I'm around him?"

"Um, you act as if you don't have the first clue. Because you don't. You have your grandmother's suggestion, which hardly makes a good case on its own. Plus, with all the inn stuff behind you, you shouldn't have reason to ever see him."

"He'll be in Bristol when we all go up for Cooper's missionary fare-well. I can't avoid being around him then."

"But you'll be with Jamie the entire time. There won't be room for weirdness if you and Jamie are always together. Let this one go, Lane. Focus on Jamie. He is right for you. I'm feeling it."

I smiled. "You're right. I know you're right."

"Now tell me again about the concert," she said. "Oh my word—I have to find something to wear."

Jamie: Birthday date was a success.

Simon: I'm glad.

Jamie: Yeah, I owe you one. Things are feeling pretty serious.

Simon: That's great, man. I'm happy for you.

Jamie: When are you headed home? Want to ride up with me and Lane?

Simon: Cooper asked if he could haul some of his stuff in my car, so I'm driving. Thanks though. I'll be there by Friday night.

Jamie: We're riding the Creeper on Saturday. Did Mom tell you? You want to throw your bike on the back of the jeep? The rack will hold one more.

Simon: That works. Thanks, man.

Chapter 15

Lynette Hamilton was a hugger. Big hugs. Squeezing hugs. Hugs followed by more hugs. By the end of dinner our first night in Bristol, any insecurities I might have felt about meeting Jamie's parents had been hugged right into oblivion.

Katie dropped onto the living room sofa beside me. "I promise she eases up with the hugging once she gets to know you."

I laughed. "I don't mind. It's nice feeling so accepted."

"True," Katie said. "As far as in-laws go, I think we've gotten really lucky. Oh, I mean, sorry. I just totally presumed. Things are headed that way though, right? It seems like they are."

Good question. Things had been good in the weeks since our birthday date. Better than ever before. But as quickly as my doubt had dissipated, as soon as we were back at home and into our regular routine, they popped right back up again. I really wanted our relationship to feel right. But it was like there was a tiny sliver of wrong I couldn't ignore. A splinter in my foot that I couldn't necessarily see but could definitely feel.

"How quickly did you know with Dave?" I asked.

She scrunched her eyebrows. "I don't know. Dave didn't propose until our one-year anniversary, which is probably a little longer than I needed to know, but he wanted to be sure."

"A year? My parents were engaged in three weeks."

"Wow. I was nowhere near sure three weeks in. Funny how couples are all different."

Yeah. Funny but also encouraging. Because I didn't have to be sure right now. It made it a lot easier to feel okay about ignoring a splinter.

Jamie's mom stuck her head into the living room. "We're cutting the cake. You girls want to come have a slice?"

"Lane wants cake," Jamie called from the kitchen. "Always offer the cake!"

I smiled. "He knows me so well."

* * *

"Okay. Here's how it's going to go." Jamie shifted his bike around so he was facing the group. "We're divided into teams of two. Mom and Dad, me and Lane, Dave and Katie, and Cooper and Simon. Just like in a high school cross country meet, the place that each person finishes becomes their score. We'll add up the combined score of each team, and the lowest number wins the day."

I glanced sideways at Cooper, who sat on his bike beside me, and raised my eyebrows. "Is he serious?"

Cooper nodded. "Oh, he's serious. All the brochures and travel guides in the world call the Virginia Creeper a leisurely, low-key bike trail through the mountains, but that doesn't matter to Jamie. We're riding? That means we're racing."

"He's always been this way," Dave said. "Growing up, everything was a race."

"Walking through the mall," Cooper said.

"Finishing homework," Dave added.

"Saturday chores," Cooper said.

"Even passing the sacrament around the chapel on Sundays," Dave said. "He always tried to hit the back pew first."

The idea of an impatient, twelve-year-old Jamie hurrying people through the sacrament bread and water so he could be first to finish almost made me laugh out loud. "Suddenly the intensity of our soccer games makes perfect sense."

"Lane!" Jamie called from the front of the group. "You're with me."

It had been awhile since I'd been on a bike, but I'd been told the Virginia Creeper really *was* a leisurely, low-key bike trail, so I wasn't too worried about it. I'd seen two other groups start out since we'd hit the top of the trail that had had small kids in wagons pulled behind their parents' bikes, so if they could handle it, surely I could too. I waved and rode my bike up to where he stood waiting for me.

"Here's the game plan," he said. He was adorable when he was fired up. "We'll try and stay together as long as we can, but if something happens and we get separated, whoever's in the front needs to pull ahead. The faster that person finishes, the less it'll matter if the person in the back gets held up. Got it?"

"So basically, if you fall off your bike and break your arm, you're telling me *not* to stop and help but keep going so we can win."

He leaned over and kissed me, turning his head completely sideways so our bike helmets didn't bump. "You're speaking my language, baby."

"What if I get a flat tire? I have no idea how to change a tire on a bike."

He blew out an exaggerated sigh. "I guess if you get a flat tire, I'll stop and help you."

I laughed. "Okay. Let's do it."

Even though we were technically racing, it was impossible for the race to be too cutthroat. The trail was full of families and other groups, older couples, little kids. We were constantly navigating our way through and around other cyclists. Which was fine with me. It was a gorgeous trail, especially in October. The normally green forest was rich with bright oranges, reds, and yellows. I had to resist the urge to climb off my bike and gather up the prettiest leaves. Even better, the weather had finally started to turn, and a slight chill filled the air. The day felt crisp and clean and vibrant and totally worth slowing down to look around a little.

Over cake the night before, I'd fielded question after question from Jamie's dad. He reminded me a lot of Simon. He had an easy way of conversing and a genuineness that put me immediately at ease. And it was his blue eyes that Simon had inherited. The rest of the brothers all had their mother's brown eyes. We'd talked about basketball—he'd been a student the years my dad had played on BYU's team—and about Puerto Rico. Both parents served Spanish-speaking missions, as did Simon, so it was fun to hear the three of them break out their very rusty Spanish.

It was the first time in months the family had all been together, so Katie and I also spent a lot of time watching the brothers interact with their parents. They were gentler around their mother than when it was just the four of them back in Chapel Hill. It made it easier to see their regard for one another—and their unabashed loyalty to their family.

I asked Jamie that night before settling into the basement bedroom I was sharing with Katie if the brothers had ever fought over girls when they were growing up. He'd answered immediately and with firm conviction. "Never," he had said. "I dated the more sporty girls." He gave my shoulder a nudge. "Dave did too, but he was more cheerleader, while I was more soccer/swimmer/runner. Simon was old enough we didn't really care about who he dated, but I'm guessing they were all boring and bookish so it wouldn't have mattered anyway."

"Bookish girls are boring? I'm a bookish girl."

"But you're also a sporty girl," he said. "That saves you."

There was the splinter. Fine. I was a sporty girl. But I didn't love that Jamie didn't acknowledge much beyond that.

He slowed his bike in front of me. We'd been alone on the trail for a couple of minutes, no one in sight ahead or behind. "Did you see that?" Jamie asked. "She ran completely off the trail."

"She who?" I asked. "I didn't see anything."

Seconds later, a pink helmet popped up out of the brush. The rest of the girl—probably no older than nine or ten—emerged, tugging her bike back toward the trail.

I stopped in front of her. "Are you okay?"

She yanked at her handle bars. "Stupid bike. I think the chain came loose."

"Did you hurt yourself when you fell?"

"I don't think so." She looked at her hands, then brushed some leaves off her knees. "The ground was pretty soft where I hit."

I dismounted and leaned my bike against a tree so I could help her get hers back on the trail. "You sure you're okay?"

She nodded.

"Are you riding with your family?" Jamie asked.

"I raced out ahead," she said with a sniff. "But they should be coming soon."

"Probably that couple we passed awhile back," Jamie said. "Does your dad have a kid seat on his bike?"

Another nod. "That's my baby brother, Benjamin."

"That was longer than a few minutes," I said. "You must have *really* raced ahead."

"Benjamin was making them go *so slow*," she said, her final words full of dramatic emphasis. "And I am super fast. I couldn't help it."

"What do you say I help you get your chain back on?" I said. "My name's Lane."

"Ivy," she said. "It's nice to meet you."

I gestured toward the trail. "Hey," I said to Jamie. "You go ahead. I'll wait with her till her parents show up."

"I'll help with the chain first," he said.

"I don't need to wait for my parents," Ivy said. "I can ride by myself."

"You know what?" I handed her bike over to Jamie, who had it fixed in a matter of seconds. "I'm sure you can. But I'm guessing your parents are really worried about you. I think we better wait for them. Just so they know you're safe."

She sighed. "Fine."

"Go on." I urged Jamie again. "Dave and Katie are only a few minutes back. I'll catch up as soon as Ivy is back with her parents."

"You sure?"

"Seriously? You tell me this is leave-me-in-the-ditch-with-a-broken-arm level racing, but you're worried about leaving me now? I'm fine. I'll be fine. Go keep our lead."

He grinned and climbed back onto his bike. "You're my favorite."

"Is he your boyfriend?" Ivy asked as we watched him pedal away.

"Yep. His name is Jamie."

"My mom says I'm too young to have a boyfriend. There's a boy at school who likes me, but he told me not to tell anybody so I don't think he really counts."

I chuckled. "Probably not."

A few more minutes and Dave and Katie breezed by, followed closely by Jamie's parents and Cooper. That left only Simon still behind me. Fantastic. Cooper waved from the trail, slowing down long enough to shout a hurried, "You okay?"

I waved him on. "Totally fine. I'll be riding again in a minute."

"There's my mom," Ivy said. She waved both her arms over her head.

"Ivy Grace." The woman pulled up to a stop in front of us. "If you ever ride off like that again, I swear . . ."

"She took a little bit of a tumble," I said. "Her chain came off, but we've got it fixed now. I don't think she was hurt."

"Lane wouldn't let me ride until you caught up," Ivy said.

Her mom looked at me, eyes wide, and mouthed a silent "thank you," then turned her attention back to Ivy. "I think Lane must be really smart. I know you want to ride fast, Ivy, but you have to stay with me and your dad, kid. It's either that, or we stop right now and walk the rest of the way."

"According to my map," I said, "that's about twelve more miles."

"That's a long way to walk," Ivy's mom said.

Ivy huffed, her arms folded tightly across her chest. "Fine. I won't ride ahead. But can we please try and ride a little faster?"

A man pulled up beside us. Ivy's dad, I presumed, based on the baby seat attached to his bike. "You found her."

"Our friend Lane here helped her after a fall and wouldn't let her leave till we showed up."

"The hero of the day, then," the dad said.

"It's not a big deal," I said. "I just didn't want her to be alone."

"Thanks again," the mom said. "Ivy, ready to go? If you promise not to speed off, we'll let you lead the pack."

She wheeled her bike up to the front. "I promise." She turned back and waved at me. "Bye, Lane."

"Bye!" I watched them ride off, giving them a little bit of space before I started back up myself. Not that it mattered. Not ten feet after I started pedaling, my back tire started shaking so badly I had to stop riding again. I pulled over to the side of the trail and bent down to look at the tire to see if I could tell what was wrong.

"You okay?"

I turned and saw Simon approaching.

"The tire's shaking. I don't know what's wrong." Seconds later, a loud bang sounded close to my head. I jumped back and fell into the dirt. "What was that?"

Simon climbed off his bike. "That was your tire."

"Are you serious? What on earth happened?"

He leaned down and looked at the back wheel. "Hard to say. Sometimes they just blow."

"Can you fix it?"

He nodded, then retrieved the repair kit off the back of his bike. "I've got a spare tube." He stood my bike up. "Here. Can you hold this up?"

I took the bike. Something was up with Simon. He seemed . . . annoyed. Testy. So not like his usual chill self. "Where's Jamie?"

"He's up ahead. We got split up."

Simon stopped and looked at me, frustration creasing his eyebrows. "I know he's competitive, but he left you behind on the trail?"

"No, it wasn't like that. I stopped to help this girl, and we didn't both need to be there. I told him to go ahead."

"Just because you told him to doesn't mean he should have." His shoulders were tense, the veins in his arms standing out as he crouched down and wrestled the new tube into the tire. He literally looked like he wanted to break something. "I mean, there's friendly competition and then there's downright rudeness. Sometimes I wonder where Jamie actually falls."

Something big was going on inside Simon's brain. That much was perfectly clear. I'd never seen him so perturbed. I reached out and touched his arm. "Simon."

He stilled under my touch, his jaw clenched.

"What's wrong?"

He sank back onto his heels, stewing in silence for a long moment before finally shaking his head. "I'm sorry. Forget what I said, all right?"

"I don't care about what you said. I want to know if you're okay."

He kept his eyes down as he continued to work on the bike. "It doesn't matter." He pulled out a CO_2 compressor and filled the replacement bike tube, then shoved everything back into the repair kit. "There." His words were sharp, each syllable punching the air with its own tiny burst of force. "Now it's fixed, and you and Jamie can ride off into the sunset and live happily ever after." The disdain in his voice was almost tangible.

"Simon. Stop and tell me what's wrong."

He turned his back, running his hands over his face before resting them on his hips. His shoulders rose and fell with each breath, his entire body rigid with anger I had no way of explaining. Finally, he gave his head another weary shake, turning only enough for me to hear his voice. "I'm sorry, Lane. This isn't your fault. Just . . . bad timing. Please forget I said anything. Your bike is good to go."

I took a step forward, wanting to reach out, touch him again, do something to ease the tension in his face. I wanted to fix *him*. Make him feel better. Make whatever was wrecking his insides disappear as quickly as humanly possible. But Simon wasn't mine to fix, and remembering as much gave me pause.

I stopped in my tracks, wrapping my arms around myself, my hands tucked under my arms—my only defense against any errant touching. "I'm not leaving you like this. Not unless you tell me what's going on."

He sighed, seeming to consider. Finally, he reached for his phone and scrolled through a couple of screens before handing it over. "We've been out of cell range for a while, but a few miles back, there was coverage enough for this to come through. Go ahead. Press play."

It was a voice mail from Karen. I raised my eyebrows, my finger hesitating over the Play button.

"You said you wanted to know why I was angry," Simon said. "Just listen."

My stomach sank as the message started. Karen was British—something I hadn't expected—her voice clear and deep with a lyrical quality that made me think I would have liked her had I met her in person. That was, until I listened to her words. That ended any trace of actual *liking*.

"Simon. I'm sorry I didn't catch you in person. Listen. There's been some stuff going on. Big stuff, really. And I know I should have talked to you sooner. It just never seemed like the time was right. We've been so remote, you know, with no cell service much of the time. Anyway, the thing is I've met someone. He's one of the archeologists who came onto the dig last month, and well, after everything, I think he's the one, and he says he feels the same, so we've decided to get married. I suppose we saw it coming, didn't we? We both knew our relationship wasn't going anywhere. So sorry, Simon. You deserve better than this, but, well, things happen, you know? I hope you can understand. Give my love to your family, and best of luck. I really do hope you're well and happy."

I lowered the phone from my ear and handed it back to Simon. "I'm really sorry, Simon."

A group of riders approached from behind us. We moved over, scooting our bikes so we were completely out of the way. Simon leaned against the smooth bark of a birch tree, his earlier anger fully dissipated. "I shouldn't be surprised, really," he said. "Things have been . . . off, I guess, for so long. I just figured once she was home we might be able to work through stuff."

"I can't believe she broke up with you in a voice mail."

He scoffed. "No joke."

"And I can't believe she didn't tell you sooner. Dating someone is one thing, but engaged? That's hard."

"I've even talked to her," he said. "Since she met him. We've talked, and she acted like nothing was up. That's the hardest part. I'm telling her I love her while she's . . ." He stared at the ground without speaking, and I found myself wishing, again, that I could reach out and comfort him in some way. I leaned against the same tree, our shoulders touching like two corners of a square. "Simon. Someone like that—she doesn't deserve you. You're such an amazing guy. You're thoughtful, generous, kind. You see whole people. I think that's what I like most about you—you don't see labels or stereotypes; you just see people." The truth of those words hit me hard. And not just because I felt like Simon hadn't stereotyped me. I recognized it in his interactions with others too, in the way he spoke about people. He didn't judge. "Some girl is going to be really lucky to be on the receiving end of all that."

His mouth curved up into a regretful smile. "Not Karen though."

I nudged him with my shoulder. "And that's her loss."

He took a deep breath. "Listen, I'm sorry about what I said earlier. I was angry, but I shouldn't have snapped at you or said anything about your relationship with Jamie. That was . . . lame."

"Don't even worry about it. It's already forgotten."

He pushed off the tree. "I think we are officially in last and almost-last place."

I groaned. "Don't remind me. Jamie's gonna wish he picked a different partner."

He chuckled and shook his head. "No. I doubt he'll ever think that." His eyes met mine, holding my gaze a second longer than necessary. I turned away, moving toward my bike, but his voice called me back. "Lane."

I looked back, wishing he didn't make my stomach feel knotted.

"Thank you for listening, and for . . . making me talk about it. It helped."

"Don't worry about it."

"And . . . thank you also for what you said. It's maybe the nicest thing anyone's ever said about me."

I shrugged my shoulders. "It's the truth."

He took a giant step toward his bike—which felt very much like a giant step *away* from me—and cleared his throat. "Should we go? I promise I'll let you take the lead."

We didn't see anyone else from the group until we hit the bottom of the trail. They were all sitting at the outdoor tables of an ice cream place, halfway through dessert, when we finally rolled in. Jamie looked from me to his brother and raised his eyebrows. I took off my bike helmet and dropped onto the bench beside him, leaning in to give him a quick kiss on the cheek. He offered me a bite of his ice cream, which I gladly took.

"What happened?" he asked. "We were about to head back up the trail to look for you."

"I blew a tire."

"Did it pop?" Cooper asked. "I heard a bang and wondered if that's what it was."

I nodded. "Right in my face too. I nearly had a heart attack." Simon settled on the bench across from us. "Luckily, Simon was still behind me when it happened. He had a spare tube and replaced it for me."

"Hey, thanks, man." Jamie gave his brother a high five. "I'm glad we restocked all the repair kits last night."

"Not a problem," Simon said. "Who ended up winning?"

"We did," their parents said in unison. "First and second place right here, baby," Lynette said. "All you young and tough boys can eat that for dinner."

Dave tossed a napkin at his mother's head. "Yeah, yeah," he said with a grin. "Don't let it go to your head."

* * *

The rest of the weekend was more of the same. Lots of joking and laughter but also moments of tenderness that made me love the Hamilton family as a whole in serious ways. After church, I watched as each brother, throughout the afternoon, found a moment to sit down with Cooper individually. I don't know what they talked about—advice, I guessed, from three former missionaries to a brand-new one—but whatever their words were, it was touching to see it. To recognize their regard for one another.

We drove home Monday morning, leaving Cooper behind for two final days with his parents before heading to the Missionary Training Center in Johannesburg. Time alone in the car with Jamie was much-needed relationship validation after the weird moment I'd had on the trail with Simon. Something had happened inside of me when Simon had suddenly become free of the protective bubble his relationship with Karen had provided. His official off-limits status had always made it much easier to dismiss any potential spark or connection or whatever it was that had happened when he'd looked at me like he'd looked at me on the trail. Now that was gone, which made being around him feel dangerous in ways I couldn't explain. But Jamie was real. And he was mine. And though I'd voiced my misgivings to Randi about some facets of our relationship, we'd had a great time over the weekend. We were good together. Things had been really good.

Just across the Virginia/NC border, we stopped at a Dunkin' Donuts. "You want anything?" Jamie asked. "I was thinking some hot chocolate would be good."

I stared. "Right now?" October was almost hot-chocolate weather, but it was still sixty-five degrees outside. I mean, yes, I drank hot chocolate year-round, but I was weird.

"Why not?" He shrugged his shoulders. "I've been wanting to try the hazelnut. I've heard it's good."

I smiled. "It's my favorite." See? Good together. No, not just good. We were *great* together.

Cooper: I'm signing off, brothers. I wish you all a good two years while I'm gone.

Dave: Same to you, little brother.

Simon: You're going to be great, Cooper.

Jamie: Not as good as I was, but you'll do.

Cooper: Know what I realized?

Cooper: You could ALL get married while I'm gone.

Dave: Pretty sure mine's a done deal, bro. No could, just will.

Cooper: Well, yeah. And I've accepted that. But if Jamie marries Lane, and Simon marries Karen, then I will be a groomsman for NONE OF YOU. Dude. This is bad.

Jamie: Don't worry. Karen and Simon are on the five-year plan. You'll be back before they ever get hitched.

Dave: Ha. True.

Simon: Not true. Karen and I broke up.

Jamie: For real?

Simon: No. I'm kidding. You know I'm such the joking type.

Jamie: Sorry man. That's terrible. What happened?

Simon: She's engaged to someone else.

Dave: Ouch.

Cooper: Yeah. Awful. Why didn't you say anything?

Simon: Just happened over the weekend. But, hey, on the bright side, Coop, you'll probably be back in time to be my groomsman.

Jamie: Without Karen in the picture, you'll probably be home and married before HE is.

Simon: Thanks for that, Jamie. Your vote of confidence means so much.

Jamie: Anytime, bro. You know I got your back.

Chapter 16

IT WAS A GOOD THING we'd had such a good time in Bristol. Otherwise I'd have never made it through the rest of October. Jamie was gone almost the entire month. He kept insisting things would get better, and I believed him, but the interim was killing me. Absentee boyfriends weren't any fun.

I stayed busy at work, though the entire feeling of work had changed since Ida had left. She'd disappeared shortly after her initial conversation with Simon, flying out west to spend time with her family and to discuss, I assumed, the future of Thornton's legacy. She'd stayed away longer than anyone had expected, leaving us all in an uncomfortable holding pattern. Only Simon's semiregular appearance in the office gave us peace of mind. When Ida left, she'd temporarily turned over the monetary functions of the inn to him, authorizing him to take care of things while she was gone. As long as he was still showing up, we at least trusted we were going to keep getting paychecks. When I pressed him for details, Simon assured me he was no longer working for free and that Ida was compensating him nicely for stepping in when he already had a full workload. That part made me happy, but I was still nervous. He insisted his role was only temporary, which meant change was coming. I had no idea what that change was going to be.

Ida didn't return until the end of October. It felt like an eternity had passed since I'd seen her last. The week before Halloween, I found her in the rose garden, sitting on the little wooden bench below the tree I'd spent so many summers climbing. The limbs were all but completely bare, the mud-brown leaves swirling and crackling at our feet.

"I don't know why Carlos hasn't gotten all these leaves up," Ida said as I approached.

I sat beside her. "I like that he leaves them a few days. It makes it feel more like fall to have them blowing around everywhere."

"I guess I like that part too," she said. "You know, I used to sit out here when I was pregnant with the boys? I'd bring a book and sit for hours under this tree, making Thornton do all the work inside. It was my escape."

"It was always one of my favorite places too. Except I'd read while sitting *in* the tree."

She laughed. "How have things been, Lane? I hope you've managed okay without me."

"We're all happy to have you back, but it's been all right. We have another wedding this weekend that's pulling together nicely. That's helped to keep everyone's spirits up. Having something big to work on."

"You've probably all been terrified you were losing your jobs."

"Yeah, there's been a lot of that," I said. "But Simon coming around helped. He always seemed to have things under control."

"That man is a godsend," she said. "He's been wonderful. When he told me where things stood, I thought for sure we were going to shut things down and give up, but he made a few simple recommendations that kept us at least turning enough profit to keep the doors open."

I nodded. I'd seen Simon's recommendations happening all over the hotel. The restaurant's limited hours. The cutbacks with staff in every department.

"He's the reason the inn's still open. Everyone should know that. His wisdom is what saved us."

"Does that mean you're going to stay and keep the inn open?" I tried not to infuse too much hope into my voice, but I couldn't hold it back completely.

She turned to me and sighed, then shook her head. "I can't do it anymore. Not with the debt and all the problems Thornton left behind. I think I've decided I have to sell."

I nodded. I'd seen enough clues to know it was coming, but it still hurt.

"I want you to know how hard it feels to say so," she said. "I can't stand the thought of ever letting this place go, but when I think about a little house in Colorado close to my grandchildren, that sure does sound easier than running this place into the ground."

I took a deep breath. "I can't fault you for feeling that way. It makes sense."

"I don't want you to feel like this is your loss, Lane. The inn was a sinking ship before you ever came on board. There wasn't anything you could have done."

"I do know that. I still wish there was something I could do now."

"You keep right on doing what you're doing. Whoever buys this place will see how vital you are. I can't imagine them not wanting to keep you on staff."

"I hope so," I said. "Because I really don't want to go anywhere else."

The next afternoon, Ida's youngest son flew in and spent three days wandering the property with a guy I could only assume was a commercial real estate agent and someone they only identified as a consultant. Thankfully, I spent the last half of the week prepping for Chloe's Saturday reception, which provided just enough distraction to keep me from noticing all the assessing and appraising happening all over the inn. The following Monday, Ida made the announcement. The inn was officially up for sale, and she was actively pursuing interested buyers.

By Halloween, I was ready to escape the unknowns of my life. Work was the worst, not knowing who would buy and what they would do with the property. But the angst in my relationship with Jamie was only slightly better. I'd been waffling back and forth all month between feeling like things were great and thinking things were seconds away from crumbling. Jamie would show up with a novel he thought I might like—Ariana Franklin's *Mistress of the Art of Death* was a pleasant surprise—and I would feel seen and heard and understood, but then he'd disappear to California and ignore me for a week, texting nothing but soccer stats and pictures of the ocean, and I'd be scratching my head again. California. That was the biggest source of angst. Was he moving? Not moving? For all my pressing, he would commit to *nothing* and avoided the subject whenever he could.

I had done so much pondering on both issues I was ready to forget all of it and party my way to Atlanta for a couple of days with Randi and my beloved BOYBAND 2.0. The plan was to drive down early Wednesday morning so we had two full days together before the concert on Thursday night. After that, I'd drive up to Raleigh in time for Dave and Katie's rehearsal dinner on Friday and the wedding on Saturday.

In that regard, all the upheaval at the inn worked to my advantage. Ida and her sons had decided to keep bookings at a minimum until the transition—whatever that was going to be—was complete so my job responsibilities were scaled *way* back. It made taking several days in a row off really easy.

Wednesday morning before the concert, I was moments away from leaving, my vintage BOYBAND T-shirt safely packed in my overnight bag, when my phone rang.

"Hello?" I answered.

"Lane? *Eres tú?*"

I immediately switched into Spanish. "Abuela? *Cómo estás?* How are you?"

"I'm very well, thank you for asking. Your mother tells me you have a boyfriend."

I put down my bags and sat on the couch. Of course. The boyfriend would be the first thing she mentioned.

"I do, Abuela. And I've been meaning to talk to you about that. No more sending men to see me."

"I have no idea what you're talking about."

"Don't you play coy with me. Someone named Jason showed up just last month. Told me you'd given him my name and number and the name of the inn where I work."

"Jason." She paused. "Oh, yes. Jason Middleton. He was a nice young man. And tall. Tall enough even for you."

"I just turned twenty-six, Abuela. These boys you're sending are barely twenty years old. No more, okay? I'm dating a really nice man now."

"Tell me about him, then. Is he a member of the Church?"

"Of course he is. You know how important that is to me."

She cleared her throat. "Did he serve a mission?"

I could almost see her sitting in her living room in Arecibo, a stubby pencil in her hand, marking check boxes down her list of "requirements for Lane's husband." I wasn't necessarily down with the opinion that a mission was some sort of a guarantee. Like it was the only measuring stick for good character, but I respected Abuela too much to argue.

"Yep. He did."

"And he's a nice man? He has a good family?"

"He's very nice. I've met all his family, and they're wonderful too."

"I can't wait to meet him. You'll bring him, won't you? To Thanksgiving?"

"I don't know, Abuela. He has family in Virginia. He might be going home. I'm not sure what his plans are."

"Virginia is very close to North Carolina."

"Yes, it is."

"But Puerto Rico is very far away. Please, *mija*. Bring him for me. I am an old woman. Let me meet him and see for myself that he loves you."

"Okay. I'll talk to him. I'll see what I can figure out."

"Ahh, perfect. I'll call your mother. I will cook!"

I smiled. My mother was a good cook and had raised us on a lot of the traditional Puerto Rican dishes she'd grown up with back in Arecibo. *Arroz con gandules, mofongo, tostones*. But she'd also been influenced over the years by my very Southern father, who loved corn bread and greens, fried chicken, biscuits and gravy, and sweet-potato pie. Mom had loved learning from Granny Grace how to make the food Granny had raised her family on, and Mom had become a sort of hybrid cook—pulling elements of the two cultures together into one very happy kitchen.

But Abuela in the kitchen meant a return to the heart of what I loved most about my Puerto Rican heritage. Time in the kitchen was as much about love as it was about the *sofrito*—the seasoning Abuela put in everything. Memories of her standing in her kitchen scooping the homemade sauce into ice cube trays so she could freeze it and pop out a cube whenever she needed one, filled my mind. She loved to cook for us. And I loved that she loved it. "Can we make *pasteles*?" I probably sounded nine years old blurting out the question like I did, but longing for home and nostalgia for the meat-filled pastries we'd made every time we'd visited Abuela washed over me with such strength it was almost painful.

"Of course we can. You'll help. And John. And your boyfriend too. Even your father will help."

"I can't wait to see you, Abuela."

"I can't wait to meet your young man. I hope he's worthy of you, Lane. You deserve the very best."

"Thank you, Abuela. I promise he is. You're going to love him."

•••

Simon: Had a meeting at the inn today and stopped by the kitchen.
    Lane loves crème brûlée.
Jamie: Got it. Thanks.
Simon: You know, YOU could do this research just as easily.
Jamie: Not from California. Long-distance relationships are terrible.
Simon: Yes, they are. I agree with you there.
Jamie: Give me a book to mention. What could I have read on the
    flight home?
Simon: If I give you a suggestion, are you going to read it?
Jamie: Probably.
Simon: I don't like this game.
Jamie: Come on. Last time I ask for help.
Simon: It will not be the last time.
Jamie: Probably not. But you'll help me anyway? What's the last thing
    you read?
Simon: Cost Management: A Strategic Emphasis
Jamie: That's not funny.
Simon: You asked what I read.
Jamie: Not helping.
Simon: Tell her you read Fountainhead. *Ayn Rand.*
Jamie: I've heard of that one. What's it about?
Simon: On the surface, it's about architecture. But it's more about
    passion. Living for what you really believe in. I'm not sure if
    Lane has read it, but if she has, she loved it.
Jamie: You're sure?
Simon: Yeah. I'm sure.

Chapter 17

My BOYBAND BOYS DID NOT disappoint. And Randi didn't either. I'd only managed to bring a T-shirt bearing the band's names and faces. Randi had tracked down a full ensemble. Even her leggings had little BOYBAND 2.0 insignias stitched all over. We looked completely ridiculous, but it was still amazing—everything I had imagined and more. When we left the arena, I could hardly talk for all the screaming we'd done.

We walked toward the car arm in arm, still singing with our worn-out, croaky voices to the songs humming through our heads. "There will never be a band like them," Randi said. "I don't even think they look that different all grown up. Except for Corban. Sad he's the only one who's bald."

"He's still cute though. The beard makes up for it."

Randi pulled out her keys. "Do you remember where we parked?"

I looked around. "This way, I think. Over in the corner."

We found the car and climbed in, deciding we needed a run for cheeseburgers before we headed back to her apartment.

"You know I have two trays of pistachio macarons in my freezer, right?"

"What? I did not know this. How have I been staying in your apartment for two days without knowing this very important piece of information?"

"I guess I forgot about them. But hooray! Now we know, and we can eat them all tonight."

"Two trays? In one night?"

She shrugged. "Maybe we ought to skip the cheeseburgers?"

I pulled into the line of cars waiting to exit the arena parking lot. "I don't want to skip the cheeseburgers. I haven't had any real food tonight, and I'm starving."

"Fine, fine. I'll eat a burger. So give me a boyfriend update. Did you talk to Simon earlier today?"

I shot her a sideways look, wondering if she realized what she'd just done. "You mean Jamie?"

She gave me a quizzical look. "Right. Isn't that what I said?"

"You said Simon."

Her eyes went wide. "Did I? That's so weird! Why would I have done that?" She leaned back in her seat. "Maybe it's a sign, Lane. An echo of things to come!"

"An echo comes after something that's already happened. Besides, you told me to run far away from Simon and focus on Jamie."

"You're right. I did. So, Jamie, then. How's Jamie? Did you talk to *him* today?"

"Just briefly. He's back in NC and spending some time with Dave before the wedding this weekend."

"Oh, that's right. You told me the wedding was coming up."

"Yeah. It'll be good. Dave and Katie are really great for each other."

"You think Jamie might propose?"

"What, to me?" I finally pulled out of the parking lot and into the still slow-moving traffic circling the arena. At least we were going *somewhere.*

"No. To your grandma. Of course to you. Who else would he propose to?"

"I haven't really thought about it. We've barely spent any time together all month."

"It's a wedding though. You know how weddings make people. Everyone's happy and in love. I'd give it some thought. It wouldn't surprise me if he's planning something."

I shook my head. "I don't think so. I think he'll be focused on his brother this weekend. Plus, he's got this ballroom-dance thing with the maid of honor. There's going to be a lot going on."

"Hmm. Maybe you're right. Do you think it'll happen soon though? Are you getting the vibe?"

An interesting question. But an easy one to answer. We were never together. "Vibes are tough when there's two thousand miles separating you."

"You just need to move out there already. Go for it."

"You want to hear something awful?"

"Always," she responded.

"I really don't want to move." It was the first time I'd said as much out loud, and a sudden weight felt like it'd been lifted off my chest. I didn't want to move back to California. I loved North Carolina. I loved being closer to my family. And I'd *just* moved back. I was nowhere near ready to move again.

"Seriously? Those are big words, Lane. He's moving for sure, isn't he?"

I sighed. "He hasn't told me yet. All signs seem to be pointing in that direction, what, with how much time he's spending out there, but he still says nothing is final. The business deal is final, but the *move* isn't necessarily so. They're still discussing whether or not an East Coast office is a reasonable possibility."

"So, wait. The two of you aren't talking about what this means to your relationship?"

"No. Weird, isn't it? He's completely avoiding the subject. And I guess I am too because if he asks me if I want to move, what am I going to say? No?"

"If that's how you feel, yeah."

"I think I'm waiting for something to happen that will make moving seem worth it. Something will click, and then I'll know he's the one and I should move."

"Well, it's definitely too big a step to take if you don't feel that way."

"Right?"

Twenty minutes later, we settled into her living room, burgers, sweet-potato fries, and two dozen macarons filling the table in front of us. "I'm so happy right now," I said with a sigh.

She reached for a macaron, her burger still wrapped neatly on the table before her. "I want to see a picture of Simon."

I grabbed my own macaron. "Why?"

"Just because. Does he look like his brother? Is he better-looking? These are important questions."

It was a dangerous vein of thinking, comparing the two brothers, but I dug my phone out of my purse and pulled up my Facebook account anyway. I searched through my friends until I found Simon's profile. His picture was from the back—him on a mountain somewhere—and was totally ambiguous. It could have been *anyone* in the picture. Slightly annoying but also totally Simon. Unlike Jamie's profile picture that looked like he was a dang J.Crew model. I clicked on his photos and searched until I found a good one, then handed the phone over to Randi.

"Wow. He is cute." She scrolled through a few more pictures. "I think he's cuter than Jamie. He looks more . . . I don't know. Real, I guess."

"That's my boyfriend you're knocking. Jamie looks plenty real."

"No, I know. I can't explain it. Maybe I just like his looks a little more."

She couldn't explain it. But I probably could. The word that came to mind totally unbidden and quick enough that I was ashamed to even acknowledge it, was *depth*. Simon had some. Lots of it. When I looked at the few pictures he had of himself on Facebook, that was what I saw.

"So how's it been with Simon lately?" Randi asked. "Do you ever see him anymore?"

"Why are you asking? You keep bringing him up, but you told me he was off-limits."

"I did say that, but . . ."

I didn't love her hesitation. It always meant she was gearing up to say something hard.

"But what?"

"But I'm not convinced your heart's really in this thing with Jamie. And I *think* it's because of Simon. If he's the better guy for you, I want to talk you through it."

I shook my head. "No. That's not how it is. I've barely seen him lately. At the inn a handful of times, but he's there on business, so it's been brief and neutral. We haven't really talked since we were in Bristol with his family."

"I guess with Jamie gone so much you're not exactly hanging out with his family members without him."

"Exactly. That would be totally weird."

"Okay. If you say it's not an issue, I'll believe you," Randi said.

A few hours later, I stretched out on Randi's couch and tried to sleep, but my brain wasn't cooperating. No matter how hard I tried, I couldn't shut it off.

I thought first of Jamie. By acknowledging Simon's depth, was I implying I thought Jamie was shallow? When I broke down the evidence, he wasn't. We'd talked about *Fountainhead* the last time he'd called. You couldn't talk about *Fountainhead* if you were shallow. I made a few more tally marks in his favor. He ran a successful business. Had meaningful relationships with his family. Plus, he loved *me*, which had to say something.

It should have said everything I needed to know about our relationship, but I wasn't convinced it did. I was afraid that while Jamie himself might not be shallow, our relationship very well could be. And that wasn't a good thing.

I huffed, annoyed with my current train of thought, and turned over, pounding my fist into my pillow. Would I even be having doubts if Simon weren't in the picture? If he were the one getting married in two days, if we'd never spent any time together, would I be overanalyzing Jamie's flaws?

I *said* it wasn't an issue, but the more I thought about it, the more I realized it was. Mostly because *I couldn't stop thinking about it.* Still, everything with Simon was pretty nebulous. Vague notions from Granny Grace or moments of connection I'd tried to ignore. Broken down into individual moments, it didn't add up to much.

But there *was* something more significant. Something I had yet to admit, even to myself. But lying there in the dark, staring at Randi's ceiling, wishing I'd stopped at macaron number six instead of ten, the truth was too blatant to ignore.

I *liked* Simon.

Maybe I'd fallen in love with Jamie, but I'd noticed his older brother in a way I probably shouldn't have. And everything felt more confusing because of it. I had to be careful. I couldn't let my guard down around Simon—not even a little.

As a counterpoint to the argument, did it even matter if Simon was the reason for my doubt? If Jamie really *was* the right man for me, would any man, brother or not, be enough to lure me away?

My phone chimed with an incoming text, so I rolled over, curious to see who it was. It sat facedown on the coffee table beside me, its light reflecting off the glass tabletop and bouncing back up toward the ceiling. I reached for it, happy to see a text from my brother, John.

Little sister! Just got your voice mail. Are you still up?

I glanced at the clock. It was almost 2:00 a.m. *Crazy, but true,* I texted back. *I'm still up and so happy to hear from you!*

His response came through immediately. *Can I call?*

I hurried off the couch and onto Randi's front porch, dragging a blanket behind me. In her four-hundred-square-foot apartment, you could talk from one corner to the other in a normal speaking voice and not miss a single word. I didn't want to wake her up.

I answered John's call on the first ring. "Johnnie!" I pulled the blanket around my shoulders to keep out the chill. Georgia was warmer than NC, but it was still 2:00 a.m. at the end of October, and I was in pajamas. Definitely blanket-worthy circumstances.

"It's good to hear your voice," he said. "How are you?"

I couldn't stop smiling. It had been way too long since we'd last spoken. "I'm so good. How are you? How's work?"

"Hard. But rewarding. I scrubbed in on an intrauterine fetal surgery today. Fixed a baby's heart before she's even been born. It was amazing."

"I can imagine. Are these generally the hours you keep? I can set my alarm for 2:00 a.m. if it means you'll be able to call me more."

"That's a decent plan. I'm still at the hospital even now. With surgery scheduled first thing in the morning, it seems silly to go home."

"At least go stand on the roof and get a little sunshine."

"I miss the North Carolina sunshine. Feels like there isn't as much of it up here."

"So come home! Are you coming for Thanksgiving?"

"I'm going to try."

"Abuela's coming. Mom bought her ticket already."

"Ahhh," John groaned. "I guess I'll be there for sure, then."

"Why don't you sound excited?"

"I got a voice mail from cousin Armando."

"Is that Valeria's son?"

"Mm-hmm. He lives in Arecibo right across from Abuela, and he's very concerned about her making the trip."

"Why? What's going on?"

"It's her health. That's why he called me. She had a series of ministrokes a few months back. She's been fine, but they're all worried about the strain of travel."

"Does Mom know about this?"

"Not yet. Armando sent me her doctor's information, and I took the liberty of calling this afternoon to get a doctor-to-doctor opinion. While she advised against it, she was encouraged by the prospect of me being with Abuela and just suggested we take it really easy and make sure she gets plenty of rest during her stay."

I heaved out a sigh. "I just talked to her a few days ago."

"How did she sound?"

"Great. Excited. Maybe a little tired, but she's eighty-four. I guess I expect her to sound a little tired."

"If Mom already bought her plane ticket, Abuela's mind is made up, and I doubt we can change it. We'll just have to take care of her. Make sure she's happy. And mentally, we need to prepare ourselves. I doubt she'll make the trip again."

I pulled in a sharp breath of cold air. John's words hit me hard. Abuela had *always* been there. Life without her was a reality I didn't want to imagine.

As an adult, I hadn't been great about making the trip to see her. We'd gone consistently as kids, but after our last trip as a family, the summer after I graduated from high school, I hadn't been back. To be fair, she'd been to the States twice in the seven years since then—once to surprise my mother for her birthday and again two years later for my college graduation. That last time, she'd told me, "Next time, I'll come for your wedding."

Now *next time* had become *this time*. I couldn't give her a wedding by Thanksgiving. But maybe supplying a boyfriend wasn't asking too much. "I guess I really need to bring Jamie home with me, huh?"

"If she's expecting to meet him, I wouldn't want to disappoint her if I were you."

"It's all she talked about when she called. And really, I guess I want her to meet him. Maybe it'll stop her from giving my contact info to the missionaries."

"She's still doing that?"

"Yep."

He laughed. "Man, you have it worse than I ever did."

"Don't rub it in."

"This might be it, Lane. Abuela isn't getting any younger. I know it feels like a lot of pressure, but her hopes hinge on you. If you can make it work, I'd bring him."

"I'm sure he'll come if I ask him. It's just all . . . a little complicated right now."

"What's complicated?"

"Life. Love. Everything."

"Okay. Spill it, sis. Spare me no details."

I curled up into Randi's porch swing, my blanket still pulled tightly around me, and launched into a detailed account of my love life, even down to the nitty-gritty of my conflicted feelings regarding Simon.

"I can't figure out why he even keeps coming to my mind," I said. "I really do love Jamie. It annoys me that I keep thinking about Simon at all."

"Sometimes there's no rhyme or reason for what our heart feels," John said. "Have you thought about asking Simon how he feels?"

"What, about me?"

"Sure. I don't want to diminish your feelings here, but it's possible you're making it all up, right? If Granny Grace hadn't planted the seed of doubt, suggesting Simon had feelings for you, would you be thinking about this at all?"

"I don't know. I think maybe yes. We've had these moments, John. Nothing major. Just looks mostly. But there's definitely a connection. It feels real."

"So talk to him. If it's one-sided, you can let it go and make a decision about Jamie and California without Simon as an outside influence. If it isn't and he has feelings for you, well, then you factor that in when you're making your choice."

"Except it won't matter if he has feelings for me. Simon would never betray his brother."

"Even if you and Jamie break up? After some time, surely . . ."

"I don't know. I seriously doubt it. And honestly, I don't know if I'm willing to risk it. My relationship with Jamie is good. It feels foolish to even be voicing doubts."

"I'm going to channel Mom for a minute, okay?"

I groaned. "Uggh. Fine."

John raised his voice and mimicked our mother's Puerto Rican dialect almost flawlessly. "It's not like you don't have some choice in the matter, young lady. Focus on the relationship you want, and dismiss the inconsequential feelings. Let your mind lead your heart, not the other way around."

I couldn't stop laughing. It was perfect. *Perfect!* "That was so awesome."

"Thank you. I've been practicing."

"She would die if she heard you."

"And I thank you for keeping my talents hidden. But, Lane, it isn't bad advice. Don't let your doubts mess stuff up. If you've got a good thing with Jamie, focus on that. Especially since finding a new boyfriend before Thanksgiving might be tough, and you cannot come home unescorted."

"Don't remind me."

"Does Mom know about your man trouble?"

I shifted the phone from my left hand to my right, pulling my now-freezing left hand under the blanket. "Don't call it trouble. That makes it sound way worse than it is. And no, Mom doesn't know anything other than that I'm dating someone and it's getting kind of serious. And I'd like to keep it that way, please and thank you. I'll keep your secrets if you keep mine."

"That's what I'm here for."

I yawned. The late hour was finally catching up with me. "It's late, John. I think I need to get some sleep."

"You and me both," he said. "I've got a date with the OR in just a few hours."

"When are you ever going to stop working so much?"

"Never. I'm having too much fun."

"Is that what doctors are calling it these days? Your patients are lucky to have you."

"I'll see you in a couple of weeks?"

I sniffed, my nose suddenly running from the cold. "Sounds good. Love you, John."

I could hear the smile in his voice. "Love you too, little sister."

Simon: Brothers. Got an e-mail from Cooper asking that I add the following message to the thread so he isn't left out of the wedding celebrations: Congratulations to Dave, the first of us to fall. May you be happy and prosperous and gain fifteen pounds from Katie's delicious cooking so you will be slow and easier to beat on the field.

Dave: A poet, that one.

Jamie: Are you nervous?

Dave: Not at all. Just excited.

Simon: I need to ask a favor. Of both of you.

Jamie: Shoot.

Simon: I'm bringing a date to the rehearsal dinner.

Jamie: Dude. Way to rebound.

Simon: That's why I brought it up. I know it's soon after the breakup. Please don't make it a big deal.

Dave: We've got your back, man. But are you ready to date again?

Simon: Probably not. But loving someone who can't love you back stinks. The distraction helps.

Jamie: Don't play her though, man. That's not okay.

Simon: I would never do that. It's just a date. And she's nice. Who knows if it'll go somewhere. But just don't react. Jamie—I'm looking at you.

Jamie: Noted. I'll be on my best behavior.

Chapter 18

I HATED BEING A THIRD wheel.

It wasn't really by anyone's choosing, but since I wasn't in the wedding party and everyone else I knew was, I spent a lot of time at the rehearsal dinner hanging out on my own. Or for the most awkward moments of the night, hanging out with Simon's date, Melia. Exotic, lovely Melia who was totally rocking a high-waist, black pencil skirt and killer red heels. I watched Simon and Melia from the opposite end of the large private dining room the Hamiltons had rented for the dinner and tried to convince myself the burning in my chest wasn't jealousy. Because I had no right to feel jealous. Not even a little.

"How long have they been dating?" I asked Jamie about halfway through the dessert course.

"This is the first I've heard of her," Jamie told me. "So it can't be long. He says she's a grad student at Duke."

"I guess it's good to see he's moved on from Karen."

"I'm not so sure. Feels a little rushed to me. He asked me not to make a big deal about it though, so he must really like the girl."

My stomach tightened. "You think?"

"He texted me and Dave both and asked us to lay off the teasing. That's got to mean he likes her, right? And doesn't want us to embarrass him."

"Huh." So I guess that cleared up one potentially awkward conversation in my future. No reason to even think about talking to Simon *now*. "Did you talk to your mom about Thanksgiving?"

Jamie nodded. "That I did. Don't worry. She was cool about it. I'm all yours for the entire holiday weekend."

I smiled. Make that two things to strike off my worry list.

* * *

The next night at the reception, I found myself sitting alone with Simon. Jamie was off talking to an old high school friend, and Melia, whom he'd brought along to the reception as well, was . . . somewhere else. I didn't look around to find her.

"How are things at the inn?" Simon asked.

I shrugged my shoulders. "Still up in the air. It's officially on the market, so we're just waiting at this point to see if it gets any interest."

"I think I saw you in the garden last week. Talking to Ida?"

"Really?"

"I can see the garden from my front porch."

"Oh. You should have waved."

"It looked like a pretty serious conversation."

I shrugged. "She was just telling me all the reasons she's decided to sell. And I'm glad she did. It helps me understand her side of things."

"You definitely sound a lot more at peace about everything."

"I don't know if I'd go that far. I'm still totally stressed about who the new owners might be."

"That's understandable. I don't think you have any reason to worry though. Winding Way is a great property. You'll get a good buyer. I'm sure of it."

"Thanks. You know, I used to play in the gardens at Winding Way all the time as a kid."

"Really?"

I nodded. "The rose garden was my favorite. I'd crawl over the south garden wall with my books and read for hours in the big tree that shades the bench. I finished a lot of books in that garden."

"What did you read?"

"What books?"

He nodded.

"Normal little-girl stuff. Little House on the Prairie. Nancy Drew mysteries. Anne of Green Gables. Want to hear something funny though?"

"Of course."

"I always carried one of my dad's old books with me whenever I went to my tree. It was the book he was reading when he met my mother, so I figured if I was going to meet my prince, it'd be good luck to have it with me."

"Dare I ask what the book was?"

I sighed a happy sigh. "Gabriel García Márquez. *A Hundred Years of Solitude.* It was an original print edition, in Spanish even. You want to hear the story?"

He leaned forward, his elbow on the table. "More than anything."

"Okay. Here's how it happened. My dad first met my mom through a mutual friend and was really impressed. He knew she was from Puerto Rico, so to impress *her*, he found a novel written in Spanish at a used bookshop and took it to the library. He sat a few tables over from where he knew she liked to study and just waited for her to show up and take notice. It took three days of him visiting that same table for his plan to work. When she did finally notice him sitting there, his nose buried in a Spanish novel, she immediately called him out, sure he didn't speak a word of Spanish, much less read it. He admitted she was right, said he'd only been trying to impress her and get her attention, then he asked her to dinner. She accepted, and the rest is history."

"You have to admire your father's persistence."

"He said he never doubted for a second. She was it. He just had to be patient enough for her to figure it out too."

"Did you read the book when you carried it to your tree?" Simon asked. I loved that he called it "my tree," just like I had. "*A Thousand Years of Solitude* is some pretty heavy reading for a little girl."

"I didn't. Not until I was much older. But now it's one of my favorites. Because it's brilliant but also because it's a part of my history."

"It's one of my favorites too. I've never read it in Spanish though."

"I've read both. Hard to say which I love more. The translation was beautifully done."

"Do you still have it? Your dad's book?"

I frowned, holding my hand to my heart. "Now we must tread carefully. This is hard, *hard* to speak of."

"I'm not sure I want you to go on."

"I left it on the subway in New York."

"Oh! That's painful."

"It still kills me to think about it."

"I can imagine. Did it bother your dad when you lost the book?"

"Not at all. He says the book was simply a means to an end and he'd rather hold on to Mom than some book. I think it was just my childish romantic brain that gave it significance."

He shook his head. "I don't think it was childish at all."

I loved the way talking to Simon made me feel—like I was interesting and deep and . . . *valued*. But it was also making my head hurt. It seemed as though every time I felt convinced Simon wasn't an issue, some conversation between us, some look or gesture would scramble my insides all over again, dashing my certainty into a thousand different pieces. It was exhausting.

Seconds later, Melia showed up at the table. She dropped a hand on Simon's shoulder and made eye contact with me, a possessive gesture that made my insides burn. Seriously? After two dates, she was all protective and defensive?

"I guess I should go find Jamie," I said pointedly.

Simon shot me a look, apology evident in his eyes. I gave my head a slight shake. It was fine. He was fine. Melia was fine. I was just *fine*.

* * *

Twice over the next couple of weeks, Jamie and I hung out with Simon and Melia. Both times, it was awkward.

Melia was . . . odd. When she wasn't giving me the stink eye, which Katie insisted I was making up even though I'd caught it happening more than once, she was sweet. *So* sweet. But she didn't get Simon. And none of us got her. She *had* to have a brain in her head since she'd gotten into graduate school at Duke, but it's like she avoided all potential conversation that might require her to use it. It was the weirdest thing I'd ever seen. Even Jamie noticed. It became a game to see if we could get her to discuss what she was studying, but she somehow managed to shift the conversation away from herself and onto something else every single time. We half wondered if grad school was a cover story and she was really spending all her time at the nail salon. Her nails were always gorgeous. Perfectly manicured to match her outfits. Total craziness.

It was only out of respect for Simon that the rest of us kept our mouths shut. The only good thing that came out of their weird, mismatched relationship, at least the only good thing for *me*, was that Melia's presence made it much easier for me to ignore my Simon-related doubts and focus on my relationship with Jamie. I was a terrible person for even thinking it, but with Simon shifting back to unavailable—to the untouchable Hamilton brother he'd been once before—it was so much easier for me to breathe.

* * *

Thanksgiving week, Jamie called while I was on my way home from work. "Hey," he said. "How are you?"

"Totally stressed," I told him. "The inn sold. Today. Just like that. They still have to finalize everything, but the offer was made and accepted, and the new owner is paying cash, so it's going to go through really fast. Like before-Christmas fast."

"Wow. Any idea what to expect?"

"I don't know anything for sure. April did some digging, and if it's who we think it is, it's a company that owns a lot of hotels up and down the East Coast. Which is probably a good thing."

"Winding Way is a great inn," Jamie said. "It makes sense someone would want to capitalize on that."

"I hope you're right."

"Hey, are you home yet? Can you come over?"

I was seconds away from pulling into my driveway, but his place wasn't that far away. "Sure. Is everything okay?"

"I just need to talk to you about something."

"Should I be scared? Your voice sounds like maybe I should be scared."

"Not scared. Well, not too scared. We'll talk when you get here. Love you, bye." He was gone before I had the chance to respond. I grumbled at my cell phone, then tossed it onto the seat beside me. Whatever he needed to talk about, I felt sure I wasn't in the mood.

I found Jamie at his kitchen table, his laptop open in front of him, his phone pressed to his ear. It was weird walking through the house knowing he was the only one who still lived there. Dave had moved in with Katie after the wedding since she hadn't been too keen about bunking up with her husband's twin brother. With Cooper gone, that left the whole house just for Jamie.

He motioned me into the kitchen as he ended his call. I sat but kept my jacket on. He'd said scary news. I kinda felt like I needed an extra layer of protection. He put down the phone and looked at me, his face sheepish and sad. "Hi."

"Hi."

"Please don't hate me."

"Please don't give me a reason to hate you."

He took a deep breath. "I can't go home with you this weekend."

I stared. He was joking. He had to be joking. "Jamie. My eighty-four-year-old grandmother flew all the way from Puerto Rico so she could meet my boyfriend. You can't not come."

"I know that. And I've been on the phone for hours trying to figure out a way to still be there, but . . . Lane, there's a guy coming from Japan. This is *huge*. We've been trying to break into the international market on our own for months, and Byron just made it happen. Set the meeting up, invited him out. And he's coming. I can't miss this."

"Let Dave meet with him."

"Dave and Katie are having Thanksgiving with her family—their first as a married couple. Plus, he can't talk marketing like I can. He's too . . . technical. This guy needs to be wooed. That's what I'm good at."

Ha. Yeah. That was the truth. "When's the meeting?"

"Thursday morning."

"Are you serious? *On* Thanksgiving?"

"It's not a holiday in Japan."

"But Byron was the one who set up the meeting! Does he not have any respect for your personal life? For your family?" I hadn't had the pleasure of meeting Byron yet, but I'd already decided. He was not a man I expected to like.

"Lane, if it were any other meeting, you know I'd skip it. But at this stage, everything is so critical."

I stood. "I really can't talk to you right now."

"Please don't be upset."

I spun around to face him. "Are you serious? Jamie, this has been on the calendar for weeks. It's really important to me. Abuela probably won't make the trip again, ever. And the main reason she's coming is so she can see her grandchildren—see *me*—happy and settled. Do you know how many missionaries she's given my phone number to? How many men she's had call me, sure they were going to be the one to win my heart? In her mind, I am ancient and alone and will never get married unless she continues to intervene. This was my chance to show her I'm fine. I'm happy. And look, I have this amazing man who loves me and wants to take care of me."

"I do love you."

"Then come with me."

He dropped his head into his hands. "I can't, Lane. I'm so sorry." Some small part of me knew this wasn't entirely Jamie's fault. There was a little bit of hero worship going on between Byron and him, which was expected considering the circumstances. It made sense, even if it was annoying, that Jamie would jump through Byron's hoops. But this. This was big and hard, and I was having a difficult time wrapping my head around it. He'd been gone *so much* lately. This felt like one more way he was putting distance between us.

Suddenly, all the not knowing regarding our relationship felt like too much to handle. For the first time, I wondered if maybe Jamie was having doubts about us. Curse my overconfidence. I'd been dealing with my own doubts without even considering the possibility that maybe the reason we weren't talking about his potential move was because he didn't want to. "Can you please talk to me about California?" I blurted out.

He kept his eyes down, his jaw clenched.

"Jamie, it's the giant elephant in the room, and it's making me crazy. I feel like we're trapped in this weird middle ground. Are you moving? Are you staying? Do you even want me to be a part of that decision? Right now you're putting this business move before everything else. And I get that. But you have to start talking to me. I literally have no idea what to expect. It's like a game of chance whether or not I'm going to get to see you from week to week. You're here, then you're gone. You're spending Thanksgiving with me, then you're not. It's exhausting. And suddenly all I'm imagining is your doubt. Because if you didn't have doubts, you'd be talking to me about this."

He took a breath like he was going to speak, then huffed, shaking his head.

"What is it?" I said. "What are you not saying?"

"I don't have doubts." He held up his hands, palms up, a gesture of surrender. "I just haven't wanted to push you. I didn't want you to feel pressured to make this huge life decision before you were ready. Before *we're* ready. Everyone says I'm impulsive, that I make decisions quick. I didn't want to do that to you. I . . ." He shook his head. "I thought I'd scare you off."

"What's scary is wondering if your boyfriend isn't talking to you about his plans because he's not sure he wants you to be a part of them."

"That's not it. I promise, Lane." He squared his shoulders. "Here's the truth, all right? I'm going to California. For sure. It's a done deal. And I don't want to go without you. I've just had no clue how to tell you that. That's big, you know? I didn't want to put that kind of pressure on you this early on."

"But, Jamie, you should have told me. As soon as you knew, we should have talked about it." Even as I said the words, I felt the wisdom in his restraint. If he'd come to me six weeks earlier and said, "Hey, how about you move to California to be with me?" I'd have probably panicked.

He stood and crossed the kitchen to where I leaned against the counter. He took me by the arms, gently turning me so I faced him head-on. "You're right. I should have told you sooner, and I'm sorry I didn't. Can we talk about it now?"

I'd just told him it was what I wanted. To talk about it. But suddenly the whole conversation felt too overwhelming. There was no way I could adequately express everything that was going on inside my brain. All the doubt and worry over the past month—doubts about the depth of my relationship with Jamie, about moving, about potential feelings for Simon—had set the stage for a perfect storm of emotion. Mix in the disappointment of Jamie not coming home for Thanksgiving, and I was a complete mess. There was no way I could have any kind of objective conversation about California with my emotions already so churned up.

I pressed my forehead into the heels of my hands. "I don't want to talk about it right now."

"You don't want to talk about California right now?"

"About anything. Any of it. I think I just need some time to process."

He nodded, though I could see the disappointment in his eyes. "Time to process. I'm not sure I know what that means."

"I need to process! Make sense of what I'm feeling. And *stop* feeling so angry about you bailing on Thanksgiving. I'm just not in the right mind-set to talk about something as big as moving across the country." It wasn't the entire truth, but for the sake of our discussion, it had to be enough.

He took a step back. "Okay. I can respect that."

I reached for my keys on the kitchen counter, where I'd dropped them on my way in. "I think I'm going to go."

He ran his hands through his hair, his agitation clear. "Lane, wait." He caught my hand and pulled me into a hug. I let him wrap his arms around me, but I didn't hug back. I just stood there, my arms tucked between us, my cheek leaning against his chest. "You do know how sorry I am, right?"

I nodded. "I know."

"I don't want you to give up on us because of all this, okay? Thanksgiving stinks, I know, but I'll make it up to you. I promise. And then we can look forward. *Move* forward. California would be great for us, Lane. I know it would."

I shifted out of his arms. "I'm not giving up on anything. I just need a little time."

His shoulders slumped, but he nodded his head. "I understand."

"I'll call you later, okay?"

"Okay."

Before I was even out of the kitchen, Simon appeared in the doorway. "Oh. Hey," he said.

"Where'd you come from?" Jamie said. "I didn't hear you come in."

"I came in through the basement. Dave borrowed my tools before he moved out and never gave them back, so I dropped by to pick them up. What's up with you?"

Jamie stood frozen, his hands resting on the table behind him, looking from me to Simon, then back to me again. I could almost see the wheels turning in his brain. Something was up.

"What is he doing?" Simon whispered to me.

"I have no idea."

Jamie finally moved, a smile stretching wide across his face. "Lane. I think I just solved our problem."

"What problem?" Simon asked.

"What are you doing for Thanksgiving?" Jamie asked, his eyes boring into his brother.

"Me?" Simon asked. "Nothing. Going home, I think."

"Want to go to Asheville instead?"

"Jamie, what are you doing?" I said.

He took a step forward. "It's perfect. He goes to Thanksgiving with you and pretends to be your boyfriend. He meets Abuela, everyone is happy because Lane is happy, and then after the first of the year, you guys break up and you're back with me."

"Back up," Simon said. "Why aren't you going to Thanksgiving with Lane?"

"Because he's going to California for a meeting with Byron." I didn't even try to keep the bitterness out of my voice.

"Seriously? On Thanksgiving?"

"I know. It stinks. But we can still fix this." Jamie looked at me. "It's not like I'm asking you to take a stranger. This is Simon. You guys are friends. It'll be easy to pretend like you're in love."

I stood there frozen in one spot, paralyzed by Jamie's words. I had to stop him. There was no way I could agree to *Simon* pretending to be my boyfriend for a single minute, much less an entire weekend. Like an old-school movie reel, my mind flashed through all the moments I'd ever shared with Simon. All the tiny sparks I'd felt between us, the looks, the conversations. It was like someone turned a mirror on my own life, bringing into sharp focus the fact that such a weekend could *never* happen. Instead of dousing sparks with water, an uninterrupted weekend with Simon had the potential to do the exact opposite. Granny Grace's warning roared in my brain. *You want to avoid trouble with the one brother? You stay far away from the other.* But how could I explain that to Jamie? It was impossible. My mind started scrambling for other reasons—reasonable reasons—to thwart his plan.

Simon crossed his arms. "Jamie, it's a bad idea."

Good. At least he and I were on the same page.

"Why? It'll totally work."

"What about social media?" I asked. "There are pictures of us out there. How would we explain that?"

"Lane, you never post anything on social media. Your Facebook status still says single."

"Are you serious?" I pulled my phone out of my pocket and opened Facebook to check.

"Yep. I just checked the other day. There are no photos of you and me together on Facebook, and if your mother is anything like mine, that's all she uses."

"Doesn't Lane's family already know your name?" Simon asked. "How would we explain her boyfriend suddenly becoming someone different?"

Jamie's face fell. "That's a good point."

"Except . . . they don't know your name." The words tumbled out before I could stop them. Why was I trying to help?

"You've never told them my name?" Jamie asked. My words couldn't have done much to bolster his confidence.

"Well, no," I said. "But you haven't met my mother. Our relationship is complicated."

He frowned.

"My brother knows your name, if that matters," I added.

"That's enough, then, right?" Simon said. "Your brother would know something was up."

"Actually, John would probably help us pull it off if we needed him to." *What is happening?* It was like my words were functioning independently of everything logical inside my head. "He gets it. He's got the same family I do."

"Then for sure we can make this work. If we've got a man on the inside, it's a done deal," Jamie said.

Finally, my brain managed to rein the rest of me in. "No. It's not a done deal. I don't want this. I don't want to spend the entire holiday pretending." As I said the words, my chest constricted, and my heart started to pound. Maybe my brain didn't want to pretend. But my heart totally did.

"Lane, think about your abuela. Think about how disappointed you'll be if you have to disappoint her."

Abuela. Her last trip. Her failing health. Her anticipation and hope for my happiness.

I looked up at Simon. He looked . . . miserable. Like he wanted the ground to open up and swallow him whole. "I can't ask that of Simon, Jamie. To give up his entire Thanksgiving weekend to play charades. It's not fair."

"But it's more than that. He gets to spend the weekend with you, and, I mean, I know I'm biased, but you're pretty amazing. What do you say?" he said, turning to his brother. "Will you do it?"

Simon took a breath and gave his head a slight shake like he was forcing off his misery. "If Lane is comfortable with it, I guess I'm willing."

Talk about emotional whiplash. I knew taking Simon home for Thanksgiving was a bad idea. So why was I happy he'd agreed to do it? Never had I felt such discordance between my head and my heart.

"Will, um . . ." My voice cracked. I cleared my throat. "Will Melia care?"

Simon huffed out a laugh. "Ha. No. We aren't seeing each other anymore."

"What happened?" Jamie asked.

"You know how she'd never talk about grad school?"

"Yeah," Jamie said. "We had a game going to see if we could get her to mention it."

"Don't think I didn't notice," Simon said. "It drove me crazy. Not your trying, just the fact that she'd never say anything."

"What was up with that?" Jamie asked.

"I called a guy. An old classmate. He works in the admissions office at Duke." Simon shook his head, a smile playing on his lips. "She's not enrolled."

Jamie's eyes went wide. "She made it all up?"

"All of it. She works in a nail salon in Carrboro."

"I knew it!" I said. "I knew she couldn't have perfect nails like that unless it was her job."

"I don't have anything against people who work in nail salons," Simon said. "But I don't like being lied to."

"Poor Melia," I said. "I hope she's okay."

"It all comes down to you, Lane," Jamie said. "Melia isn't a problem, and Simon's willing. What do you say? Want to save Thanksgiving for your abuela?"

I held up my hands in a gesture of surrender. "Okay. Let's do it."

* * *

I paced back and forth across Granny's living room floor, worrying a pathway into her carpet. I'd tried to call Randi—she was much better for this type of thing—but she hadn't answered, and I was desperate for a sounding board.

Granny sat on her sofa, her feet propped up on the coffee table with a pillow underneath, and listened while I walked her through the entire scheme. "Don't you think your abuela would understand?" Granny said. "If you told her the truth?"

"Maybe. Probably. But she'd be so disappointed. And her health isn't great. I don't want to make things worse by making her sad."

"I guess it's good luck the man standing in is a man who's caught your eye a time or two."

I had known it wouldn't take long for Granny to make that point. After all, she'd been the first to suspect there was something going on between Simon and me. At least, she'd suspected there was potential for it.

I made another pass in front of the sofa. "I'm trying not to think about that part," I said.

"Child, you're going to run holes in my rug if you don't come sit down."

I stopped my pacing and dropped onto the sofa beside her.

"Why aren't you thinking about that part?" she asked. "With all the wondering you've done about Simon, maybe spending some time with him will help clear things up," Granny said.

"I thought you told me to stay away from Simon. Brother relationships and family loyalty and all that."

"I did say that. But you went and ignored my good advice, and now here we are. Better to make the most of the opportunity than to squelch it based on principle."

I leaned in closer to Granny so I could put my head on her shoulder. "Granny, I'm scared."

"Of what?"

"That I might really like him. I don't know what to do with that if I do. I really *don't* think Simon would ever betray his brother. Not for me, not for anybody."

She reached over and took my chin, tilting it upward until our eyes met. "You know what happened when your mama told me she was having a baby girl?"

I shook my head.

"I got down on my knees and said, 'Lord, you better send some extra wisdom to old Grace. I got a feeling this one's going to be a handful.'"

I laughed despite my effort not to. "You did not!"

"Listen to me, Lane. I'm about to give you some of that extra wisdom."

I sat up, and she reached for my hand, holding it softly with her own. "You say Simon wouldn't betray his brother, and I reckon you're right about that. But what makes you so sure that if Simon loves his brother enough to sacrifice his own desires for Jamie's happiness, that Jamie doesn't love *his* brother the same way? You've heard me say it before, child. Sometimes the heart wants what the heart wants and there's nothing we can do to stop it. If you're determined to go through with this, at least go with your heart open. See what happens. Sure, it's a risk. But God knows you, and He knows those brothers too. You might be surprised, if you put a little more faith in Him, to see where that faith might lead."

A tear spilled over, dripping down my cheek and onto her worn, weathered hand.

"You're going to be all right, Lane. You just wait. It'll all be just fine."

*Jamie: Anyone free to take me to the airport tomorrow morning? Lane's
      got a work thing. So she can't.*
Dave: No can do. Katie and I will already be gone by then.
Simon: What time is your flight? I can take you if it's before 10.
Jamie: Flight's at 8:15, so that will work. What's at 10?
Simon: That's when Lane is picking me up.
Jamie: Oh, right. That.
Dave: Um, what? What for?
Jamie: I hate everything about this.
Simon: It was your idea. I feel no guilt.
Dave: About what? What is going on?
*Jamie: I can't go to Asheville with Lane, but her grandma is coming all
      the way from Puerto Rico to meet me.*
Dave: So Simon is going instead?
Jamie: Pretending to be her boyfriend.
Dave: Oh, dude. This is so good. Simon and Lane. I love it.
Simon: Is it really that hard for you to imagine?
Dave: Yes. Yes, it is.
Jamie: Nobody imagine anything. It's temporary.
Simon: I'll take you to the airport in the morning.
Jamie: Thanks.
Simon: You're welcome. And don't worry. I'll only kiss Lane twice a day.
Dave: Ha, ha.
Jamie: So help me, Simon . . .
Dave: I'm so sad Cooper is missing this.
Simon: Me too.
Jamie: I hate you both.

Chapter 19

I'D NEVER BEEN TO SIMON'S house. Which felt weird considering I was picking him up to take him home for the weekend, where he would meet my family and pretend to be in love with me. When I pulled into his driveway, I noticed just how close he was to the inn's gardens. He'd told me his property bordered the southeastern edge, but I guess I'd imagined a more distant border. He could have thrown a rock from his front porch and hit the garden's pathway. No wonder he'd seen Ida and me talking in the garden. I walked across the grass, charmed by a different view of the gardens I'd loved for so long.

"It's nice, isn't it?"

I spun around. Simon stood on his porch, his hands pushed into his pockets. He was wearing dark jeans, an untucked button-down shirt, and a blazer. More casual than the suits I'd normally seen him in, but it was a look that suited him.

"It's lovely."

He walked down the steps and crossed to where I stood. "The gate's down there, at the corner." He pointed.

"Okay, if I lived here, I really would walk to work every day."

Simon gave me a quick tour of the rest of the house before we left. It wasn't very big, but it was full of clean, modern lines and space so well appointed it didn't feel small. The décor was far more than I expected of a bachelor pad. It was minimal but still intentional. And there were books everywhere. Funky bookends of all different styles filled the mantelpiece, the bookshelves, and the table behind the couch. "You decorate like I do," I said. "With books."

"Yeah, I figured it was better than antlers or those weird singing-fish things."

I grinned. "Or cats."

"Definitely better than cats." He shrugged his shoulders. "So. I guess I'll grab my bag, and we can go."

I gripped my keys a little tighter. "Sounds good."

Things were quiet the first few minutes of the drive. I navigated the car to the highway and headed west toward Asheville, nothing but some casual small talk filling the silence between us. Finally, Simon cleared his throat like he wanted to say something but then froze, his mouth hanging open.

I glanced his direction. "You okay?"

He gave his head a slight shake as if to clear his thoughts. "Sorry. I was trying to think of the most appropriate way to start this conversation."

"Simon, I think we're far past appropriate with the whole charade we've cooked up for this weekend. Whatever it is, just say it."

He smiled. "Well, that's just it. I wonder if we shouldn't set some . . . ground rules. No. Ground rules sounds so formal. I just want to make sure I behave like you would expect me to. Do we hold hands? Should I keep my arm around you? And what's our story? How did we meet? How long have we been dating? I'm guessing people will ask those questions, so we probably ought to figure out the answers."

All very good questions. "Right. Okay. Let's start at the beginning. We met on the soccer field right after I moved in. We don't even need to lie about that one."

He nodded. "Good. And we started dating right away?"

"Sure. We can even talk about how you helped me out at the inn, and because we spent so much time together, falling in love was really easy."

"Yes. Good. That works."

"Holding hands is great," I said. "And an arm around me every once in a while would be nice. Don't hover though. We have to be casual enough that people believe we've been dating for months. In tune with each other but not overly infatuated."

"I can do that."

It came to my mind, not for the first time, just how big a thing this was. How generous Simon was for going along with the whole crazy plan. "Thank you for doing this, Simon. For me and for Jamie too. I know how crazy it must feel." He looked up when I mentioned Jamie's name, our eyes meeting for the briefest of moments, then he looked down at his hands.

I turned my focus back to the road, wondering if he was going to say anything. He looked like he wanted to, so I continued to wait.

"Don't think anything of it," he finally said. "My brothers are a lot of things, plenty of things I don't like. But the one thing Hamiltons have never lacked is loyalty. Jamie in particular, for all his insults, would do anything for me. I don't doubt that for a second. It's only right I do the same for him."

"Well, thank you for making such a noble sacrifice," I said.

He smiled. "Sacrifice, indeed. You're pretty terrible company, Lane. Spending four days with you is going to be rough. For Jamie, I can endure. But I don't have to like it."

"Very funny. Did he make it to the airport okay this morning?"

"Yeah, he did." He paused. "You know this is really hard on him, right?"

"I know. He's told me he's sorry five million times. I've told him it's fine, but . . ."

"He doesn't believe you?"

I shook my head.

"But he should?"

I looked at him. "Why does everyone doubt me? I get it. His work is important right now."

"I guess Jamie gave me the impression there's a little more at stake."

So that was what he was getting at. My *future* with Jamie. "What, because of the move?"

"How are you feeling about it?"

I sighed a weary sigh. "I don't know how I feel. I really wish he didn't have to go."

"I remember you telling me you didn't love living in California. Are you still feeling that way?"

"I don't know what I'm feeling. I'm changing my mind daily. I keep hoping something will stick, but so far, the only thing I know for sure is that I still don't know what to do." There was a lot I wasn't saying. How much it still hurt that Jamie had kept me in the dark about California for so long, even if his reasons were well-intentioned. How much it hurt that even when he knew what was at stake, he still couldn't prioritize me over his business. I'd told Jamie and Simon I was fine, and I wanted to believe I was, but I still felt the sting, no matter how reasonable I tried to be.

In a way, it was like there were two relationships on trial for the weekend. The fake one Simon and I had to convince my family was real. And inside my own heart, my real one with Jamie. I told myself I just had to get through the weekend with Simon, then I would have the emotional bandwidth to sort out how I truly felt about Jamie. But I couldn't ignore it—the huge California-shaped cloud looming over my head. Nor could I ignore the Simon-shaped *person* sitting next to me and the role he might play in the sorting out of my feelings. Whether I wanted him to or not.

A question bounced around the back of my brain. I shouldn't ask. Simon had just spoken of his loyalty to his brother, so asking might put him in an uncomfortable position. But he also might have insight I could benefit from. And seeing as how I was about to make a huge decision, I really wanted to ask. "Can I ask you something about Jamie?" There. Damage done. I'd committed.

"Sure. Anything."

"Sometimes I feel like I'm dating two different versions of the same man."

"Okay."

"Jamie is impetuous and impulsive. Not in a bad way. He just knows what he wants, and he goes after it. I can relate to that. I'm like that in a lot of ways, but he's a little like a barrel rolling down a hill, you know? He just goes and does without thinking, trusting he'll hit the bottom eventually, thrilled at how fast he's managing to go on the way."

Simon chuckled. "That is a perfect description of Jamie."

"But other times, he seems so thoughtful. Like he's slowed down and observed the things I like and the music I listen to. It's so sweet when it happens, but, honestly, it always kind of surprises me when it does because he's not really like that with other people. I don't want to sound like I'm painting him in such a negative light. It's not that he's not considerate. He'd do anything for anyone. I know that. But he's not always the most observant guy. So there's a dichotomy there. These two different sides of his personality that don't necessarily mesh."

Simon shifted in his seat. "Maybe he's more observant with you because of how much he cares about you. He's trying harder because he loves you."

"Yeah. That's what I keep telling myself. But I don't want him to feel like he has to be someone he's not."

"I think he just wants to impress you."

"I know. And I appreciate it. He's done some amazing things for me." I glanced his way. "He told you about my birthday, right? It was incredible. But it still felt . . . I don't know how it felt."

"I'm guessing there's still a question in there somewhere."

"Right. I did say that. I guess I'm wondering what Jamie has been like in the past. Is this typical girlfriend stuff you've seen him do before?"

He ran his hand over his jaw. "I'll say this. I've never seen Jamie care so much or work so hard to make a woman happy like he has with you."

"Really?"

He nodded. "Really."

My cell phone rang before I could say anything more. The Bluetooth in my car picked up the call. My mother. Risky, answering her through Bluetooth, considering Simon would hear our entire conversation. I glanced at my phone sitting in the center console, comforted to know I could make a fast switch if need be.

"*Bueno*? Mama?"

"Lane? Are you on your way?"

"We are. We should be there by lunchtime. How is Abuela?"

"Oh, fine, fine. Everything is fine, but, Lane, I need to warn you."

"You're on speaker phone, Mom. Simon's listening."

"Oh. Hello, Simon. Nice to *finally* have the chance to say hello." I glanced at Simon and rolled my eyes.

"Hello, Dr. Bishop. I'm looking forward to meeting you in person."

"Mmm. He has a nice deep voice, Lane. Very nice."

"Mom!"

"Where was I? Oh yes. There's something I need to tell you. Nothing major. Just a small little detail that I may have mentioned to my mother when we were discussing you and Simon."

"What kind of little detail?"

"You know how she pressures me, Lane."

"Uh-huh."

"And you know how persuasive she is."

"Mama. What did you say to her?"

"It's just that she was talking on and on about how a young woman's choice is never really made until she has a ring on her finger. Did you know she invited three men to my engagement party with your father? Three! 'Backup,' she called them. In case I changed my mind at the last minute."

"Please tell me she's not turning my Thanksgiving into a speed-dating event."

"No. She's not. Though you're lucky we're not in Puerto Rico. If we were, it might be a different story."

"So what did you tell her about Simon and me?"

She sighed. "I told her you were already engaged."

"What? Why would you do that? We're not!"

"I told you. She kept going on and on about how important it is for you to get married and asking what I was doing to help you and how serious were you with this boy, and, Lane, it was like it was me all over again. I don't want her to do this to you. I love my mother. And I know she loves you and that is where her concern comes from, but she's a little crazy. If you're actually engaged to this boy, I think she may dial it back a bit."

I huffed. "Is that your professional opinion?" My mother was even-tempered, reasonable, and wise in nearly every sense—an incredible psychiatrist who counseled people out of damaging, destructive relationships on a daily basis. But she was full-on nutty when it came to dealing with her own mother.

Mom huffed right back. "Don't pull the professional card on me. This is your abuela we're talking about. There is no medical degree that covers how to handle her."

Simon and I exchanged glances. Engaged. I mean, we were pretending all weekend anyway. What difference did it make if we took things one step further?

"Oh no," Mom said. "I just thought of something. Lane, put Simon on the phone."

"He's on the phone. We both are."

"I know that," she said. "Just him."

Simon raised his eyebrows in question. I shrugged—I had no idea what she wanted—but gestured to the phone in the center console.

He picked it up. "Okay. It's just me now."

I watched and waited while he listened, a smile playing around his lips the entire time. "No, I do appreciate you mentioning that," he finally said. He nodded. "I wasn't planning on it, but I think we can work something out for this weekend." He paused again. Another nod. "Okay. I'm looking forward to meeting you too." He hung up the phone and dropped it back into the center console. "So," he said. He cupped his hands over his knees. "You want to get married?"

"I cannot even begin to imagine what you think of my family."

He shrugged. "Everybody's got a little bit of crazy, right? It's not a big deal."

"What did my mother ask you?"

"She wanted to make sure I wasn't planning on proposing this weekend for real."

"Ohhh. Because pretending to be engaged would ruin it."

"Exactly. She also asked if we could swing by a jewelry store and pick up a fake engagement ring. I guess she doesn't have one you could wear?"

I thought for a moment. "Not that would fit me. She's tiny."

"So we'll get one, then. There's bound to be a jewelry store between here and Asheville."

"We don't need a real jewelry store. I'm sure we can find some cheap costume jewelry somewhere."

"So I can look like I bought you something cheap? No way. I'll spend the money, you wear the ring for the weekend, then we'll stop and return it on our way home."

"I guess that could work. This feels totally ridiculous though, just for the record. I want to make sure you hear me say that. I am baffled at the absurdity of my own life right now."

Simon grinned. "I'm having fun." He pulled out his phone and opened Google Maps. After a few clicks and scrolls, he held it up. "Um. There's a Walmart in seven miles."

"That's your idea of not cheap?"

"I was being funny. There's not really anything between here and . . . Marion? Is that a good place to stop?"

"If we're stopping in Marion, we might as well just stop in Asheville. There will be plenty to choose from there."

"Can we go downtown? There's this place . . . I've only been there once, but it has the greatest chocolate. Not hot chocolate. It's . . . man, I can't remember what it's called."

"The French Broad Chocolate Lounge? Liquid truffles."

"Yes! That's it. That place is awesome."

"Okay. Downtown it is."

We drove in silence for a few minutes. Simon was probably cataloging a list of reasons for why I was a crazy person, but all I could think of was what it would feel like to wear an engagement ring—*Simon's* engagement ring—on my hand.

Simon cleared his throat. "So there's one member of your family we haven't talked about yet, and I feel like we should."

"Yeah? Who's that?"

"Is your father going to know we're only pretending to be engaged? Because, here's the thing. If I had proposed for real, I'd have never done it without meeting your father first. Does that make me old-school?"

"A little. I like it though. And knowing my father, he would appreciate the gesture."

"He's going to know, right? Even though this is all made up, I still want him to think I'm a nice guy."

"I'm sure Mom filled him in. He's been around Abuela enough. He'll take this all in stride."

"Anything else I should know before I meet him? He's still going to think I'm your boyfriend, right? Even if he knows the engagement isn't real?"

"Yes. The only person who knows the truth besides me, you, and Jamie is John."

"Okay."

"Don't worry about my dad. He can be intimidating when you first meet him, mostly because he's so tall and imposing, but he's a total softy. Once he smiles, and he smiles at everyone, you'll feel like you've been best friends for years."

"I wish I played basketball."

"Do you play at all? Like if you shot around in the driveway, would I be totally embarrassed to call you mine?"

"Completely. I don't even think I can dribble."

I shot him a look.

"Don't look at me like that. I *lived* on the soccer field."

"What about football? There's a game on Thursday morning—an Asheville Ward Thanksgiving tradition. Are you up for it? Just flag football. No tackles."

"Your dad plays?"

"Oh yes. He plays and coaches and refs and yells and generally likes to tell everyone on the field what to do."

"Geez. I hope I'm on his team."

"If John's home by then, he'll watch out for you. You'll love John."

Simon sat up straighter. "How did he respond when you first told him about our plan?"

"He thinks we're crazy, but he's cool with it. He for sure won't blow our cover."

I filled the next half hour talking about Bishop family culture. All the traditional Puerto Rican food we would include in our Thanksgiving dinner. The decorating for Christmas that would start literally seconds after the table was cleared. Our traditional drive up onto the parkway to see the mountain views and take a family photo and our trip to the Biltmore Estate to see the annual tree lighting. It made me anxious to get home, to see and be with my family.

Oddly, I didn't expect it to be awkward, despite the realities of having a fake fiancé along for the ride. In my mind, imagining Simon with my family felt natural. So much so that if I let myself forget about the pretending, even for a moment, all that was left was excitement.

* * *

We parked in downtown Asheville in the garage on Biltmore Avenue. I hadn't been downtown in a long time. The same familiar energy filled the air and reminded me of how much I loved where I had grown up. The food, the people, the sights and sounds of the city—it was a fun place. I pulled my deep-purple wool coat around my shoulders, happy for the protection against the cold November wind. We walked up to Pack Square, where a group of living statues stood on the corner, a crowd of observers gathered around. We watched until the statues shifted their pose, then we moved past, heading toward the jewelry store on Patton Avenue.

"I wonder how long it takes to get into all that body paint," Simon said once we were out of earshot.

"No joke. And for real, what do they do when they need to scratch their nose?"

"They don't, I guess. Except for when they shifted on purpose, I didn't see a flinch from any of them. How do they stay warm?"

I turned around and looked back up the sidewalk. "Maybe we should go back and ask them all our questions. Think we could make them flinch if we do?"

Simon chuckled. "If Cooper were here, he'd be heckling."

"He seems a lot like Jamie," I said. "Not the heckling, I mean. Just in general."

"A nineteen-year-old Jamie would have heckled. Age and experience have been good for him."

I nodded. I could see that. Made me kind of glad I'd never met nineteen-year-old Jamie.

"And yes," Simon said, "Cooper is a lot like him."

We stopped on the sidewalk in front of the jewelry store we'd mapped out in the car. Simon opened the door. "After you."

The store was busy. Which made sense the day before Thanksgiving, but still. It only added to the awkwardness of fake ring shopping. I told Simon we could get the most inexpensive one, but he insisted the ring had to be something I felt good in. We settled on a simple round stone set in white gold with two emeralds on either side of the diamond. It wasn't crazy expensive, but it still made me cringe when Simon pulled out his credit card.

"Well, if it isn't my favorite baby sister."

I spun around. John stood in the doorway, a dark-blue scarf wrapped around his neck, his collar pulled up high. I hadn't seen him in more than a year, and the sight of him standing there nearly made me cry. I rushed into his arms, literally leaping off the ground to hug his neck. John was nearly as tall as our father. He even made my five foot nine seem tiny. He lowered me to the floor. "What are you doing here?" he asked.

"I, um . . ." I turned and looked back toward Simon, who was standing behind me. He stepped forward, handing me the engagement ring, then extended his hand to John.

"I'm Simon Hamilton," he said.

"Ah. The fill-in boyfriend. John Bishop. Nice to meet you."

"Fill-in fiancé, actually." I slipped the ring on my finger and held up my hand. "Mom called this morning. She told Abuela we were already engaged, so we're here to perpetuate her lie."

John looked at my hand, then raised his eyebrows at Simon. "I'd like to see the ring you buy when it's the real deal."

I lowered my voice. "We're going to return it after this weekend. It is gorgeous though, isn't it?"

John shook his head, then looked at Simon. "I have no idea how you wound up in the middle of all this, but you are one good friend."

I smacked John's arm. "What are you even doing here? I thought for sure we wouldn't see you until tomorrow."

"I wanted to check on Abuela and make sure she'd handled her flight okay, so I came a day early. I just had lunch with a friend and happened to see you on my way back to the car."

I put an arm around him, hugging him again. "It's so good to see you."

"You look good, Lane." He looked at Simon. "It's your brother, right? The real boyfriend? I hope he's taking good care of her."

"I don't *need* to be taken care of."

They both ignored me. "Jamie is a good man. I can promise you that," Simon said.

John nodded. "Good." He turned back to me. "Hey, guess who I ran into outside? You remember Emma? From church? She lived over in Hendersonville and played the violin?"

"Yeah. We hung out at girls camp every year. She got married over the summer, didn't she? To the famous piano player?"

"Elliott Hart. I met him. They were together, heading up to the Chocolate Lounge. You might still catch them if you want to say hi."

"We were headed there anyway. Come with us." I led the way as we all filed out of the jewelry store and headed back toward the square. The living statues had relocated to a different corner, but a guy with a guitar, a harmonica, and a foot drum had taken their place. He sang Christmas songs, which made me unexpectedly happy. I pulled my coat a little tighter. "I love this time of year. If only it would snow, everything would be perfect."

"We've got plenty of that in Chicago," John said. "You should come see me."

"Why? So I can hang out in your apartment alone while you live at the hospital?"

"It's not all that bad. I slept at home . . . three times last week. That's pretty good."

Emma and Elliott were coming out of the Chocolate Lounge when we got there. Emma smiled wide when she saw me and stepped forward to give me a hug. "Lane! It's been so long! It's so great to see you," she said.

"You too! I'm sorry I couldn't make it to the wedding this summer. I was right in the middle of a move, and I couldn't get away."

She waved away my excuses. "Don't even worry about it. This is my husband, Elliott." She grinned at the word *husband* like she still wasn't used to saying it out loud.

I shook his hand. "It's great to meet you."

"Likewise," he said.

I realized almost too late that I needed to introduce Simon. Which meant I needed to introduce Simon *as* someone. And probably not a "fill-in fiancé." I was home, with people who went to church with my parents and needed to believe Simon was the real deal. "This is my boyfriend, Simon," I blurted out.

Emma gave me a funny look. "Um, that diamond on your hand says more than boyfriend."

I froze, looking at my hand like I didn't know what she was talking about.

"It only happened yesterday," Simon said, coming to the rescue. "I guess we're still getting used to the new status."

"Sorry. Yes. Fiancé." I looked at Simon. "I swear you shouldn't read anything into that." I took a step closer and wrapped an arm around his waist. He pulled me close, his arm resting across my shoulders. It was the first time we'd really touched. *Ever.* Maybe handshakes and a random touch here and there, but never a hug. Never anything this personal. Aside from the delicious waves of heat the contact sent coursing through my body, what I felt more than anything was safety.

"You guys are a really cute couple," Emma said. "Congratulations."

We said our good-byes, then settled into a back booth of the Chocolate Lounge, Simon leaving John and me alone while he went to order for all of us.

John leaned across the booth. "What. Was. That?"

"What was what?"

"What was the way you looked all glowing and happy in the arms of the guy you are not supposed to be in love with?"

"I was not glowing and happy."

He only raised his eyebrows, his look saying just how much he didn't believe me. "Are you sure?"

I hesitated. "Yes?"

"Oh, Lane, what have you done? You were supposed to let that spark die!"

My shoulders slumped. "I have no idea what I've done, but it keeps getting messier and messier. I swear when I'm with Jamie I love him. I'm happy. Most of the time, anyway. He's a great guy."

"Wait a minute. What's with the 'most of the time, anyway' disclaimer? Why are you qualifying your happiness?"

"I'm not."

"You just did."

I huffed. "Fine. Things have been tougher lately. He's been working a lot and spending all his time across the country, and we're just not feeling as connected."

"That was a problem when we talked last month too."

I nodded. "Yeah. It's been going on awhile. And now he's moving for sure, and I have no idea where that leaves us. You remember how much I *loved* living in California."

"Help me understand here, Lane. Are the two issues exclusive of each other? Things are rocky with Jamie, so you decided to take his brother for a test-drive? Or things are rocky with Jamie because you'd *rather* be with his brother instead?"

"I'm not test-driving anybody. Simon coming to Asheville was Jamie's idea. He set the whole thing up because he felt so terrible for having to bail himself. And it all happened so fast; what was I supposed to say? Please, no, not him. I may have a crush on him, and that could be bad news for us?"

"So you're admitting you have a crush."

I sighed. "Please don't say anything. I'll figure stuff out. I'll talk to Jamie when I get back home, but for now I just have to get through this weekend."

Just get through the weekend.

Surely I could manage that.

Jamie: How's it going?

Simon: Fine. Lane's family is nice.

Jamie: Have you met the crazy grandma yet?

Simon: She isn't crazy. She likes me. I speak Spanish.

Jamie: Ugh. Am I going to have to learn Spanish for this lady? How are Lane's parents?

Simon: Her dad is huge. But nice. Her mom is tiny and intense. But also nice. Have you talked to Lane at all?

Jamie: Just through texts. I think she's afraid to talk to me since you're there. Who does that make me?

Simon: True.

Jamie: Thanks for doing this, man. I owe you one.

Simon: It's fine. I'm having a good time.

Jamie: Not too good a time though, right?

Simon: You're the one who asked me to do this.

Jamie: I know. It felt like a good idea at the time. But . . . I wish I was there.

Simon: Lane wishes so too.

Chapter 20

SIMON DROPPED ONTO THE COUCH beside me. "Hey."

I closed the book I'd been reading. "Hey. How was it?"

He rolled his head around as if to stretch his neck, then dropped it back onto the cushion behind him. "Intense."

"Uh-oh. Not bad intense, I hope?"

"No, it was good. We bonded. Even if we had to hold the stupid ball with our hands."

"Bonding is good. Did your team win?"

"Of course we won." My father paused in the archway that led into the family room, where I'd been reading. "When have you ever known me to do anything but win?"

I shifted and reached to the side table where I'd left my phone. "I don't know, Dad. Let me just pull up this season's basketball schedule. I'm thinking . . . Who was the team you played last week? It was close, wasn't it?"

Dad lunged into the room and grabbed a pillow he then tossed directly at my head. "You watch it, young lady."

I tossed the pillow back at him with little grace or aim. It landed far and wide, about three feet left of where he stood. He looked at me, then at the pillow, then back at me. "It's a good thing those soccer goals are so wide." He looked at Simon. "This is why she'd have never made it as a basketball player."

"Dad!"

He grinned. "Your young man did well today, Lane. He's fast. Scored the winning touchdown."

I looked at Simon, my eyes wide. "You score the winning touchdown and all you say is 'It was intense'?"

"Fine," Simon said. "I was awesome. Happy now?"

"Yes. Yes, I am."

"How's the cooking going?" Dad asked. "I'd have made you come and play had I known you'd be sitting around here."

"I haven't been sitting but for the past ten minutes. Abuela worked us like crazy this morning. She's making a true Puerto Rican feast."

"It took her three years before she cooked like this for me." Dad looked at Simon. "You're lucky she's taken to you so fast."

Simon shot me a sideways glance, and my stomach tightened. "I feel lucky," he finally said. "She's an amazing lady."

"As long as her cooking doesn't stop Maria from baking a sweet-potato pie, I'll agree with you." My dad smiled at us both, glancing over his shoulder in the direction of the kitchen. He leaned forward. "I know this engagement isn't for real just yet"—he paused but continued to nod his head, his smile warm and sincere. He looked at me—"but I think this is a good match for you, Lane." Then he turned to Simon. "I can tell you care for my daughter, Simon. I want you to know you have my support." He stood and walked toward the kitchen. "I'm going to say hello to your mother."

I let out the breath I didn't know I'd been holding as I watched my dad walk into the kitchen. I leaned my head back onto the couch. "This is wrong," I said quietly.

Simon didn't respond. He stood, running a hand through his hair with a sigh. "Do you mind if I borrow your car?" he asked. "I'm going to go for a drive."

* * *

Simon was gone an hour or so. By the time he came back, I was so wrapped up in final dinner prep I couldn't do more than wave from the kitchen. I didn't see him again until he came down for dinner showered, clean-shaven, and looking really, really irresistible. I carried a platter of turkey into the dining room and set it close to my dad's plate, then moved to stand next to Simon.

"Hi," I said softly. "You okay?"

He smiled, looking at me in a way he never had before. Like he'd taken down a wall. His eyes were warm, his gaze intense. He reached forward and took my hand, his thumb rubbing across the top of my knuckles. It made my breath catch. We'd touched, even hugged a few times around the family.

We were putting on a show, after all. But this didn't feel pretend. He smiled a half smile and nodded. "Yeah. I'm good."

Abuela came up behind us, her smile cutting deep creases in her weathered face. She looked at me, then laid a hand on my cheek before reaching up and kissing me right where her palm had been. Her deep-brown eyes glistened as she turned, doing the same thing to Simon, touching his face, then kissing him on the cheek. He had to lean down so she could reach him. When she finished, she wrapped her arms around us both and squeezed us into a three-sided hug.

"Um, I think you guys just got married," John said from across the room. He spoke in Spanish so Abuela would understand too.

She waved a dismissive hand at John but didn't break her smile, then turned back to us. "It's just my way of saying I'm happy for you," she said.

Dinner didn't disappoint. As a US territory, Puerto Rico still honored Thanksgiving as a traditional holiday, so much of the expected menu still graced our table—just with a little more flair and, if you asked Abuela, flavor. The turkey was roasted and stuffed with *mofongo*. There were *arroz con gandules*, *tostones*, and my cherished *pasteles*, which we'd stayed up late making the night before. All of us had filled the kitchen, just as Abuela had hoped, trimming the plantain leaves, cooking the pork with *sofrito* and a rich adobo sauce, then wrapping them up assembly-line style until we had enough for Thanksgiving and several dozen extra to freeze. Of course, there was also my dad's sweet-potato pie, a green bean casserole, and a Jell-O salad I'd made from Granny Grace's recipes. The fusion of the two sides of my family into one collective meal made me happy, as did the people surrounding the table. It had been too long since we'd all been together.

Before dessert, *dulce de leche*, bourbon pecan, or pumpkin pie (or all three if you're me), Abuela reached for my hand. "*Mija*," she called me, short for *mi hija*. My daughter. "Tell me when you first knew you loved Simon."

My Thanksgiving dinner turned to cement in my stomach. It felt horrible to lie, especially when Abuela seemed so sincere.

"Don't be shy," she urged. "We all love a good love story."

"I don't know, really. I guess it happened gradually."

"I can tell you when I knew," Simon said.

I looked up, trying to catch his gaze. He didn't need to do this. I wanted to tell him as much, but he seemed intent on avoiding any eye contact with me. He focused instead on Abuela, and she smiled her encouragement.

"One afternoon, I stopped by the inn where Lane works to drop off some paperwork. I'd been helping her with some accounting needs the inn had, but this time around, she didn't know I was coming. I thought it might be fun to surprise her during her lunch break, only she was the one who ended up surprising me. I found her in the middle of her office, shoes kicked off to the side, dancing."

I covered my face, silent laughter making my shoulders shake.

"Dancing?" my dad asked. "To what?"

Instead of answering, Simon started to sing. "You'll get me back! You'll get me baa—acck." His voice was high-pitched and awful, an intentional fake out since I'd heard him sing with his brothers before Cooper had left on his mission.

I gave his shoulder a playful shove. "You are terrible."

Abuela giggled right along with us. "You loved her dancing?" she asked Simon.

"No. Her dancing was terrible. But I loved that she would dance. That she was willing to let stuff go and have fun. I need more of that in my life, and I think that's what I recognized. That being around her will always make me a better person."

"Amen to that," my dad said from the other end of the table. He raised his water glass. "To love that improves and inspires us."

John, sitting directly across from me, raised his glass to me, his eyes like lasers burning questions into my brain.

What is going on?

Does he really mean the things he's saying?

What on earth are you going to do now?

I could only shrug my shoulders. Because I had no earthly idea.

Jamie: *Dude. I can't get Lane to answer my calls. Is she avoiding me?*
Simon: *I am just the pretend boyfriend. Not the for-real go-between.*
Jamie: *Is she okay?*
Simon: *She's fine. She's with her family. Remember, she hasn't seen her grandmother in years.*
Jamie: *Just ask her to call me, would you? Or at least text.*
Simon: *Fine. I'll tell her you asked about her.*

Chapter 21

I THOUGHT MAYBE DINNER WOULD be the last of it. No more talk of inspired love to complicate things even further, but I was wrong. Family tradition required postdinner activities to proceed as planned, which meant we all worked together to decorate for Christmas. The only thing worse than my mother sitting Simon down to see all thirteen Christmas ornaments plastered with my face—one for each year of school I'd completed—was John getting out the mistletoe. *Mistletoe.*

He was behind Simon when he pulled it out of the box, so only I saw the look on his face—the look that said *Oh my yes, we're going to use this tonight.* I gave my head a slight shake, trying to warn him with my eyes, but it was a lost cause. He nearly vaulted over a box of ornaments to get to where Simon and I stood, then pinned the mistletoe up directly over our heads.

"Subtle, John," I said. "Really subtle."

Simon looked up at the mistletoe. He knew as well as I did that John was in on our secret, so he had to be wondering what John was up to. But it was too late for it to matter. Abuela watched us from the couch. "*Un beso,*" she called. "*Un beso!*"

There was a question in Simon's eyes when he looked at me. Should we? Did I want him to? I looked back at Abuela, who still watched, both hands pressed against her heart. I turned back to Simon and smiled, leaning toward him enough for him to know that, yeah, this was happening.

"Are you sure?" He whispered so softly I nearly missed his words.

"They're all watching," I whispered. "Kiss me." In my head, I assumed it would be something chaste, simple. Nothing more than a little peck. But Simon clearly had other plans. He touched my face first, his fingers lingering on the side of my cheek before they slid to the curve of my neck. His other hand wrapped around my waist and rested on the small of my back. It was too obvious. Surely everyone would realize we'd never done this before. But I didn't care. All I cared about was that Simon's lips were seconds from touching mine and in that moment, there wasn't anything in the world I wanted more.

Fire. That was what it felt like. Heat up and down my arms, tingling all over every inch of my skin. The kiss only lasted a moment. I mean, my grandma was in the room, after all, but it was long enough. Long enough for me to know that everything had changed and I couldn't ignore it anymore.

I took a step backward, creating enough distance between Simon and me to catch my breath. It wasn't enough. I needed air. Space. *Answers.* "I'm gonna go for a walk." I hurried to the front door and reached for my coat hanging on the antique coatrack in the corner. Simon was right behind me, but I didn't stop, not until I was down the porch steps and halfway across the lawn.

"Lane, wait!" he called out after me.

I turned around, my hands shoved deep into my coat pockets.

"Don't run away," he said.

"Why are you doing this?"

He looked guilty but not necessarily ashamed. "Mistletoe?"

I huffed in frustration. "Not just the kiss. The words. What you said at dinner. I know I brought you here to convince my family we were in love, but I guess I didn't expect you to be quite so convincing. You're messing with my head, Simon."

The way he stood illuminated by the porch light behind him, I couldn't see anything but his outline. Not his eyes or the set of his mouth. He was a shadow. "I'm sorry," he said softly. "I'm not trying to mess with you. I'm definitely not trying to hurt you."

A sharp wind rustled the leaves around our feet and tossed my hair into my face. I pushed it out of the way and pulled my scarf higher. Simon had left the house without a coat. "You should go back inside."

"Lane."

"I need a minute, all right? Tell them . . . tell them I'm talking to Randi."

He nodded, then backed up toward the house. "Okay."

I didn't call Randi. I was too keyed up to talk to anyone. Instead, I walked laps around my parents' neighborhood, wondering what on earth I'd gotten myself into. Three things were very clear. First, I'd never felt that level of intensity when kissing Jamie. Second, I was pretty sure whatever I'd felt, Simon had felt it too. And third, I had no idea what I was supposed to do about it.

John found me camped out at the playground at the end of my parents' block. He walked across the little mini field where I'd played soccer as a kid and joined me on the swing set. He was silent for a minute, his too-long legs spread out in front of him. "I feel like this is my fault."

"What?"

"You. Out here. Hiding from everyone."

"I'm not hiding."

"Mom thinks you're hiding. Simon told her you were talking to Randi, but that was close to an hour ago."

"I know. I'm sorry."

"You okay?"

"No."

"Want to talk about it?"

"No."

"Lane, I'm sorry about the mistletoe. I probably pushed it too far."

I didn't respond. He had pushed it too far, but it was good that he had. If anything, it made me confront my feelings, and for that I was long overdue.

"I guess I wanted to see if what he'd said at dinner was true. He sounded so sincere."

"So you set us up to have a first kiss in front of our entire family."

"It seemed like a good idea at the time?"

"Ha. Yeah. I'm sure it did."

"Do you think you're maybe falling for him?"

I pushed back on the swing, dragging my boots through the dirt. "I don't know. Maybe. If I let myself go there, then yes. I wanted that kiss, John. I didn't even care that the whole family was watching. When I stop thinking about all the reasons why I shouldn't be, I'm so drawn to him."

"Everyone sees it, Lane. You guys seem so in tune with each other."

"Granny Grace saw it too. She warned me even. Early on when I didn't have a clue myself."

"What did she tell you to do?"

I huffed out a laugh. "To stay away from Simon if I didn't want trouble with Jamie."

"It's definitely more complicated because they're brothers," John said.

"It's impossible because they're brothers. Simon would never do that to Jamie. He told me himself how deep his family loyalty runs."

"So you're stuck," John said. "No matter what you do . . ."

"I'm going to lose them both."

* * *

I could tell Simon wanted to talk. About our kiss. About everything, probably. It was in his eyes, in the way he watched me. But I was always one step ahead. Starting conversations with my parents. Clinging to Abuela's side like she couldn't last a minute without me. By Saturday evening, Simon and I hadn't spent more than five minutes alone. We had, however, managed to have an incredible time with my family. Shopping and out to dinner in downtown Asheville. Driving on the Blue Ridge Parkway. Visiting the Chocolate Lounge enough times to determine their lavender honey caramel truffle was absolutely the best one.

We spent the second half of Saturday at the Biltmore Estate. We toured the house, then waited in the great hall for the lighting of the Christmas tree. It was massive—nearly thirty-five feet—but I loved the gardens more. Strewn with Christmas lights, the sidewalks and pathways lined with luminarias, the gardens felt a little like a fairy tale. Fairy tales can do only so much against the cold though, which was why after just a few minutes of walking outdoors, the rest of my family headed inside, leaving Simon and me to walk the garden pathways on our own.

"Alone at last," Simon said, falling into step beside me.

I shivered, pulling my gloves out of my pocket so I could put them on. "Big wimps," I said, looking back at my retreating family.

"Let's call your parents and brother wimps," Simon said. "I think your abuela gets a pass though. It's never this cold in Puerto Rico."

"True."

"You know, she's sweeter than I thought she was going to be."

"Who? Abuela? She just has you charmed," I said.

"Completely. I guess I thought with all the talk of matchmaking, she'd be a little more . . . I don't know. Out there."

"It's probably my fault you had that impression."

"I'm pretty sure the guy just off his mission showing up at your office gave me that impression."

I chuckled. "Maybe so."

"I've enjoyed getting to know your family," Simon said. "They're great."

We turned a corner and headed back toward the house. "We have that in common, then. I love your family too."

He nodded. "Speaking of family, have you talked to Jamie lately?"

I dropped my gaze to the ground. The answer to his question was easy. Explaining why was another matter altogether.

"Lane, he's worried. Are you avoiding his calls on purpose?"

I dropped onto a concrete bench beside the pathway, the cold seeping through my clothes so quickly I immediately regretted my decision to sit. Simon lowered himself down beside me.

"I'm avoiding his calls mostly because it'd be weird to spend a lot of time talking to him when my family thinks you're him," I said.

He leaned forward, perching his elbows on his knees, looking at the ground between his feet. After a beat of silence, he turned his head, catching my eye. "Is that the only reason?"

"Don't ask me that, Simon. I'm still working through how I feel about Jamie. I know I need to talk to him. And I will as soon as I'm back in Chapel Hill. But it feels like too much to try to sort everything out now."

"Lane! Simon!" John's voice echoed across the garden. We stood, waving him over. He broke into a jog, covering the distance between us in a few strides. "Abuela isn't feeling well, so Dad's gone to get the car. We're going to head home."

"Is she okay?"

"We think so," John said. "She's asked for hot chocolate and a warm blanket, so I think she's probably just cold."

"And tired too," I said. "There are a lot of stairs in the Biltmore House, and she climbed them all." The three of us walked together toward the front of the house, where Dad was already waiting in the SUV. Mom was helping Abuela into the front seat. Simon stepped up and offered his assistance, closing the door for Abuela, then offering my mother a hand as she climbed into the back.

On the drive home, Simon and I squeezed into the very back, leaving John in the middle with Mom. Simon put his arm around me, and I leaned in, resting my head against his shoulder. It felt warm. Right. Like I belonged there and nowhere else. It was probably wrong to feel that way. Probably more wrong to sit that way. But the longer we were together, the more I found myself wishing that Simon wasn't pretending. That our time together was more than a candlelit fairy tale. Granny Grace told me the heart wants what the heart wants. My heart seemed bound and determined to prove her right.

•••

Jamie: Brothers. I have news. Serious, big, exciting news.
Dave: What time is it in California? I'm still asleep, and we're three hours
      ahead of you.
Jamie: 5:30 AM. Can't sleep. Too much on my mind.
Simon: What's the news?
Jamie: I've found a house.
Simon: Yeah?
Jamie: Just down the street from the office. In a nice neighborhood but
      still close enough to the city. Lane will be able to commute into a
      hotel without any trouble.
Simon: So you're asking her to move to California with you?
Dave: It's about time if you are. All this back and forth has to be
      killing your relationship.
Jamie: I'm asking her to marry me. I just bought the ring.
Dave: Congrats, bro. I'm happy for you.
Simon: Are you sure you're ready?
Jamie: I have to go for it. She was worried I had doubts. I have to show
      her I don't.
Simon: When will you ask her?
Jamie: Not until I'm home. Wednesday or Thursday, probably. Don't
      blow my cover. I want it to be a surprise.

Chapter 22

I BLINKED MY EYES AT the alarm clock sitting on the nightstand in my old bedroom. Well, sort of my old bedroom. The dimensions were the same; the closet and adjoining bathroom were still in the same place, but otherwise you'd never know the space had ever been mine. The second I'd left for Berkeley, Mom had redecorated, creating what she called a "tasteful, functional guest room." I didn't really care. I'd probably be mortified to sleep among my BOYBAND 2.0 posters with my boyfriend on the next floor anyway. No. My *pretend* boyfriend. I sighed. For a brief, happy moment, I'd forgotten how complicated my love life presently was.

The clock read 8:43 a.m. It was late. Later than I should have slept on a Sunday morning. But then I remembered the snow. It had started just after we'd arrived home from the Biltmore the night before. It wasn't much— only a few inches—but three inches in North Carolina was enough for everything to shut down. Even church. I could vaguely recall John sticking his head into my bedroom just past seven and letting me know. It had been blissful settling back into the covers knowing I had nowhere to be. I hadn't expected to doze back off or stay asleep so long. It felt so indulgent. And . . . amazing.

I stretched and stood, wondering if Simon was already awake. On the foot of my bed, there was a small package wrapped in brown paper and tied with thick twine. My name was written on the front. I reached for it, sitting back down on the corner of my bed.

When I pulled off the last of the paper, I gasped. It was an original-print Spanish edition of *Cien Años de Soledad, One Hundred Years of Solitude*, by Gabriel García Márquez. An exact copy of my father's book—the one I had lost. My heart started pounding. There was only one person who knew just how much the book meant to me. But what was he trying to say with the gift? What did it mean?

I opened the front cover and read the inscription there, which was written in a light, loose script. *It is enough for me to be sure that you and I exist at this moment.* It wasn't signed or dated. It could have been Simon who wrote it, but it was a used copy of the book. It just as easily could have come with the inscription.

I pulled my hair back into a ponytail and shrugged into my sweater before hurrying down the stairs, my new book clutched closely to my chest. I needed answers. And quick.

Simon didn't strike me as a guy who could sleep in—he was too pragmatic for that—so I was surprised when I didn't see him in the kitchen having breakfast with everyone else.

"Good morning, *mija*," Abuela said. "Are you hungry?"

"Not yet. Have you seen Simon this morning?"

"I don't think he's up yet," Dad said.

"I'll go see." I hurried to the basement steps just off the kitchen. If there was ever a place one might sleep later than expected, my parents' basement was it. It was fully finished and was a nice space, but it was a true basement. No windows anywhere. Dad had set up a projector and turned it into a giant movie room when we were kids, and we'd used it well. More than once, we'd stumbled up the steps, bleary-eyed from hours-long movie marathons, surprised to see sunlight shining through the kitchen windows.

The overstuffed sectional in the center of the room had served as Simon's bed for the weekend. It wasn't particularly glamorous, but he'd had his own bathroom and more privacy than he would have enjoyed had he stayed upstairs and shared a bedroom with John. As I neared the bottom of the steps, I could hear Simon talking. I stopped, unnerved by the tone and urgency in his voice.

"If you don't tell her, I will. It doesn't feel right, you taking this next step under false pretenses."

False pretenses? What on earth?

"It shouldn't make a difference at all," Simon continued. "If Lane loves you, none of that stuff will matter. But you do have to tell her."

My heart started to pound. He was talking about me, but what stuff? What wouldn't matter?

"I never said you lied," Simon said, his voice sharp. "But you did pretend to be something you're not. And Lane deserves to know what's really you and what isn't. Think about it this way. The concert tickets. The poetry. Talking about books. That's the Jamie Lane is used to. It's what she expects because that's what you've shown her. But I'm not going to be around to funnel information to you forever. What happens when you're on your own and Lane is disappointed when she figures out you don't actually know who Billy Collins is? It's time to start being you, man. And you need to come clean about what's happened so far."

I sank to the steps, the reality of Simon's words buzzing like angry bees in my brain.

The concert tickets.

The poetry.

The books.

None of it had really been Jamie.

The most frustrating part? Everything suddenly made *so much sense.*

I'd said I felt like I was dating two different versions of the same man, and I was right. Jamie on his own, and Jamie listening to Simon. All those things that came out of left field—it was Simon all the time.

"I need to go," I heard Simon say. "Just think about it, all right?"

I stayed there, sitting on the stairs. Thinking. Processing. Anger building as each second passed. They'd lied to me. Both of them. Like it was all some sort of game.

"Oh, hey." Simon stopped at the foot of the stairs. "What are you . . ."

I wiped a tear off my face and shook my head. I wasn't ready for words.

"Oh no," Simon said. He cursed under his breath and turned around, pushing his head into his hands. He came back to the stairs, almost frantic. "Lane, please let me explain."

"So." I swallowed. "Was this weekend like field research? Jamie couldn't make it so he sent his research guy to dig up some dirt, maybe get some ideas for Christmas presents?"

"No. Of course not." He sat down a few steps below me.

"I feel so stupid," I said, more to myself than to Simon. "Like I've fallen for one giant prank."

"It was never meant to be a prank," Simon said. "Jamie wanted to impress you. He wanted you to think he was the kind of guy you could connect with."

"But it wasn't real. Was it? Was anything he did or said ever just him?"

"Of course it was. He's a good man, Lane. You know the real Jamie. The competitive, impetuous, dynamic, charming Jamie. That's him." I did know that Jamie. And he was adorable and talented and fun to be around. But the Jamie who kept me hanging on, who kept me pushing my doubts aside wasn't *that* Jamie. It was the thoughtful, observant Jamie who would talk to me about books and poetry and notice things like what kind of hot chocolate I liked. *That* Jamie? It was Simon. Which made the sting of betrayal even worse. All the time Simon had spent with me, the interest he'd shown, the easy way he'd talked to me. Not even that could feel real anymore. Our entire friendship felt counterfeit—like I was nothing but a project.

"Jamie never read *Fountainhead*," I said—a statement, not a question.

"No. He didn't," Simon said.

"He doesn't know Billy Collins, and he didn't pick out Ariana Franklin." Simon sighed and nodded.

"Nikki Giovanni. And the concert tickets. Both ideas that came from you."

"Yes."

"Is there more?"

"Those are the big things," he said. "The rest were small. Observations. Stuff I noticed about what you like to drink and what kind of desserts you like. It wasn't anything significant."

I stood and walked into the basement. I needed movement. Distance. Space. "Everything is significant, Simon. Do you know how many times I doubted, wondered if my relationship with Jamie had the depth I wanted, when all of a sudden he would swoop in and do something or say something that pushed my doubts aside? That side of Jamie was the side that kept me hanging on. And it was never really him." I thought of mine and Simon's conversation in the car on the ride to Asheville four days before. "I . . . I even told you how I was feeling! In the car on the way here, I told you I felt like Jamie was two different people, and you didn't say anything. You let me puzzle it out, knowing full well I actually was dating two men the entire time."

"It wasn't that blatant," he said. "It was always Jamie. I gave him advice every once in a while. That's it."

"But you said it yourself. He was pretending to be something he wasn't. To like stuff he didn't like."

"I know. You're right. That's why I told him he needed to be honest with you."

"What about you? You didn't feel like *you* needed to be honest with me?" I unfolded my arms and pulled out the book I'd been hiding inside my sweater. "Did you give this to me?"

He sighed. "Oh, Lane, I—"

"What were you trying to say? Was it from you? Or was it supposed to be from Jamie? Another one of your tricks to make me think he actually knows who I am?" Thoughts were tumbling through my brain at lightning speed, but rather than overwhelm or confuse me, it felt more like things were finally clicking into place—giving me the whole picture that had been eluding me for weeks.

"It wasn't supposed to be from Jamie."

"Simon, all the stuff that I liked the most about Jamie was the stuff that came from you. When I combine that with the way you've been treating me this weekend, looking at me, talking about me. When I think about that kiss, how am I supposed to feel? It's felt real, but now I'm not so sure. And with this"—I held up the book—"I have no idea what you want me to feel."

He ran a hand through his hair and forced out a heavy sigh. "Lane, the book was a mistake."

I looked up, pain piercing all the way to my gut. "What?"

"Wait. I need to tell you something first. I need you to understand. Every single second I was with you, it was me. I asked you things because *I* wanted to know, expressed interest because *I* really was interested. It was all real for me, okay? I hated funneling information to Jamie. I never thought it was a good idea."

"Then why did you do it?"

"I shouldn't have. I definitely see that now. But he's my brother. He asked for my help, so . . . I helped."

"And neither of you stopped to think about what this might do to me?"

"A thousand times I thought about it. I was actually planning on telling you everything. And the book was the start of that. You were going to find it when you woke up and then come find me, and I was going to tell you. But then—" He paused and closed his eyes, his hands balled into fists at his sides.

"Then what?" I prodded, wanting him to finish his sentence.

He moved his hands to his hips, his head hanging low on his shoulders. He finally looked up to meet my gaze, his eyes full of resignation. "Then Jamie told me he's going to propose, Lane. He wants to marry you. He texted this morning to let me know."

I took a step backward.

Marriage.

California.

Marriage.

It was too much to wrap my head around. "So you changed your mind."

He nodded. "I tried to convince myself I could do it, but it wouldn't . . . He's my brother, Lane. It wouldn't be right."

I wiped the tears off my cheeks with the back of my hand. "Where does that leave me, Simon? I feel like I've been toyed with in the worst kind of way, and what am I left with? I can't be with Jamie, not after this. But I can't be with you either." I looked at the book he'd given me, then handed it back. "I think you need to take this back. I'm ready to go home."

* * *

Another upside to North Carolina snow? It never stuck around long. By three on Sunday afternoon, most of it had already melted. Enough, at least, that the highways taking us back to Chapel Hill wouldn't be a problem.

Simon and I kept our smiles on while we said good-bye to my family. It was possible, even likely they'd heard fragments of our argument floating up the stairs to where they'd been sitting in the kitchen. Thankfully, no one had brought it up.

Only John mentioned something when he gave me a hug good-bye. "You owe me a phone call," he'd whispered.

I nodded. "Soon," I told him.

Simon offered to drive on the way home. I agreed without a word, just tossed him the keys and moved to the passenger side of the car.

I leaned into the seat, staring out at the side mirror as the mountains grew smaller, their muted winter blues and grays blending into the matte November sky.

"Lane, please talk to me," Simon said after nearly an hour of silence.

"No," I said simply. "I don't have anything I want to say."

Dave: Yo. Where is everyone? This thread has never been dead this long.
Jamie: I'm flying in tomorrow. How was Thanksgiving with the in-laws?
Dave: Good. Did you get the specs I sent over on the new app?
Jamie: Yep. Sorry I didn't respond. Was caught up with Byron when they came through. They look great though.
Dave: You popped the question yet?
Jamie: Not yet. Seeing her tomorrow night. Simon, you still good to get me from the airport?
Simon: Yeah. I'm planning on it.

Chapter 23

FIRST THING MONDAY MORNING AND through the first half of the week, I buried myself in postholiday work at the inn. Arriving early. Staying late. It worked to my advantage for a couple of reasons. One, the new ownership visited three days in a row, mapping out the steps needed for a healthy transition. It was encouraging to meet them and see their enthusiasm and optimism regarding the inn's future. And it helped to let them see *me* putting in the hours at work, committing myself to a job well done every single day. Two, staying busy was the only way I could keep myself from randomly bursting into tears.

I hadn't seen or spoken to Simon since we'd gotten back into town on Sunday evening. I still had his ring and needed to return it, but I couldn't think of any situation where seeing him wouldn't make me feel worse. Finally, on Wednesday evening, after I'd worked a retirement party in the ballroom, I sent Carlos through the rose garden to Simon's house with a thick manila envelope I made him promise he wouldn't open and wouldn't give to anyone but Simon. In person. Leaving it on the doorstep was not allowed. With all the assistance Simon had provided before the inn was sold, it must not have seemed an unusual request. Carlos didn't even question.

He came back a few minutes later empty-handed. "Did you see him?" I asked. "Did you give it to him?"

He nodded. "Why do you look like you swallowed a bumblebee? I gave it to him. He said to tell you thank you."

"Thank you. Is that all he said?"

Carlos furrowed his brow. "Yes? Should I have asked him something else?"

I shook my head. "No. Sorry. It was just an important . . . document. If you gave it directly to him, I'm sure things are great."

A few minutes later, a text popped up on my phone.

Thanks for the ring, Simon texted.

I responded right away. *I'm sorry we didn't return it before we left Asheville. I should have remembered.*

They were closed because of the snow anyway. It's fine. They have a sister store in Greensboro. I can return it there, his text read.

Sorry again for the trouble.

How are you? he asked.

It was a loaded question. And one I had no idea how to answer. I was still confused. Still hurt. Still angry.

I'm working on being okay, I texted back. It was the truth, after all. I was working on it. And I'd already decided on the first thing I needed to do before I could really feel right again.

I had to break up with Jamie.

I waited up for him Thursday night. His flight was delayed, so what had originally been scheduled as dinner turned into "maybe we can still grab dessert," then finally "too late for food, but we need to see each other anyway."

It was 9:45 p.m. when he finally showed up.

I met him at the door. "Hey, you," he said, pulling me into a hug. "I missed you."

Despite his traveling, he still smelled like California—like sun and salt and ocean breeze.

"I've missed you too," I responded. "How was your trip?"

His eyes danced. "So good. I can't wait to tell you about it."

I knew in my gut if Jamie started talking before I did, he wouldn't stop, barreling forward into a proposal I didn't want. If I could avoid it, sparing us both the awkwardness of that serious of a rejection, I had to try. I squeezed his hand. "Let's go sit down."

We moved into the living room, and I said a silent prayer that my fortitude would be enough to get me through the next half hour. I wouldn't deny I'd been somewhat of a mess the past few days, but at least on this point, my conscience was clear. Jamie wasn't the man for me. For all my warring emotions, that truth had settled into my heart, and I knew it was right. I didn't want a relationship full of doubt or uncertainty. I didn't want grand gestures to convince me to hang on. I didn't want to need convincing.

I'd spent a good deal of the drive back from Asheville thinking about what had led me to go after Jamie in the first place. It was Simon who had approached me after the game. Simon who had complimented my playing and offered me water. And yet I'd looked right past him. To be fair, I'd been told he had a girlfriend, which he had. But more than that, I'd let my competitive spirit drive me forward. Jamie was a conquest. The untouchable, undateable brother. He was the grand prize, and I was a girl who hated to lose. It wasn't a fun realization to make. It made me feel shallow—more superficial than I wanted to be. Which was precisely the problem with my relationship with Jamie. We were happy because things remained surface level, nothing but a few manufactured connections to take us deeper.

I don't know how I thought he would react to the breakup. Remembering how annoyed he was over lost soccer games, I probably should have anticipated a bigger argument. But when I told him how I felt, I was totally blindsided by his anger.

"Do you realize how much planning I've done?" he said, his voice raised. "I found us a house, Lane. It's close to hotels for your work, and it's in a great school district. What am I going to do with a house if you're not in California to share it with me?"

"You never asked me if it's what I wanted. You did all that planning without talking to me at all."

"When you said you needed time to process, I thought you just wanted to be sure about moving. I didn't think you were questioning our entire relationship."

"It feels like I'm questioning everything lately. But, Jamie, really think about it. We haven't been speaking the same language for weeks. We're not connecting. Not like we should be."

"But we have fun, Lane. We've never even had an argument. I feel like this is really coming out of nowhere."

"That doesn't alarm you at all? That we've never argued? How invested are we, really, if we haven't ever felt anything strongly enough to fight about it? I don't think you know me nearly as well as you think you do."

A conversation I'd had with Simon while walking through the Biltmore House came to mind. He'd been asking me questions, trying to get me to tell him things he didn't already know about me.

"Okay," Simon had said. "Here's what I've got. You love to read poetry—Billy Collins for his love of ordinary subjects, Longfellow for his passion, and Nikki Giovanni both because she writes revolutionary words and because she helped pave the way for other black artists and authors. You love chocolate but more as an accent than the main ingredient. You have a ridiculous yet somehow still-adorable obsession with BOYBAND 2.0. You play a mean game of soccer. Your favorite color must be turquoise because one, you have two different scarves, both turquoise, and two, it's the color of your toenails. You love to read books that touch you on a soul-deep level. You love Puerto Rican food more than anything ever cooked in the States, with the exception of Granny Grace's chicken and dumplings."

I'd been blown away by his thoroughness and perception. Sure, much of what he'd mentioned we'd talked about, but other stuff he'd figured out because he'd paid attention. He cared about details like I did, which allowed him to see me like I wanted to be seen, in a way that despite his best efforts, Jamie never could. Jaime had been wrong for me from the start. It had just taken us a long time to realize it.

After twenty more minutes of arguing, Jamie was finally subdued, and I was completely drained. I reached over and touched his shoulder. "Hey. You okay?"

He gave me a long, hard look, then breathed out a weary sigh. "I think I will be." He started like he wanted to ask something more, then hesitated before blurting out a question. "Is there someone else, Lane? When you went home, did you meet someone?"

I wasn't sure what to make of the fact that it didn't even occur to him to consider Simon. It could be that he simply trusted his brother's loyalty, but more than that, I think he'd *never* considered his older brother an actual threat. Jamie never lacked confidence, not on the soccer field, not in business, not with women, and I'd seen him mock his brother more than once regarding those particular aspects of his life. It was like he had a blind spot when it came to Simon. Because he was quieter, more reserved, and much less of a showboat, he was discounted. It made me sad—so much so that I almost wanted to tell Jamie what had happened with Simon just to jostle his perspective. But I couldn't do it. Simon wasn't the reason we were breaking up. Saying anything more would create a rift between them that didn't need to exist.

"No. This is just about us. No one else."

He nodded his head slowly, then stood from the couch. "I guess I should go."

"I'm so sorry, Jamie."

He leaned down and kissed me on the cheek. "I'm sorry too, Lane."

* * *

I pushed my toes against the end of Granny's couch and pulled the blanket a little tighter against my chin. It had been snowing for three days, this time enough to really make a difference. Thick, heavy snowflakes had accumulated quickly and essentially shut down the city. Though, snow or no snow, I'd probably still be hibernating in Granny's family room. Breaking up stunk. And I felt a little like I'd been through two of them. One with Jamie, and one with Simon.

"Lane? You still in here?" Granny peeked in from the kitchen. "Are you hungry? I made some soup. And there's leftover cornbread in the bread box."

I sat up and stretched. Soup and cornbread sounded amazing. Granny had been a patient listener the past few days. She'd nodded and hmm'ed and aha'ed in all the right places. She'd let me cry and pout and had handed me mugs of hot chocolate and bowls of ice cream and pieces of fried chicken. Sometimes all at the same time. But I could tell she was getting tired of my moping. I couldn't blame her, really. *I* was getting tired of my moping.

It had been just under a week since I'd had any contact with either of the Hamilton brothers, save a few text messages. Jamie was likely at home packing up his house, getting ready for his big move to California. I could imagine him pacing around, annoyed that the weather was slowing him down. I was glad he was planning to move. I didn't bear him any ill will. I wanted him to be happy, and he would be once he'd made it to the West Coast.

I could imagine Simon too, holed up at home, working a little, reading. I wanted to see him and felt a swell of sadness I couldn't push aside. We'd had one more text exchange since I'd given him the ring.

I heard about the breakup. I'm sorry, he'd texted.

It was the right thing to do, I responded. *How's Jamie?*

Dejected. But resolute. He seems to be moving forward-ish.

That's good.

His next message came through over an hour later. *Lane, I'm sorry about my role in all of this. That you ended up getting hurt. More than anything, I'm so sorry we didn't meet under different circumstances.*

The subtext of what he didn't say pulsed behind his words. *Jamie's my brother. He's broken, and I won't make it worse. But if he weren't . . .*

It killed me. Because the more I thought about Simon, the more I realized how much I cared about him. All along, he'd been the one seeing me, understanding what would make me happy. Without having to really think or try or pretend, we'd always connected. That I'd ignored the obvious for so long in the guise of saving my relationship with Jamie was almost too much to process. But then, truly, what would it have mattered? They were brothers, and Simon had proven he'd never turn his back on his brother.

In the kitchen, Granny had the table set and was already ladling the soup into bowls. She handed me one and then the other. I breathed in, savoring the aroma of the spicy corn chowder, before setting them on the table. "Corn chowder *and* corn bread?"

Granny paused and leveled a stare right at me. "There's a foot of snow on the ground outside. You been to the store lately?"

I leaned forward and kissed her on the cheek. "I wasn't complaining. I'll eat your cornbread with anything." I filled my glass with water while Granny filled hers with sweet tea, then we both sat down. "How are things at the inn?" she asked.

"Quiet. There are a few stray guests left over from last week, but most everyone cancelled their reservations because of the storm. There's supposed to be a wedding on Saturday in the ballroom. Hopefully the roads will be clear enough by then."

"Have you met the new owners yet?"

"Early last week. From what I can tell, they seem really nice."

"Are they going to keep you on?"

"I don't know. I think so. I'm sure they'll make some changes, corporatize everything, but that's probably a good thing. There are a lot of things at the inn that could use improving."

"As long as improving doesn't mean firing you."

I took a bite of soup. "I don't think it'll come to that. I know the inn. And I've had enough experience at bigger hotels that any changes they implement shouldn't be totally foreign territory."

"Well, that's good. I wasn't too keen on the idea of you moving away now that I'm finally used to you being here."

I put down my spoon. "It took you this long, huh?"

She chuckled, her grin wide. "You're a handful, Lane. There's no denying that."

I crumbled my cornbread into my soup and scooped up another bite. "I'm pretty sure that's what Grandpa used to say about you."

Her chuckle turned into full-bellied laughter. "That he did."

I was nearly done with my soup when she asked me if I'd talked to Simon. She'd had a few moments of gloating when I'd given her the rundown on what had happened. Claimed she'd known it all along. It was fine to let her have her fun, but I didn't like talking to her about him. Because she failed to see how he'd done anything wrong. And I wasn't ready to let him off the hook. "You still haven't talked to him?" she said as she rinsed out her bowl.

"It's only been three days since you last asked me that."

"Really? Only three?"

"I'm not giving in, Granny. What would it accomplish? Even if we both wanted it, we can't be together. It's not worth the heartache of calling him up just to talk about something we can't have."

And so began my fast from the Hamilton brothers. An icy November thawed into an unseasonably warm December. I spent almost all my time at work, coordinating with the new ownership, growing more and more confident in my role at the inn. I worked through Christmas. New Years. Oversaw and executed lavish parties and elaborate meals, observing from the sidelines as people lived their happy lives. I found a sort of detached peace through it all. I was alone, yes, but there was simplicity in solitude. I worked, I exercised, I ate with Granny Grace. And in my lowest moments, I agonized over how I was going to tell Abuela my engagement was off. She was expecting an announcement in the mail. Had asked about it multiple times, mostly through my mother. I was sick over the thought of disappointing her.

John's reassurances went a long way in making me feel better. He reminded me over and over again that Abuela loved me. That she wanted me to be happy and I shouldn't be scared to tell her the truth. But I couldn't do it. Probably because somewhere in the innermost recesses of my heart, I hoped there might be a future for Simon and me after all.

Once, in late January when winter had finally descended on North Carolina in all its frigid glory, I bundled up in my wool coat and turquoise scarf and left my office for the gardens. I wound my way back to the rose garden, a place I'd been avoiding for weeks. I stood in the corner, hidden behind the leafless branches of my favorite tree, and stared at Simon's house. It was late afternoon, so he probably wasn't home. But I wished he were. Time had dulled and dissipated my anger. All that was left was longing.

I realized with a keen sense of regret that I missed him more than I had ever missed Jamie.

It became a frequent walk for me. Once, maybe twice a week. At first I timed my outings so I knew he wouldn't be home. But then, as time passed, I started walking later in the afternoon, closer to dinnertime, when he might be arriving home from work. I wasn't sure I wanted to talk to him. I had no idea what I would say. But I did want to see him.

It was the end of March, on a Tuesday afternoon. I'd just finished a long meeting with a wedding planner who had very specific requests for the reception space, and my brain was done. I'd grown to appreciate the benefits of taking a walk through the gardens to clear my head, which was my very specific goal that afternoon. For once, I hadn't even given Simon a thought.

Until I hit the corner of the rose garden that offered a vantage point of his porch and saw him standing there in front of his door. He wore a suit and an overcoat and held a stack of what looked like letters in his hand. His mail, probably. He sorted through them, his face passive. It was such an ordinary thing to be doing. Looking through his mail. But it made my breath catch anyway. My reaction was visceral—felt all the way in my bones. The detached peace I'd cultivated and enjoyed the past few months evaporated in a moment, replaced with a longing so intense I nearly fell to my knees. I needed him. Wanted him. *Loved* him.

I took a step backward, leaves crunching under foot. He turned at the sound. We made eye contact across the yard, though neither of us moved. We just stood there. Staring. Finally, I lifted a gloved hand and waved. He waved back, offered a hint of a smile. And then I turned and walked away.

I did my best to wipe away the tears before I was back at the inn. But my efforts were fruitless. I ran into Carlos at the back door.

"Hey, you okay?" he asked.

I sniffed. "I'm fine. Just getting a cold, I think."

He furrowed his brow. "I don't believe you." It wasn't surprising he didn't believe me. We'd gotten to be good friends over the past few months. When he'd started coaching his daughter's indoor soccer team, he'd asked me to help, and I'd readily agreed. I'd needed things to do outside of work, aside from church and endless hours of Netflix binging. Assistant coach to a team full of ten-year-olds was a pretty great gig.

"I'm fine, Carlos. Just thinking."

"You were walking in the rose garden again. Did you see him?"

I scowled. He wasn't supposed to ask me questions like that. "See who?"

He cocked his head. "You are not so hard to read, *amiga*." Carlos had gotten bits and pieces of the story as our friendship had grown. "Why don't you just go talk to him?" He held open the back door, and I followed him into the inn's office space.

I scoffed. "So many reasons. I don't even know what I would say."

"You still worry about Jamie?"

I nodded. "I do. It hasn't been that long. Plus, I don't even really know how Simon feels anymore."

"You just said it hasn't been that long."

"No, but it still feels scary."

"Sure it does," Carlos said. "The best things always do."

Jamie: Hey. I'm on your front porch. You got a key hidden somewhere?

Simon: You're in NC? When did you get in?

Jamie: Just now. Finally here to empty the storage unit behind the old office. Can I crash at your place?

Simon: Of course. Key is on the back porch, wedged under the bird feeder.

Jamie: Got it. Thanks.

Simon: I'll be home in an hour.

* * *

Jamie: Simon. Why didn't you tell me about Lane?

Simon: What are you talking about?

Jamie: I found the book. And the card. Are you seeing her?

Simon: No.

Jamie: Were you ever seeing her?

Simon: No. I never gave her that card. Please, Jamie. Let's talk about this in person. I'm coming home right now.

Chapter 24

My DOORBELL RANG AT 5:14 P.M., three nights after I'd seen Simon from the corner of the rose garden. No one ever rang my doorbell. I was back in my bedroom, changing clothes for soccer practice. "Just a second!" I called from the hallway. I threw my shirt on and hurried to the door.

Jamie.

I didn't really know who I'd been expecting, but it definitely wasn't him. "Oh my gosh! What are you doing here?" I reached up and gave him a hug, which he returned with a broad smile.

"It's good to see you. Can I come in?"

I stepped out of the way and let him in, then followed him into the living room. "How are you? How's California?" We sat on opposite ends of the couch. He had a bag with him, like a gift bag but simple. Brown, unmarked.

"California's great. Things are . . . Things are good."

"I'm really glad. That's really, really good." Internally, I cringed. Maybe I should've said "really" a few more times.

"Are you playing soccer?"

I looked down at my jersey. "Oh. I'm coaching. Carlos's daughter, Javie, is on an indoor team, and I'm helping out."

He nodded. "That's great."

"Yeah. It's been good for me, I think."

"So I, um . . ." He reached for the bag. "I found something. At Simon's house. And I think you should have it."

I sat up a little straighter. When Jamie pulled out the copy of *Cien Años de Soledad*, my hand flew to my chest, a reflex to try to still the crazy pounding of my heart. He held the book, looking at it for a long moment before handing it to me. "This was always meant to be yours, Lane. There's a card inside the front cover. Sorry. I know it wasn't meant for me, but when I found it, I didn't know what it was. So I read it."

I read over the inscription one more time—the words that had floated through my mind countless times since I'd first read them. *It is enough for me to be sure that you and I exist at this moment.* I swallowed. "Did he—"

"Did he write the inscription?" Jamie asked.

I nodded.

"I asked him. He did. What's it from?"

"It's a line from the novel," I said, my voice barely above a whisper.

My hands shook as I pulled out the card. I looked up at Jamie. "I'm not sure I can read this."

"You can," Jamie said softly. "And you really should."

I shook my head. For him to be the one giving me this felt all kinds of wrong. "But for you—"

He cut me off. "Lane. I'm fine. Just read it."

I took a deep, steadying breath, then opened the card, the seal of the envelope already broken. It was simple paper, folded in half, the date— November 30, two days after Thanksgiving—inscribed at the top.

Lane,

There are a thousand reasons why I shouldn't give you this note. I have tried with all I have in me to keep from doing so. Respect for my brother and for you and the feelings you share have compelled me to remain silent. But I can't do it anymore.

Longfellow, a poet I know you love, loved his wife for six years before she accepted his proposal. At one point in that painful span of time, Longfellow tried to rid himself of his affection, to put off what he believed was fruitless, pointless, and never to be returned. Like Longfellow, I have tried. Told myself it can go nowhere. Which may be true, even now that I'm telling you the truth. But I am compelled to tell you anyway. The story I told at dinner about first falling in love with you is true. I loved you that day in your office, and I love you now, still. Every minute I spend in your company sends me from one extreme to the other. Exquisite joy for how much I love to be around you, followed by sharp pain that you aren't mine to love.

I thought it would be enough. To influence and suggest. To help Jamie see you as I see you. But I realize now I have made a mess where no one can win without someone else getting hurt. For that, I will always be sorry. If

it's too late and my words are unwelcome, I'm sorry for adding this burden of knowledge to your shoulders. In the end, I want only your happiness.
   Always, Simon

I read the letter, then read it again. And again. It read like poetry. Like it belonged in a nineteenth-century novel. I wiped the tears from my eyes.

"You didn't know?" Jamie asked.

I shook my head no. "I . . ." My voice cracked, so I swallowed and started again. "I suspected, but I didn't know for sure. We never talked about it."

"I should have seen it sooner," Jamie said. "He noticed things. Knew things about you that I never picked up on. In hindsight, it makes so much sense." He huffed a laugh. "Honestly, I can't believe I didn't figure it out. I feel like a jerk. Sending him to spend the weekend with you. Asking him to pretend when really he was in love with you the whole time." Jamie shook his head, self-incrimination emanating from his face.

He didn't seem worried, but I didn't want him to think he'd been betrayed by me or his brother. "Jamie, nothing happened that weekend. We kissed under the mistletoe because my family was watching, but that was it. It didn't have anything to do with why you and I broke up."

"I know." He reached over and took my hand, giving it a reassuring squeeze. "Simon told me. Not about the kiss. He left *that* part out. But he told me nothing happened, and I believed him." Jamie took a deep breath. "I trust him, Lane. He didn't give you that letter because I told him I was going to propose and he is a man who will never take the last Pop-Tart."

I sniffled a laugh.

"He will always think of others before he thinks of himself," Jamie said.

"You're family. It was the right thing to do."

"Maybe. But it isn't the right thing anymore."

"Jamie, you're being really gracious about all of this."

He chuckled. "It's fine. I've made peace with our breakup. You were right. About everything."

"Yeah?"

"Yeah. Turns out I've met someone."

I smiled. "Really?"

"She's great. Different. Different from anyone I've ever dated. She knows nothing about soccer. *Nothing.*"

"That does sound different from what you're used to."

"She's into horses. Owns them. Rides them. Shows them. I don't know what it's all about. But I'm loving learning about her world and what she's passionate about. We're having fun."

I raised my eyebrows and gave him a stern look.

"But not just having fun," he amended. "We're talking too. About everything. We even had a fight last week."

I smiled. "That's good. I bet she's really great."

He reached for my other hand so he held both of mine in his, then tugged gently until I was sitting straight up, turned sideways on the couch so we were facing each other. "Lane," he said, his tone serious. "My brother is a good man. I always say he's the best of us, and I mean it. I really want him to be happy, and based on the conversation he and I just had, I'm pretty sure he could have written that letter yesterday and every word would still be true."

I closed my eyes, my grip on his hands tightening.

"By any chance . . . I don't know . . . It's probably a long shot . . . but did you maybe happen to fall in love with him too?"

I started to laugh. And cry. And generally make a mess of myself. Through my tears and more snot than I would have preferred, I managed to nod my head yes. "I did. I really, really did."

Jamie smiled. "Should we go find him?"

"Right now?"

"I mean, you might want to wipe your nose first and change out of your soccer jersey, but yeah. Let's go."

I tossed a pillow at his head. He caught it, a playful grin on his face. "Come on," he said. "I know where he is. This is going to be fun."

I texted Carlos to tell him I wasn't going to make it to practice after all, then spent ten minutes cleaning myself up before following Jamie to his jeep. I was reeling. My heart racing. My mind buzzing. I was going to see Simon. Talk to him. Tell him the truth. I held the book and letter in my lap. Clutched it, really. Like it was a lifeline I hadn't known I'd needed until I'd had it in my hands.

Jamie got on the highway heading toward Raleigh.

"Where are we going?" I asked.

"Into the city," he replied. "Simon had a dinner meeting with a client. But . . ." He glanced at his watch. "He should be finishing up about the time we get there."

"I'm not crashing his meeting."

"Oh, come on. It'll be fun."

"Jamie."

He grinned. "Fine. We can wait for him outside the restaurant." He rolled his eyes. "If you want to be *boring*."

I shook my head at his theatrics. "How's Cooper?"

"He's good. Really good. His letters are great, and he seems like he's doing well."

"And Dave?" I realized how much I'd missed hanging out with the brothers. With their entire family.

"Oh! He and Katie are expecting a baby."

"Really? So soon?"

"Well, they say it only takes once."

"Well, yeah, but . . ."

"It was a total surprise. A first-class accident, I've been told, but they're still excited."

"Are they settled in San Diego? They like California too?"

"Yep. They're doing great."

Twenty minutes later, we pulled into a parking garage in downtown Raleigh. Jamie got out and motioned for me to join him. "Come this way."

"I told you I'm not storming the restaurant. This is crazy!"

"I know what you told me. But if we sit in the car, he could finish and leave and we'd never see him. We have to at least get into position, where we can see what's happening."

"Fine. But so help me, Jamie, if you're leading me into a trap . . ."

We exited the garage on foot and rounded the corner. "No traps," Jamie said. "Look. That's the restaurant. He's in there, which means he's eventually going to come out that door."

"How do you know he's not going to be meeting all night?"

"I guess I don't, really. But this is Simon we're talking about. He's not exactly a party animal."

"What if his client is a woman and she's beautiful and they end up talking for hours?"

He rolled his eyes. "His client's name is Frederick Gordon. Sound like a beautiful woman to you?"

I huffed. "You never know."

Five minutes turned into ten, then fifteen, then twenty. There was a bench on the sidewalk with a great view of the restaurant's door, but it was too cold to sit still. Or maybe I was just too worked up to sit still.

"Lane, if you don't stop pacing, I'm tying you to this bench with your shoelaces."

"I'm wearing boots. I don't have shoelaces."

"Then I'll use *my* shoelaces. Come and sit. Please."

I froze. "There he is."

Jamie stood. "Which direction is he going? Does he see us?"

"I don't think so. He's still talking to his client. Oh gosh, this was a bad idea."

"Stop it. It's not a bad idea." Jamie turned me to face him. "Hey, I'm going to get out of here."

"You're not staying?"

"Do you really want me to stay and witness whatever moment this is going to be for the two of you?"

Good point. "No. I guess not."

He leaned forward and kissed my cheek. "I'm happy for you, Lane. For both of you." He disappeared into the parking garage, and I turned back to find Simon. He stood at the corner, waiting for the light to change so he could cross the street. I took a step back into the shadow of the building behind me, willing my nerves to calm the heck down.

When he made it across the street, I stepped forward and called his name. "Simon."

He stopped in his tracks. "Lane? What are you doing here?"

I had no words. Rare for me, but everything I thought to say sounded too shallow, too silly for how intensely I felt. He was there in front of me, and for the first time, there was nothing to stop me from making him mine. I did the only thing I could think of—the only thing that felt right: I walked toward him, driven by momentum and will and love, and kissed him, pulling him close against me, holding his face with my hands.

In a second, his arms were around me, anchoring me to him, his lips returning the kiss with a fervor that made me glad I had him to lean on. When we finally parted, breaking the kiss, he kept his arms in place, holding me tight.

"Hi," he said, his voice soft.

"Hi." I pulled the book out of the oversized pocket of my coat, the open letter on top. "Oh, wow," he whispered. "I guess you've been talking to Jamie."

"It is enough," I whispered, "for me to be sure that you and I exist at this moment."

He leaned his forehead against mine. "That's my favorite line from the book."

"Well, now it's mine too."

He grinned. "Man, I love my brother right now."

I laughed. "Me too. But not as much as I love you."

Simon leaned in and kissed me again.

And then again.

And then again.

Dear family,

Thank you for all the updates.

I have much to say about Africa this week. The work is hard, but we've seen a lot of good the past few days, so I can't complain. I'll get to all that very important spiritual stuff soon enough but not until I give Simon a massively huge high five. You should probably go ahead and build a permanent trophy case for the golden soccer ball. With Lane on your team, the rest of us don't stand a chance. I'm curious though. Did you and Jamie have an actual fight over this? Like, was there blood? I'm sorry I missed it if there was. I'm happy for you, however it happened. Lane's cool. I'm glad she'll be a part of the family.

So I know you're not technically engaged yet, so no pressure. But if you do start to talk wedding dates, I'm thinking fall of NEXT year would be great. Just throwing that out there. In case you're interested in having the handsomest of the Hamilton brothers in any of your photos.

I'll write more soon. I love you all. Keep the letters coming.

Peace out from Africa.
Elder Hamilton

About the Author

Jenny Proctor was born in the mountains of Western North Carolina, a place where she still resides and considers the loveliest on earth. She and her husband stay busy keeping up with six children and a growing assortment of pets. She loves to hike with her family and spend time outdoors, but she also adores lounging around her home, reading great books or watching great movies and, when she's lucky, eating delicious food she didn't have to prepare herself. To learn more about Jenny, visit her web page at www.jennyproctor.com.